MISSION IMPOSSIBLE

Suppose you learned that your best buddy—a man who, by all rights, should be dead—is alive, a prisoner in a brutal Vietnamese camp for undocumented POWs. Suppose you've been offered a quarter of a million dollars to get him out. . . .

If you're Jack Callahan—former Green Beret, sometime mercenary—you recruit four of the best men money can buy. You put them through weeks of gruelling training until you have a razor-sharp fighting team. You spare no expense to get the best equipment available on the international black market. You prepare to hit the enemy where he least expects it—in a parachute drop too dangerous for any sane man to attempt. You plunge down, your face blackened for night fighting, your nerves raw and humming. . . .

And you make out your will in advance.

"VIVID AND BELIEVABLE . . . TAUT ADVENTURE."
—*Publishers Weekly*

"GALVANIZING . . . [WILL] JOLT READERS INTO *INSISTING* THAT THIS QUESTION BE RESOLVED."
—*Booklist*

MISSION
M.I.A.

J. C. Pollock

A DELL BOOK

Published by
Dell Publishing Co., Inc.
1 Dag Hammarskjold Plaza
New York, New York 10017

We gratefully acknowledge permission to quote from
"Let's Find Our Missing Men" by Major General John K. Singlaub,
reprinted by permission of *The American Legion Magazine,* © 1980.

Dell ® TM 681510, Dell Publishing Co., Inc.

ISBN: 0-440-15819-2

Reprinted by arrangement with Crown Publishers, Inc.
Printed in the United States of America
First Dell printing—January 1983

For my wife, Barrie.
All the good things in my life
have happened since we met.

ACKNOWLEDGMENTS

I am deeply indebted to Sergeant Major Daniel Lee Pitzer, USA (Ret.), for his help with this book. Through countless hours of taped interviews he patiently and thoughtfully granted all my requests for information and technical advice. A highly decorated combat veteran of the Korean and Vietnam wars, he served fifteen years with the Green Berets, and was a prisoner of the Viet Cong for four years. With his professionalism, dedication, integrity, and courage, he is the embodiment of the principles upon which Special Forces were founded. To know Dan Pitzer is to admire and respect him. To have him as a friend is an honor and a privilege.

I also wish to thank the following Special Forces personnel for their valuable contributions. Listed below are the units with which they served in Vietnam.

Command Sergeant Major Henry D. Luthy, USA, Recon Platoon Commander I Corps Mobile Guerrilla Force. Company Commander II Corps Mike Force. Member of seven A-Teams in various Corps areas.

Master Sergeant Kenneth E. McMullin, USA, Platoon Commander II Corps Mike Force. Team Leader Recon Team Nevada MACV/SOG (Military Assistance Command Vietnam/Special Operations Group). Member of the assault group of the Sontay raid to rescue American POWs in North Vietnam.

Master Sergeant Bobby J. Tuggle, USA (Ret.), Operations and Intelligence MACV/SOG. IV Corps, Seven Mountain Area, Chau Lang Forward Operational Base.

Master Sergeant William M. (Bata Boot) Bennett, USA (Ret.), HALO and SCUBA instructor Special Forces Training Group. MACV Recondo School, Nha Trang.

A note of thanks to Special Forces Command Historian Beverly Lindsey, and to Dan Pitzer's lovely wife, Marti, for her gracious hospitality.

It is a shocking and tragic fact that today more than 2,490 American servicemen remain unaccounted for from the Vietnam War.

All but a few have been declared "presumptively dead" by the Department of Defense. Since the war's end in May 1975, the grim roster of POWs—prisoners of war—and MIAs—missing in action—has relentlessly been whittled to near zero. The bureaucracy often seems more interested in "normalizing" future relations with Hanoi than in demanding a full accounting of our POWs and MIAs as called for in the 1973 Paris peace agreement.

From Vietnamese refugees have come scores of eyewitness accounts of groups of emaciated Americans, some in chains, being led under heavy guard along jungle trails or through villages to unknown destinations. Some of the firsthand sightings were reported as late as this year (1980)—five years after the fall of Saigon and seven years after the return of 566 American POWs from Hanoi, supposedly the last of our survivors. (It is noteworthy that 13 French prisoners captured at Dienbienphu were not released by Hanoi until 16 years later.)

Countless hours of testimony have been taken from refugees claiming to have seen American captives. As of May 10, 1980, the Defense Intelligence Agency was checking out 370 "live sighting" reports alleged to have been made since 1975. Of these, 222 were said to have been firsthand sightings and the remaining hearsay. Exhaustive interrogation sessions, including polygraph tests, have convinced even skeptical U.S. authorities that many of the refugee reports are valid.

Major General John K. Singlaub, USA (Ret.)

August 1980

Every man who wears the Green Beret today owes a measure of his pride to those who went before him.

Heroic in spirit as well as deed, they fought and they died; they served with honor and integrity, and in the end were denied and denigrated by lesser men.

But the final victory is theirs—they know what they are: *a special breed of men*.

MISSION
M.I.A.

1

Quang Tri Province, Vietnam
August 1981

The chirping calls of crickets and tree frogs, the cries of lizards, and the whining hum of mosquitoes diminished as the gray predawn light washed slowly over the small jungle clearing. A cold mist filled the air and at the edge of the clearing the dense jungle, moisture-laden from the daily drenchings of the monsoon rains, dripped heavily on the underbrush from the triple canopy of trees reaching heights of a hundred feet or more.

In the center of the clearing a sturdy eight-foot-high bamboo fence enclosed a cluster of thatch-roofed huts, and, to the uninitiated, a group of what appeared to be animal cages. The cages, resting on logs a few feet off the ground, were roughly ten feet square, constructed of thick bamboo poles nailed and tied together with ropes. The roofs were covered with leaves and bark and the door to each cage was secured with a clasp and padlock. The occupants were not animals, but men—or vestiges of men.

15

Prisoners of war at a small subcamp in the heart of the mountainous jungles of Vietnam.

Master Sergeant Frank E. Detimore shivered convulsively and brought his knees up close to his chest, curling into a tight ball. The damp night air had chilled him to the bone, unimpeded by the coarse rice mat on which he slept or the thin sackcloth blanket covering his emaciated body. He bunched the top of his light black cotton pajama uniform tightly around his neck and pulled the blanket up over his face.

"Detimore," a man whispered softly.

Frank responded quickly from his fitful half-sleep, pulling the blanket from his face. Through the mosquito netting he saw the hazy image of one of the two men who shared his cage—both political prisoners, Montagnards of the Rhade tribe.

"Must put legs in irons. Guard come soon."

Frank nodded and sat up, painfully aware of the routine and not about to mistime it, though understanding the man's sense of urgency on this particular morning.

Each cage was equipped with a long iron bar that ran the length of one end of the cage. The bar had a series of horseshoe-like clamps that fit over the ankles and held the legs in place. At night the guards locked each man in the clamps until the following morning, necessitating sleeping on either the stomach or the back for the entire night.

Eleven years ago, shortly after being taken prisoner, Detimore learned how to unlock the clamps with a piece of metal he fashioned for the purpose. Each night, after the guards were asleep, he unlocked the leg-irons, releasing himself and the others in the cage, and each morning, before the get-up gong, he locked them back in.

Frank extended his legs and sat up slowly; his joints

were stiff and sore. The Montagnard nudged the third man in the cage and gestured toward the iron bar.

Shortly after the clamps were secured, one of the Vietnamese guards approached the cage from the direction of the guards' hut. He wore the green fatigues and sun helmet of the North Vietnamese Army—the standard uniform for all Vietnamese troops since the end of the war. The enlisted guards were rotated every six months and the one nearing the cage was a recent arrival. Some were decent and some were unnecessarily harsh. Detimore had not yet determined the nature of this man.

The procedure each morning was to wake two of the prisoners a half hour early to start the cooking fire for the morning meal. This minor inconvenience was permanently designated as Frank's responsibility—a punishment meant to degrade him in the eyes of the others, for his being the acknowledged leader of the seven other American prisoners of war. The duties were shared by another occupant of his cage.

The young Vietnamese guard glanced impassively at the three men as he unlocked the leg-irons and padlock. "Go!" he ordered as he swung the door open.

Detimore slipped on his crudely fashioned tire-tread sandals and came out; one of the Montagnards followed.

The guard kept the two men in sight as they slogged through the slick red-clay mud to the stack of firewood at the rear of the compound, nodding consent when Detimore pointed in the direction of the latrine—an open hole in the ground that at times filled the camp with a repulsive stench, contributing to the constant problem of flies and mosquitoes.

The Montagnard walked abreast of Frank as they carried the firewood to the cooking area.

"You help us, Detimore?" A handsome bronzed face beneath jet black hair was dominated by intense, expressive eyes that held Frank's gaze.

Frank accepted that he would have to pay a price for his complicity in the Montagnards' escape, but his decision to help them was based on an ulterior motive as well as his compassion for the two men. He smiled at the thin, wiry man who looked much younger than his thirty-three years—almost boyish.

"Yeah," Frank said. "When do you plan to go?"

"At noon rest today," Caang said. "You make *dook braak* look away and we go."

Frank smiled at the Rhade words Caang used to describe the guards—an insulting profanity in their language, meaning monkey-peacock. He knew the chances of success for Caang and Truu, the other Montagnard in his cage, were good. They had only been prisoners for a few months and were still healthy and strong. The guards at the camp, with the exception of the two officers—who never accompanied the work details—were all former Saigon "cowboys"— pimps and black market hustlers—who had been forced into military service when the communists took over. Once Caang and Truu were ten yards into the jungle, the guards would never catch them. The Montagnards were familiar with the area and knew how to use the jungle, and most important, had family and friends to hide them.

He envied them, and had been awake most of the night with thoughts of joining them—a delusion soon dismissed by the reality of his shattered leg and the clumsy loping gait that was the most he was capable of. The wound, suffered in action when he was taken prisoner, had been improperly treated and had healed badly. His two escape attempts, nine and five years ago, had ended quickly; both

18

times he was captured within minutes. The last attempt had, in retrospect, been an exercise in futility. Had he eluded the guards, there would have been no friendly forces to escape to. He would have been an Occidental face in an Oriental world where some might have been sympathetic, but none, understandably, willing to place themselves in danger for an indefinite period of time on behalf of a man with little hope of succeeding.

His chances of getting to anticommunist forces in Laos or Cambodia were at best remote. The diet since his capture was enough to keep him alive and functioning, but in a generally weakened condition. Once a stocky, powerful man, he now weighed little more than a hundred twenty-five pounds. After years of improper nourishment and bouts with various diseases, any sustained effort would quickly exhaust him.

From the time he was captured until the war ended, he was periodically moved to different jungle camps, spending the last year of the war in a large, more permanent prison camp fifty miles south of Hanoi. Since the war ended he had been moved only twice: from the Hanoi area to a small prison inside an army base ten miles from their present location, where they had spent the past two years planting and harvesting corn and rice crops, clearing jungle trails, and doing any make-work their captors could devise.

"I'll think of something to get their attention," Frank said.

Caang gathered a handful of dry leaves and bark from the pile stored beneath the thatch-roofed lean-to covering the cooking area and placed it under the logs Frank had stacked in the fire pit. As he squatted before the shallow pit and blew on the smoldering kindling, bringing it to flames, he studied the drawn, deeply etched face of the man beside him.

"They punish you for helping us," he said, placing a blackened pot filled with water on the grate over the fire. "Bad Eye not like you."

Frank smiled at Caang's use of the nickname he and the other Americans had given the Vietnamese officer in charge of the camp. "I don't like that son of a bitch either."

"You good man, Detimore."

Frank glanced about and located the guard leaning against one of the cages. He was looking away from them. Reaching inside his shirt Frank removed an envelope and quickly handed it to Caang who just as quickly tucked it inside the waistband of his trousers.

"I want you to try and get that to a friendly journalist from the West. Do you think you or your people can do it?"

"I do it. FULRO have many contacts; it can be done."

Frank was well acquainted with FULRO—initials for French words meaning the United Front for the Struggle of the Oppressed Races—a Montagnard underground resistance group fighting their own war against the Vietnamese. Caang and Truu had been arrested for their activities with FULRO.

During the war, as the Intelligence sergeant of his Special Forces A-Team at Lang Vei, Frank had recruited and trained Montagnards and had come to know them as well as any outsider could. They brought medical aid to their remote villages, trained them to use modern weapons in defense of their people, fought with them, and slowly earned their respect and loyalty.

But they were a difficult people to understand; they

20

defined the word *inscrutable*. They were not Vietnamese and their language was entirely different, often varying between tribes less than twenty miles apart. Frank spoke fluent Vietnamese, but understood little of the Montagnard languages. They hated the Vietnamese for their oppressive policies toward them: denying them education, confiscating their land, and treating them as savages—exemplified by the Vietnamese word for them, *moi*, meaning barbarian. Under the Diem regime a concerted effort had been made to destroy their culture. They were treated with contempt, fined for wearing their loincloths, ridiculed for their religious beliefs and customs, and forbidden to speak their language.

As a result, the Montagnards were eager recruits for the Green Berets, needing little encouragement to kill Vietnamese. The distinction between the communists and the South Vietnamese was lost on them. Vietnamese were Vietnamese—centuries-old enemies, all hated.

The mixture of Montagnard and South Vietnamese troops at the Special Forces camps had been a volatile one. Frank remembered one rebellion when for some minor insult or esoteric loss of face, the ''Yards'' went on a rampage, killing fifty South Vietnamese Rangers and burning their barracks and mess hall to the ground before the Green Berets could get them under control. On other occasions, when they felt slighted, they had simply stripped off their uniforms, thrown them in a pile with their weapons, and returned to their villages. A brutal shock to an A-Team, to wake up and find that an entire company of their troops had disappeared overnight.

The majority of the Montagnards trained by and fighting with Special Forces had been FULRO members, contributing part of their American-paid salaries to the organization, a practice that the South Vietnamese had found disturbing, to say the least.

When the war ended, the Montagnards simply went back into the mountains, to remote areas of the central highlands and to their sanctuaries and training camps in Cambodia—fifty thousand armed, tough, well-trained combat veterans who hated the Vietnamese. Something for the new government to worry about.

Caang and Truu had both fought with an American mobile strike force during the war and were now involved in recruiting new members for the FULRO organization.

"The letter is for your wife?" Caang asked, placing the morning ration of rice into the boiling water.

Frank nodded. "There's a list of the other Americans here and a rough map of the area with our location on it—the one you helped me with." He thought of the irony of the prison camp's location—only twelve miles from the site of the Lang Vei Special Forces camp where he had spent six months during the war.

"Your people come get you?" Caang asked.

"Once they know we're alive, they'll do everything they can to get us out."

"Shut mouth!" the guard screamed. "No talk! Work!" Schooled in the shout and spit method of addressing prisoners, the new arrival imitated the other guards who seldom spoke to the prisoners in a normal tone of voice.

The hollow sound of the get-up gong reverberated through the camp, hanging ominously in the damp, heavy air, then moving slowly on to be absorbed by the dense jungle foliage.

The camp came alive with activity. Guards opened cages and shouted abuse at the groggy, disheveled men who stepped wearily outside to be prodded toward the latrine with stiff jabs from rifle butts.

"Go! Go!" A chorus of shrill commands followed the opening of each cage.

Some of the guards, if not sympathetic toward the prisoners, were at least unenthusiastic about administering punishment, often delivering light ineffectual blows. But if this behavior was noticed by Bad Eye or his adjutant, the offender would be sent back for further schooling and a more suitable replacement brought in.

Two of the prisoners approached the cooking area, got their bowls of rice and water, and left to sit off by themselves, away from the lean-to. They had been in the camp since 1977, and they ate apart from the others; they also worked apart, tending a small vegetable garden just outside the fence, and they were kept in a separate cage. Mahanes and Gerber were deserters from the U.S. Army who had gone over to the Viet Cong. They had fought for the enemy and infiltrated American bases to gather intelligence and set booby traps, and when the war ended and they were of no further use, they were treated as prisoners of war. The Vietnamese Army, like all others, despised traitors, even those who had served their cause.

Frank was not openly antagonistic toward them, but some of the other prisoners were not as tolerant. One in particular, Mike Donahue, had told them that if the opportunity ever presented itself, he would kill them. The camp commander correctly judged it best to segregate them.

Bill Maffey and Pete Hendricks nodded good-morning as they sat down near the fire. The two men were survivors of a Search and Rescue helicopter crew shot down over Cambodia.

Frank wasn't certain what was wrong with Maffey. He

23

functioned well enough to eat and work and take care of himself, and he could carry on a simple conversation. But he seemed to have no idea who he was, or where he was, or even what was going on around him. He smiled contentedly most of the time, and Frank decided that wherever he had escaped to was obviously an improvement over his present circumstances, and made no effort to disturb the peace he had found. Hendricks said that Maffey had found Jesus, that Jesus had taken over his mind and body. And he was sticking close to him just in case.

Lieutenant Harry Cambell entered the lean-to and filled his small wooden bowl from the pot. Sitting cross-legged next to Detimore, his eyes darted about as he hurriedly stuffed the soggy rice into his mouth with his hands.

"Frank," he whispered urgently, "I can't go back in that water today. I just can't take another day of it; those goddamn leeches are driving me *crazy*."

"Easy, Harry. Another day or two and we'll be back to clearing trails."

"I can't take another day of this shit, Frank. I'm telling you, I just can't."

"There's nothing I can do about it. I'm in there, too, and I don't like it any more than you do."

Cambell shook convulsively and choked on his food, coughing and spewing a mouthful of rice on the ground as Frank clapped him hard on the back.

Harry's complaint was about their present work detail. A bridge spanning a stream through a narrow jungle road had washed out and they were rebuilding it. Some of the men felled trees and cut logs while others stood chest-deep in cold, muddy water putting them in place. It was exhausting work and the men were showing the effects of it.

"I've got to get on the detail chopping trees," Harry said. "Maybe I can do it without them noticing."

Detimore grimaced. "The last time you tried that they gave you a vertical butt stroke. Tough it out. The leeches are worse in the woods."

Frank was worried about Cambell. In the last year his mental deterioration had increased alarmingly. Unable to forgive himself for breaking under torture by the North Vietnamese early in his captivity, he had lost all self-respect. Once a proud and confident helicopter gunship pilot, he was now a hollow shell of a man, twitching and cringing at the approach of a guard, and a constant complainer when not sullen and depressed.

Detimore noticed the suppurating boils on the back of Cambell's neck. "I'll see if Bad Eye will give me something to clean those out."

Cambell shrugged. "Why bother? They'll just crop up somewhere else."

With the end of the war their diet had improved to the point where many of the ailments and diseases related to lack of proper nourishment were kept in check, if not consistently, at least long enough for the body to build reserves to combat them when they recurred. When the small portions of chicken or pork, gotten from a local village, or fruits and vegetables were not included with their evening meal for an extended period, it was only a short time before beriberi and boils became a problem. To a man, all the prisoners were drastically underweight from amebic dysentery, and occasional bouts with malaria, which the Vietnamese still treated with quinine pills, were common and further debilitating. Some of the men were alive only because of the natural instinct to survive. They had given up hope of ever getting home.

Frank noticed the slight swelling in the hands and wrists of the Marine corporal filling his bowl from the rice pot.

"Mornin', Top," Donahue said, sitting across from him. "Another lovely day in an exotic port of call, huh?"

Detimore smiled at the gallows humor. Donahue was indomitable. He had been captured during the last months of the war, the sole survivor of a long-range reconnaissance patrol that had walked into the middle of a North Vietnamese battalion. Despite almost constant painful cramps from a stomach ailment—Frank suspected ulcers—and frequent beatings and harassment by the guards in response to his stubborn and persistent irreverence, he never showed any signs of letting his circumstances defeat him.

"Think we'll finish the bridge today?" he asked. "The way they're makin' us build the goddamn thing you'd think they were gonna drive tanks over it instead of oxcarts."

"Today or tomorrow," Frank replied, taking a closer look at the young Marine's hands, recognizing the signs of beriberi. "When did the swelling start?"

"Yesterday. It's nothin'. If these bastards would give us a few pumpkins and melons this shit wouldn't happen. I'm gonna tell that asshole Bad Eye about it tonight."

"Don't do that. He's only going to pump you full of strychnine sulfate and cause you more pain than you already have. I saw some melons over at the guards' mess area; we'll see if we can steal a few."

"Yeah, you're probably right. The last time they shot me up with that stuff I was takin' twenty leaks a day and felt like somebody had set my insides on fire."

"If it gets any worse, I'll see about getting you a B₁ shot."

"Then I'll get hepatitis from the fuckin' needle. They get you comin' and goin', Top."

"Shut mouth! Shut mouth!" the new guard screamed. "No more eat. Work now."

Donahue stared defiantly at the wide-eyed Vietnamese.

"Hey, New Meat," he called out. "Fuck off. Moron."

"Knock it off, Mike," Frank said. "We don't know this guy yet." He stood, placing himself between Donahue and the approaching guard, and gestured toward a small one-man cage set away from the others, hoping to distract the man from his purpose.

The new guard stopped and raised his rifle to deliver a blow. One of the other guards, familiar with the morning routine, spoke to the new man and motioned to Frank to go ahead. The new guard glared at Donahue and went back to join the other guards.

Detimore refilled his bowl with rice and another with water and walked over to the isolated cage.

Navy Lieutenant Dan Lucere sat in a corner of the small cage, his knees up under his chin and his arms wrapped tightly across his chest.

Detimore reached inside, removed the blanket he had placed over him the night before, and took him gently by the arm. "Come on, Dan. It's okay; it's me, Frank."

Lucere stared vacantly with no sign of being aware of Frank's presence.

Frank leaned partly into the cage and slowly pulled the helpless man toward him, getting him to his feet as he came through the door. Steadying him with an arm around his waist, he led him toward the latrine.

Lucere was a frightful sight; in worse condition than any of the men—a skeleton with gray, waxen skin stretched across it. He had been a prisoner as long as Detimore and had seen the worst of the North Vietnamese prisons. Shot down in 1970 when he was a "sideseater" in an A-6 attack bomber off the *Constellation,* he was brought to the subcamp two years ago in much the same condition he was in now. The scars covering most of his body testified to the brutal tortures he had suffered.

Finding that Lucere had no incapacitating physical injuries but was becoming less responsive every day, Frank soon realized that he had been tortured to the point of complete withdrawal. That realization was brought about one horrifying morning shortly after Lucere's arrival at the camp. Frank had come by to check on him and found a rat chewing on his face while Lucere made no effort to prevent it, or gave any indication that he knew or cared it was happening. As a result, one side of the once-handsome face was terribly disfigured.

Frank had accepted the mantle of leadership of the prisoners when Lucere was found to be incapable of assuming the responsibility, and Harry Cambell had pleadingly rejected it. The duty fell to him as the next highest ranking prisoner. He did his best to keep up morale and had taken Lucere on as his personal responsibility, determined not to let him die: feeding and bathing him, often giving him extra meat and fruit from his own meager rations.

"You've got to eat some more of this," Frank said. It was a slow process. With one hand he held Lucere's mouth open, and with the other hand he placed a wadded ball of rice at the back of his throat; then, tilting his head back, he forced him to swallow.

"Just a little more, Dan. Just a little bit more," he said soothingly to the unresponsive man. "You've got to hang in there. We'll get out of here. Get you to a good hospital. They'll fix you up good as new. Get you back to your wife and kids. You do have kids, don't you? I don't think you ever told me about them. . . ."

Detimore carried on these one-sided conversations every morning and evening while he fed Lucere. There was never any indication that Lucere heard a word he was saying, but Frank persisted, hoping to reach the battered and broken man.

Hell, he didn't know if they'd ever get out of here. He didn't even know why they were still here. Why hadn't they been released with the others? He had heard on Radio Hanoi that the war was over and a peace agreement signed. He heard the guards' radio every night. They had fought the Chinese, stopped the invasion; they were fighting in Cambodia. But there was nothing about any negotiations with the United States over POWs. Christ! Had they been forgotten? Did anyone know they were still alive? There had been demands for war reparations by the new Vietnamese government. Maybe that was it. We were their ace in the hole. This subcamp in the middle of nowhere was the perfect place to keep us out of sight of foreign visitors. It was just like these sneaky little bastards to hold back.

He wondered if the letter he had given Caang would get through; if Betty wasn't better off thinking he was dead—if his daughters would remember him. How the hell could they? Lisa was only seven and Karen nine when he last saw them on the R&R leave in Hawaii just before his last mission, and that had been eleven years ago. Eleven years! There were times he found it hard to believe he had lasted that long.

Caang and Truu sat on the grassy strip separating the stream from the jungle, eating their noon ration of cold soggy rice—the same rice cooked that morning and carried in a food pouch to the work area.

Frank climbed up the slippery stream bank and sat next to them, concentrating on unscrewing a leech from his forearm.

"Got the bastard. Head and all." He let the bite bleed for a minute, to cleanse it, before trying to stem the flow of blood. The insidious creatures secreted an anticoagulant when they affixed themselves to a host, and some of the men bled for hours after the leeches were removed. Frank usually clotted in a few minutes.

"When do you want to make your move?" he asked Caang.

"Now," Caang replied.

"Brieng not here," Truu added, referring to the spirits of violent death who reside in the sky. "Only good spirits here. They help us."

Detimore suppressed a smile, recalling his first encounter with the Montagnards' religious beliefs. The Rhade were a deeply religious tribe. Animist, like all Montagnards, they believed that good and evil spirits of their ancestors inhabited both animate and inanimate objects: rocks, trees, and streams among their favorite dwelling places. The Rhade lived in constant interaction with these animistic spirits, believing they were surrounded by them.

During his first visit to a Montagnard village, Frank had offended the village chief by inadvertently sitting on a large rock outside their longhouse. The most he could interpret from the wrinkled old man's rapid-fire, sputtering ire, was that he had sat on his grandmother.

Jack Callahan, the Commanding Officer of the A-Team, suggested a sacrificial pig might be in order to appease the angered spirit, and the old chief enthusiastically agreed—

30

upping the ante to two pigs. The next day Callahan and Frank delivered the pigs, giving the sacred rock a wide berth.

"Get ready," Frank said now as he glanced in the direction of the guards. All six of them were sitting twenty or thirty feet away, eating and chattering, occasionally looking over at the prisoners along the stream bank.

"As soon as I have their attention," he said to Caang, "take off. I'm not going to be able to distract them for long."

"I understand," Caang said. Truu nodded in agreement.

Just as Frank was about to get up, Harry Cambell came over and knelt beside him, a pained expression on his face.

"Help me get these slimy bloodsuckers off," he said, turning his back to Detimore, revealing three blood-bloated leeches between his shoulder blades.

"Not now," Frank snapped, feeling the adrenaline rising for the task before him.

"Come on, Frank," Cambell pleaded.

Detimore signaled to Donahue to join them. "Get those leeches off Harry's back," he told him.

"Lieutenant!" Cambell hissed through clenched teeth, "I'm a goddamn lieutenant, and he's a corporal. I'm not 'Harry' to him."

"Will you stop whining, *Lieutenant,* " Frank said, regretting his words as soon as he spoke them.

Donahue nodded his understanding to Detimore and knelt behind Campbell. "I'll get 'em, Lieutenant," he said evenly. "Nasty little bastards, aren't they?"

Frank stood and walked slowly toward the guards, stopping to pick up a sturdy four-foot length of bamboo. He continued walking along the edge of the jungle until he was within ten feet of where they sat, then turning to face

31

the thick tangle of underbrush and vines, he began yelling and beating the ground with the bamboo club.

"Cobra!" he screamed convincingly enough to startle the other prisoners to their feet. "Cobra! Cobra!" He pointed fiercely at the ground as the guards, at first not certain of the reason for the strange behavior, remained sitting, then jumped up and ran to where he was standing when Frank began bellowing the Vietnamese name for the dreaded, deadly snake.

"There! There!" he yelled, pointing to a spot a few feet into the jungle.

Three of the guards opened up on the spot with AK-47s, emptying their magazines into the ground.

When the shooting stopped, the guards stood at the very edge of the jungle and stared intently into the dense underbrush, straining to locate their prey, but unwilling to set foot in the suspected area.

Frank poked around with the stick. "I think I see it," he said. "You got it. It's dead."

Two of the "Saigon Cowboys" who had fired at the nonexistent snake craned their necks to get a closer look, but still kept their distance from the knee-deep tangle of vines. They smiled to each other, then turned to the other guards, confirming their kill.

Frank looked at the prisoners standing along the stream bank. Caang and Truu were nowhere in sight.

Donahue, who had understood what was happening when he saw the two Montagnards bolt for the jungle when the shooting started, winked at Detimore, and smiled.

At the end of the workday the guards assembled the prisoners in a column of twos for the two-mile march back to the compound. Frank was not surprised that Caang and

Truu had not yet been missed. The guards were inadequately trained and poorly motivated, and, he suspected, not very bright—the dregs of the Vietnamese Army.

Harry Cambell fidgeted behind Detimore, his head on a swivel, watching the new guard take the count for the third time.

"Something's wrong, Frank. Somebody is missing."

"I know," Frank replied.

Another guard, the one in charge of the detail, counted the men again, a worried look on his face as he reached the end of the column. He shouted instructions to his men who began shoving and prodding the prisoners into single file.

Donahue chuckled to himself. He nudged Frank. "Do you believe these clowns? Boy, are they gonna be in the middle of a shit storm when they get back."

"So will I," Frank said, sobering Donahue's mood. "It won't take Bad Eye long to put it all together."

This time two men made the count, one on each side of the row. Worried looks now turned to angry ones. More shouting, and two men ran back to the bridge, looking up and down the stream. Then to the edge of the jungle where the trees had been cut down. Finally, resignation and more angry shouting.

"Go! Go! Go!" the guards shrieked, jabbing the weary prisoners into double time along the narrow, deeply rutted road.

The sound of Bad Eye screaming hysterically at the senior guard carried throughout the camp. One after the other the guards on the work detail had gone into the camp commander's hut to be questioned and assaulted with verbal abuse and an occasional slap.

33

The prisoners had been locked in their cages upon returning to the camp and were denied their evening meal. Frank watched as Latrine Lips, the camp adjutant, came out of the commander's hut. The nickname, credited to Donahue, was appropriate. Latrine Lips prided himself on his extensive vocabulary of American profanities—learned while a bartender in Saigon during the war. He was an ugly little rodent of a man, inherently mean, and given to fanatical rages. His hatred of Americans was total.

He was responsible for most of the beatings inflicted on the prisoners. Any minor infraction of the rules—not responding quickly enough to a command, or not showing the proper respect to a guard—brought a flurry of kicks and punches accompanied by a steady stream of foul invective.

Donahue knew him well. "Don't worry, Top," Donahue had assured Frank when he had shown concern for him after a particularly brutal and prolonged beating, for "accidentally" pissing on Latrine Lips' boots. "I've had nuns hit me harder than that."

Frank had given up trying to convince the tough Marine that adopting a more compliant form of behavior would make his life a lot easier, not to mention longer. It was Donahue's way of coping. The hard way, but Donahue's way.

Latrine Lips shouted at two guards standing near the hut and pointed in the direction of Frank's cage.

Frank steeled himself for what he knew was to come.

"Sit," Bad Eye commanded.

Latrine Lips lost no time in shoving Detimore onto the small wooden stool in front of the camp commander's desk.

34

The short, muscular man stared hard at the prisoner before him, his left eye bright and wide with anger, his right eye drooped, cloudy and unfocused.

"You helped the *moi* escape. Yes?"

"No," Frank replied.

"Yes," Bad Eye repeated. "You draw guards away for them."

"No. There was a cobra. Your men saw it. They killed it."

"No cobra. Guards are fools. They see nothing. You helped the *moi* escape. Confess."

Frank shook his head. "I didn't help anybody escape."

"Motherfucker you confess!" Latrine Lips screamed, delivering a roundhouse punch to the side of Frank's head, knocking him sprawling onto the floor.

"Sonofabitch up on stool!"

As Frank got to his knees, a solid kick to his ribs knocked him down again.

Back on the stool, he stared blankly at Bad Eye, who glared back. Frank knew that were he to confess or not he was in for a rough night and he was determined to hold out as long as possible. From previous sessions during the early years of his captivity, he had learned that the beating and torture continued until they were satisfied, whether you gave them anything or not. If he confessed too soon, they would continue to beat him for what he had done; if he confessed later, they would beat him for not confessing sooner. They didn't want a confession, they wanted to punish him and humiliate him before the other prisoners.

Bad Eye knew how to apply torture effectively. He had done his apprenticeship in the North Vietnamese prisons during the war. Since the war ended there hadn't been much need for his gruesome skills, but when the opportunity presented itself, he relished it.

Detimore had not been tortured since his last escape attempt when he had knocked a guard unconscious, but he well remembered the merciless beatings and the pain.

Bad Eye signaled to two guards standing at the entrance to the hut. One of them was the new man, a smile fixed firmly in place. "Remove the prisoner's clothes," he told them.

"Stand! Sonofabitch!" Latrine Lips shouted, grabbing a handful of Frank's hair and jerking him to his feet.

The two guards ripped off the black pajama uniform, shoving Frank back down onto the stool.

One of the guards handed the camp commander the small notebook and pencil that had dropped out of the pocket of Detimore's shirt.

The notebooks were one of the few personal items allowed the prisoners. They were holdovers from their early years of captivity when they were lectured by political cadres of the Viet Cong, and expected to take notes. The attempts at conversion to the cause ended with the war, but every six months they still received a new notebook and four pencils. The men used them to combat boredom and for mental exercises. In one of his notebooks, Frank had composed an extensive Vietnamese–English dictionary with phonetic spellings which was circulated among the prisoners and kept well hidden.

Bad Eye opened the notebook and flipped through the pages filled with detailed drawings of a lakeside house Detimore hoped to build when he got home. A neatly folded letter wrapped in a piece of clear plastic dropped out as he reached the middle of the notebook. He unwrapped it and began reading the worn, dirty, water-stained three-page letter.

It was the only letter Frank had been given in his eleven years of captivity. It was from Betty, his wife, and he treasured it. He had read it thousands of times in the past eight years. It was his strength and salvation, his port in storm. The only beauty in his ugly world.

He knew it by heart. *I'd know if you were not alive, my darling, and I know God will watch over you and bring you home to me soon.*

Frank sat on the edge of the stool, trying to control himself, not wanting to reveal its importance to him. *You fill my thoughts and dreams as you filled my life.*

The commander finished reading the precious letter and handed it to Latrine Lips, grinning at the shaken man before him.

Frank tried, but could not take his eyes off the letter. Dear God, please don't let them take it. *I love you, Frank. I've always loved you and I always will.*

"From fucking wife. At home in bed with new man sucking cock."

Frank shook with rage. "You slimy maggot."

Latrine Lips began tearing the letter into small pieces.

Frank exploded. His first punch caught the startled man in the mouth, the second drove a thumb deep into his eye socket. Frank spun around and grabbed the stool, throwing it at Bad Eye, striking him in the head and opening a large gash across his forehead. He dived to the floor, gathering the pieces of the letter.

The new guard, regaining his composure, kicked Frank in the face while the other one pounded his head with his fists.

"Stop!" Bad Eye commanded.

The two men broke off their attack and backed away from the dazed man at their feet.

Latrine Lips got up slowly, a small trickle of blood coming from the corner of his left eye. Grabbing one of the guard's weapons, he placed the barrel against Detimore's head.

"No," Bad Eye said.

Latrine Lips hesitated, but kept the barrel in place.

"Do not kill him!" the commander ordered his incensed adjutant. "Put him back on the stool."

Latrine Lips threw the weapon across the hut and pulled Detimore to a kneeling position by his hair. The new guard helped sit him on the stool.

Bad Eye dabbed a cloth at his forehead, then tied it over the wound. "You are very foolish, Detimore. Very foolish," he said calmly.

Frank leaned forward on the stool, still groggy, and spit a mouthful of bloody saliva into Bad Eye's shocked face.

The guards attacked with a fury, raining punches and kicks on him from all directions.

When Frank regained consciousness, he found himself propped in a corner of the hut with Bad Eye standing over him handing him a cup of water. When he had finished drinking, the two guards threw him forward onto his stomach. One of them kept a foot in the middle of his back, while the other pulled his hands behind his back and clamped handcuffs on him, with the tops of his wrists together.

At Bad Eye's command, Latrine Lips tightened the special torture cuffs to the point where they cut through skin and tissue. The pain was immediate and intense.

One of the guards handed Latrine Lips a length of thin, coarse rope that he began wrapping around Detimore's arms from his elbows to his shoulders, pulling it ever tighter until it pressed against the bone. Turning him on his side, the new guard pushed on Frank's shoulder while Latrine Lips tied his upper arms and elbows together.

The pain was excruciating. His arms and hands went numb in a few moments, but the pain throughout his body continued relentlessly. He thought his chest was being pulled apart and his shoulders torn from their sockets.

The two guards pulled him to his feet and sat him on the stool.

Frank was drenched with perspiration, his mouth dry, and his breathing shallow and irregular.

"Motherfucker! Confess! " Latrine Lips said.

Frank shook his head slowly.

Latrine Lips punched his face, again knocking him from the stool onto the floor where the guards attacked with more punches and kicks. With his arms tied, he could no longer cover up to protect himself, and the attack was far more devastating. He felt a few of his ribs crack and some of his teeth shatter. But he could no longer feel the blows, so overwhelming was the pain from the ropes and cuffs. He began to pass out, but each time he came close to doing so, Bad Eye would halt the beating until he was certain his victim was fully conscious.

"You confess now, sonofabitch."

Frank tried to answer and found that his voice was little more than a hoarse whisper. "No," he managed to say audibly.

This time Latrine Lips had the two guards hold Frank on the stool while he pounded his fists into his face. Ten, fifteen, twenty times. Detimore felt none of the blows. His face was totally insensate.

Bad Eye wanted to hear him scream—more precisely,

39

he wanted the other prisoners to hear him scream. Frank knew he wouldn't be able to hold out much longer. Soon the searing, unbearable pain would dictate to the mind.

The breaking point came a half hour later. The continued beatings following each refusal to confess had become ineffectual, but the pain in his shoulders and chest could no longer be controlled by the will. Frank began to scream—endless, horrifying inhuman screams.

"You helped the *moi* escape, yes?" Bad Eye shouted.

Frank nodded his head.

"Motherfucker speak!" Latrine Lips shrieked.

"Yes," Frank answered weakly.

Bad Eye instructed his adjutant to loosen the ropes enough to allow Detimore's elbows and upper arms to come a few inches apart.

Frank felt a sudden rush of relief, then the pain returned, less intense, to surge through his badly bruised body.

"You will rest for a few moments," Bad Eye said, holding a cup of water to Frank's split and swollen lips. "Then we will discuss your unfortunate behavior."

"Goddamn Frank. Goddamn him," Harry Cambell said. "He's got us all in trouble. Now we'll all get it. Just for two lousy Yards."

Donahue had listened to Cambell's self-centered whining throughout Detimore's torture and was angered by his lack of concern and compassion for a man who had proved to be their friend.

"Goddamn Green Beanies," Cambell said. "They never think before they act. Heroes; they all want to be heroes."

"Shut the fuck up, *Harry*, you sniveling piece of shit!"

"How dare you . . ."

Donahue turned to him, shoving him into a corner of the cage. The frightened lieutenant raised his arms to protect his face. Donahue shook his head in disgust and directed his attention to the two guards pulling Detimore from the camp commander's hut.

As Frank was dragged past Donahue's cage, he called out to the young Marine in a hoarse voice. "Take care of Lucere. Don't let him die."

"I'll take care of him, Top. Don't worry."

"Shut mouth!" the new guard screamed as he punched Detimore's face.

Donahue lost control. Latrine Lips was standing with his back only a few feet from the cage. Donahue moved quickly, reaching between the bamboo bars and pulling him against the cage, clamping a death grip on the frightened man's windpipe.

"Motherfucker, huh? I'll tell you who's a goddamn motherfucker, you slope son of a bitch! I'll kill you! I'll kill you!"

A guard rushed over and slammed a rifle butt between the bars into Donahue's face, breaking his nose and knocking him across the cage, unconscious.

"Help him, sweet Jesus," Hendricks shouted. "Help him in his hour of need."

Frank was nearly dehydrated from the hours of torture. His arms and hands were discolored to a purplish black and swollen to twice their normal size. He had never been subjected to such prolonged and brutal torture. He was afraid he was going insane, and he knew Bad Eye wasn't finished with him.

When they reached the area in front of Frank's cage, Latrine Lips threw him roughly to the ground and rolled him onto his stomach. At Bad Eye's command, he again tightened the ropes to the bone.

The pain immediately reached its former peak. This time Frank had no willpower or reserves to reach for. It was only a few moments before he was conquered by the electrifying pain.

Bad Eye threw the end of a thick rope over a branch of a tree, and handed the other end, attached to a large meat hook, to his adjutant.

Latrine Lips affixed the hook to the ropes binding Detimore's arms and signaled his readiness to Bad Eye who began pulling on the rope, hoisting the screaming, hysterical man off the ground. He tied the end of the rope to the top of Frank's cage, leaving the tortured man dangling a few feet from the ground.

Frank had never known such pain existed. It burned, it stretched, it stabbed, and it tore into every inch of his body. He prayed for unconsciousness, but it didn't come. His screams soon became silent rushes of air from a parched and burning throat.

Bad Eye spoke directly into his ear. "Perhaps by to-morrow morning your attitude will have improved, Master Sergeant Detimore. If not, we can have another discussion."

Frank was vaguely aware of the get-up gong and the shouting and shoving as the guards grouped the prisoners in front of his cage. The man dangling on the end of the rope didn't even remotely resemble the man they knew. His face was swollen beyond recognition and his body covered with ugly bruises. He was unable to open one of his eyes, puffed shut partly from the beatings and partly from a night exposed to voracious mosquitoes. His mouth was caked with dried blood and greenish-yellow pus oozed from beneath the handcuffs on his wrists.

Bad Eye walked slowly over to the assembled prisoners, with his adjutant at his heels. He smiled at the grim faces.

"I will not have escapes from my camp." He released the end of the rope, dropping Detimore to the ground with a thud, and ordered Latrine Lips to release the handcuffs and remove the ropes, revealing deep gashes in Frank's arms where the ropes had been.

"Get in cage," the new guard ordered.

Frank tried to get to his feet but found his legs too weak and his arms useless. He remembered from a past experience that it would be a few days before he had complete use of them again.

Donahue stepped forward to help him and was stopped by a rifle butt in his stomach.

"No help. Watch," the guard ordered.

Frank used his legs as best he could to push himself along the ground toward the cage, but collapsed after a few feet. He tried again and again, but only became weaker with each attempt.

Bad Eye instructed the guards to move him. Grabbing his shoulders, eliciting a piercing scream, they dragged him to the cage and threw him inside.

Latrine Lips reached in the cage and removed the rice mat, blanket, and mosquito netting. "Not need for few days, motherfucker."

The new guard clamped on the leg-irons before locking the cage.

Donahue sat at the side of the lean-to farthest from the guards. He had saved half of his morning rice ration and filled another bowl with water. When the guards were engaged in conversation, he moved quickly out of the cooking area and around to the rear of Detimore's cage, out of sight of the guards. He winced at the close-up view of the battered and bloodied man before him.

"Jesus, Top. You look like hell," he said softly.

Frank turned his head and squinted through one bleary eye. Donahue's nose was bent and swollen and both eyes were blackened. "You don't look so great yourself," he said, his voice weak and raspy. "What happened?" he asked, unaware of Donahue's attack on Latrine Lips.

"Nothin'." He decided not to tell Frank about Latrine Lips' threat of having a "discussion" with him that night. He would find out soon enough.

"How's Lucere?" Frank asked.

"Same as usual. I fed him. Took him to the latrine." He placed the two bowls within Detimore's reach, spilling half of the water as he tilted the bowl to get it through the bars. "I'll bring you some more tonight. You take it easy, huh?" With that, he disappeared around the side of the lean-to.

Frank lay motionless, staring blankly at the roof of the cage. He began shaking uncontrollably, and, almost imperceptibly, tears began to flow from beneath the swollen eyelids. He had to reach deeper than ever before to call up the grim determination that had kept him alive through eleven years of a degrading, inhuman hell.

The children say good-night to their Daddy and pray for him every night. Karen is holding you to your promise of teaching her to fly-fish and Lisa will settle for a ride in the canoe. Good night, my darling. I love you and miss you.

The rain came in a sudden, drenching downpour, beating noisily on the bark and leaves covering the roof of the cage. But Frank didn't hear it. He was in Maine, in a clearing surrounded by towering evergreens on the shore of Loon Stream where it emptied into the south end of Caucomgomoc Lake. He sat before a flickering campfire, his arm around Betty, her head on his shoulder while the children's laughter carried out across the lake as they made hand shadows on the side of the tent from the light of a Coleman lantern.

2

Lieutenant General Maxwell Roberts rose from his desk chair and escorted Betty Detimore to the door of his office. A deep frown creased the brow of the tall, burly man as he clasped both her hands in his.

"I'm sorry, Mrs. Detimore. I only wish there was something I could do." The sentiment was honest and heartfelt, but the official line he had given her was not.

"This letter *is* from my husband, General. It is not a forgery or a prank."

The general nodded solemnly and opened the door. "I'll look into it, but I must tell you that we've been completely unsuccessful at verifying any of these reports."

"This is not a report, General. This is a letter from my husband, telling me he is alive and where he is. He needs your help. You owe him that. This country owes him that."

"I'll do what I can, Mrs. Detimore," he said, avoiding

the pain and desperation in her eyes. "We'll contact you if there are any developments."

He closed the door behind her and returned to his desk, staring hard at the young captain seated in an easy chair by the window.

"Goddamnit, Jacobs, I hate this. I can feel the bile rising in me every time I have to lie to these people." He flipped through the file on Frank Detimore, then slammed the folder shut. "SOG," he said. "One hell of an outfit."

"I'm sorry, General," Jacobs said. "I'm not familiar with it."

The general looked up, remembering that his young aide had graduated from West Point the year after the war ended. "No. You wouldn't be. Most of their operations are still classified top secret."

Jacobs sat silently, hoping the general would continue, knowing better than to press him for information.

Removing a cigar from the humidor on his desk, the general held it in the flame of a scratched and dented Zippo lighter emblazoned with the crest of the 101st Airborne—the unit with which he had served in World War II, winning the Distinguished Service Cross during the Battle of the Bulge.

"By definition it was a Joint Unconventional Warfare Task Force. It was designated MACV/SOG: Military Assistance Command Vietnam/Special Operations Group. Later on that was toned down to throw off the media boys, and it was referred to as Studies and Observations Group."

"Then it wasn't strictly an Army unit?" Jacobs asked, sensing that the general was in a mood to talk.

"No. For the most part it was made up of Green Berets and indigenous personnel: Montagnards, Nungs, Cambodians, and ARVN. But the Marines' Force Recon and the Navy SEALS and Air Force flight crews had a part in some of the operations. Hell, there were even CIA agents attached to it, running some of their own operations into North Vietnam.''

''What sort of operations did they run, sir?''

''Anything covert. You name it. Subversion, sabotage, psyops, prisoner snatches, recon, direct action, and things you're better off not knowing about.''

''Were most of them cross-border operations?''

The general nodded, blowing a puff of aromatic smoke toward the ceiling. ''Laos . . . Cambodia . . . North Vietnam . . . China . . . they went everywhere. A lot of brave, dedicated men who'll never get credit for what they did. Not in their lifetimes anyway. The most highly trained men in Vietnam, if not in the history of the United States military.''

''I don't recall seeing any statistics for SOG units in our casualty figures, or on our MIA or POW lists.''

''And with good reason,'' the general said, ''SOG had tremendous casualties, especially in the Command and Control units. Sometimes as high as two hundred percent. But because of their top-secret classification they hid their KIAs, MIAs, and suspected POWs in with the statistics of conventional units in other locations, to avoid any inquiries by the press. That practice is still causing problems today. SOG troops that were wounded and returned home can't get help from the Veterans Administration because they can't document the details of the action in which they were wounded.''

''Which unit was Detimore with?''

''CCS,'' the general said, rekindling his cigar. ''Command and Control South out of Ban me Thuot. Their area of operations was Cambodia . . . direct action and strategic recon patrols.''

''Any after-action report on the mission on which he was captured?''

''Still classified top secret. He was officially reported MIA after an attack on a Forward Operational Base in South Vietnam . . . and later changed to KIA. He was actually on a mission into the Parrot's Beak region of Cambodia.''

''What about the other men listed in the letter?'' Jacobs asked. ''We don't show any of them as POWs or MIAs.''

''They're probably listed as KIAs. You'll have to run a check with every branch of the service.''

''How many does that make, sir? That we're certain of?''

''With these eight . . . at least forty-two. Counting the ones in Laos. All alive beyond any reasonable doubt.''

''Do you think the Defense Intelligence Agency knows about the camp?

''They probably have satellite photos of it.''

''Then with this kind of hard intelligence, they might go in after them.''

The general shook his head. ''We're talking about Vietnam, Captain. The lard-ass liberals up on the Hill will scream bloody murder if we set one foot inside that country. The President doesn't need that kind of heat. Not now.''

''The CIA could send in an indigenous team. As they did in Laos last year.''

The general grunted. "They should have known better. We learned during the war that you can't depend on any intelligence from a totally indigenous recon team. You've got to send some 'round eyes' in with them. And that, Jacobs, is not politically feasible. One captured American is an international incident."

"Maybe the Joint Casualty Resolution people can put some heat on the Vietnamese government."

"Hell, those bastards in Hanoi are practiced inveterate liars. They'll do what they usually do: send us some Oriental remains and tell us they are from recently discovered American graves."

The general turned and looked wistfully at the collection of photographs on the wall behind his desk, focusing on an informal snapshot of himself and the surviving members of his company on VE Day. "If they'd give us some slack, we could bring those duplicitous sons of bitches to heel in one hell of a hurry."

Jacobs nodded in agreement, though unsure that the general's solution was the right one. "Then there's nothing we can do, sir?"

"Sure. We can buy them back. Would you like to take that proposal to Congress?"

Jacobs shook his head. "Maybe with the recent media coverage it will become a strong enough issue that they'll be forced into direct action."

"Don't count on it."

"I suppose we'll be hearing from the civilian MIA-POW organizations."

"That you can count on. They've got their own intelligence net, and they aren't fooled for one second by the Vietnamese bullshit and our smoke screen."

The general handed Jacobs the file folder and his notes

from the meeting. "Take this down to DIA and brief them on what we know," he said. "Mrs. Detimore is a determined woman; they'll probably want to keep an eye on her. Goddamn, I hate this!"

3

Betty Detimore stopped briefly at the Continental Inn to drop off her luggage, then walked the short distance to the Center at the bottom of Aspen Mountain. She looked out of place in her smartly tailored gray tweed suit and belted black cashmere coat amid the brightly colored ski clothing of the milling crowd.

Crossing the sundeck, she stepped onto the soft snow at the bottom of the slope and angled her way through the long double row of skiers waiting for the lift to take them for their final run of the day. She approached a short, deeply tanned man standing in front of the ski school building, and glanced at the name tag on his parka.

"Excuse me, Mr. Johnson. Can you tell me where I might find John Callahan?"

"Jack?" the man said, with an appraising look at the handsome, willowy woman before him. "Sure." He looked at his watch; it was three o'clock. "He should be down off the mountain in about half an hour."

He narrowed his eyes and squinted in the direction of the crowded sundeck. "See that big black and rust dog in the corner near the snack bar?"

Betty looked where he was pointing, recognizing the dog as a Rottweiler. "Yes."

"That's Boomer, Jack's dog. When Jack reaches the top of this slope, Boomer will leave the sundeck and come over and sit just about where we're standing now."

Betty looked up to the top of Little Nell. The skiers didn't appear much larger than exclamation points, gliding and bobbing in the distance.

The ski instructor smiled, anticipating her question. "Don't ask me how he knows. He just knows. When Jack gets near the bottom, Boomer will run partway up the slope and jump all over him. Does it every day."

Betty thanked him, grateful for the information. She wasn't certain she could easily recognize Callahan; it had been twelve years. She returned to the sundeck and found a seat in view of the dog. He was lying quietly in a sunny spot, declaratively alone, watching the mountain and ignoring attempts at friendliness by an assortment of intrusive dog lovers.

She smiled at the scene above her. A panorama of bright blue sky and sparkling snowcapped peaks and ski runs winding and plummeting through a forest of dark green spruce. The mountain was as she remembered it. The town and the people were not. A scuffle broke out in the lift line. Someone had attempted to jump the line. A chorus of angry shouts was followed by a brief shoving bout until cooler heads prevailed and the lift operator ordered a glassy-eyed young man to the end of the line.

Betty had last been in Aspen in 1959—a skiing trip with sorority sisters over spring break. The town was then less than a third its present size, the people friendly, courteous, and interesting, and the lift lines virtually nonexistent.

Over the past twenty years all of the charm and appeal had vanished. She was amazed at the number of restaurants and shops—some rivaling, a few surpassing, anything to be found on Fifth Avenue or Rodeo Drive.

The thin brown cloud of pollution that lingered over the town, trapped in the sheltered valley by the towering mountains, affirmed the old mining community's arrival into the 1980s, just as the faceless, unisex herd of sheepskin coats and cowboy hats—punctuated by an occasional full-length mink—announced the death of individuality and character.

The last slanting rays of afternoon sun began to leave the lower slopes, and Betty looked on in amusement as the less talented skiers, who seemed to be in the majority, had great difficulty adjusting to the flat light. The dips and moguls on the slope were creating a comical ballet, with four-letter-word accompaniment, of flailing arms and legs, and graceless flops and tumbles.

Those who had some talent for the sport had a problem avoiding those who didn't—the source of more foul oaths and threatening gestures. If the clumsy skiers did with their mothers what they were being accused of by those they had caused to fall, Betty mused, the next generation should be an interesting crop.

The situation could only deteriorate as more and more of the thousands of skiers finished their day and descended from the top of the mountain.

The activity on the sundeck was intensifying and the din of strained conversation, the clatter of skis, and the thump of heavy boots was reaching deafening proportions. The peacocks were on parade, primping and posturing, and jostling for position in the urgent quest for the night's companion.

"Hi. Like some hot wine?"

Betty turned to face a balding, sunburned middle-aged man who had seated himself beside her. Her eyes focused on a thick smear of white cream that outlined his mouth and covered the bridge of his nose. "Excuse me?"

"Would you like some hot wine?" he repeated, offering her the steaming white Styrofoam cup in his hand.

"Oh. No, thank you."

He shifted his position to straddle the bench and moved closer to her. "Listen, I don't usually talk to strangers," he said with a smile and a wink, "but in your case I just had to·make an exception."

"That's very flattering." She smiled weakly and stared at the array of gold chains and ornaments worn outside his turtleneck. A small gold spoon caught her eye.

"My friends and I have this supergreat house for the week up on Red Mountain, and we're having a big party tonight. How would you like to join us?"

"Thank you, no. I have other plans."

"Cancel them. This isn't going to be any wine and fondue social gathering. We have a giant Jacuzzi that'll seat twenty people easy, and we got some good stuff. It'll be wild. You can name your pleasure, if you know what I mean."

Betty bristled at the crude remark, but held her temper. The man hadn't even introduced himself, or asked her name, and he was suggesting they spend an intimate evening together. She smiled to herself at the thought of what her oldest daughter would say to him. Karen was poised and self-assured beyond her twenty years.

"I've told you, I have plans," she said with an edge to her voice.

"Whatever they are, they can't possibly compete with what I've got on my agenda. Fantasy time, honey. What do you say?"

She stared flatly at the offensive man, his face set in a wide grin. There was no doubt in her mind that he had noticed her wedding ring, and considered it of no consequence. Judging that any further courtesy extended would be misunderstood, she decided, against her nature, to put an abrupt end to their conversation.

"I'm waiting for someone, and I really prefer to do so alone. So I think it might be best if you went and found someone else to offend."

"Hey, honey. Don't get so uptight. No big deal, but you don't know what you're missing."

Betty smiled coldly. "Fortunately you're right."

It had been twelve years since she had seen her husband; twelve years of steely determination and extraordinary will-power, and despite countless proposals and a few temptations, she had remained faithful to him. She considered, but rejected, telling the man beside her that if she were inclined to cheat on her husband it wouldn't be with a coke-snorting boor who needed drugs—and by his appearance, probably mechanical devices—to satisfy a woman.

"See you around," he said, getting up and moving off through the crush of people now standing shoulder to shoulder.

Betty ignored the parting remark. Out of the corner of her eye she saw the Rottweiler move. He stood alert, furrowing the brow of his broad, handsome head, his ears pricked up and forward.

Moving to the deck railing, the dog stared intently at the

56

top of the ski run. He shook off a stray hand that reached to pet him, and cocked his head. Certain of what he saw, he leaped over the railing with an effortless thrust from his powerful hindquarters, and trotted over to the ski school building where he sat and continued his vigil.

Betty went to the railing and looked up at the mountain. There were at least two hundred skiers on the broad, rolling slope. And as they reached the bottom they were constantly being replenished from a variety of feeder runs leading onto the top of the main slope. She looked for ski school parkas and counted seven on the lower section. Boomer's alert, intelligent eyes were trained on the upper half.

A few moments later she saw the focus of the dog's attention, and understood how he identified his master.

There was no mistaking the expertise of the lithe and agile man. His rhythm and balance were undisturbed by anything in his path, and his fluid, graceful movement was distinguishable from a great distance.

Boomer emitted a high-pitched whine and began pounding his front paws in the snow. Suddenly he stood, tucked his hindquarters, and lunged forward, charging up the slope.

Betty saw a broad smile flash beneath the mirrored sunglasses as Callahan prepared for what was to come. He checked his speed, then carved a smooth turn to align himself properly, and leaned slightly forward to keep his balance while absorbing the force of the impact.

Boomer leaped high, and Jack caught the 130-pound animal in midair, cradling him in his arms as he skied to the bottom of the slope. Back on the ground, the dog began a series of exuberant leaps and twirls.

Callahan ruffled his thick coat and knelt to hug him. "Hey, Boomer old buddy. You miss me?"

Betty approached and stood quietly watching for a few moments. The tanned, ruggedly handsome face of the tall, broad-shouldered man had matured, but changed little since she had last seen him.

"Hello, Jack."

Callahan glanced up, then slowly stood and raised his sunglasses, perching them on top of his head. He stared blankly for a long moment, then his eyes brightened with a warm smile.

"Betty. How are you?" He stepped forward and embraced her, then held her at arm's length. There were strands of gray in her light brown hair, and a few more lines around her soft brown eyes than he remembered, but she was still an attractive, alluring woman. Age had only softened her beauty. "You look great."

His thoughts were filled with a rush of memories, of the time he had spent with her and Frank. In 1968 at Fort Bragg, before they went to Vietnam. It was his first tour and Frank's third. And he remembered vividly his visit to New Orleans when he returned from Vietnam; the lost and helpless look about her, and the tears as he told her the details of the mission they had been on, and how Frank had saved his life and the lives of others with them. It had been difficult for him to face her. And even now, as it all rushed back to him, he still felt a twinge of guilt that he had not been able to help Frank. She hadn't accepted the probability of his death. The Army had listed him as missing in action, but Hanoi had not released his name as a prisoner of war, and some of the men on the mission had seen his position overrun after being pounded by mortar rounds. "I would know if Frank were dead," she had said.

"God, it's been . . . twelve years," Jack said.

Betty nodded. "The last I heard, you were in Rhodesia. But when I called the Special Forces Association in Fayetteville, they told me you were here, teaching skiing."

"Seven years now. How are the children?"

Betty smiled. "The *children?* Lisa is a freshman at L.S.U. and Karen is in her junior year at Tulane. And you? Still a bachelor?"

"Yeah. I think I'm beyond hope. Boomer's the only one who can stand to live with me. Did you just get in?"

"About an hour ago."

"I didn't know you were a skier."

"I used to be, but that's not why I'm here. Something very important has come up and I need desperately to talk to you. I hope I haven't caught you at a bad time."

"No. Absolutely not. I'm finished for the day. Come on, we'll have a drink."

Jack took her arm as they walked across the bottom of the slope toward the Tippler Inn. He put Boomer on a "down stay" near the entrance and they went inside to a table in a quiet corner of the bar.

Betty waited until their drinks were served and the waitress had left, then reached over and squeezed Jack's hand.

"Frank is alive."

Callahan's first reaction was one of complete surprise, but then remembering that they had been through this before, he looked at her with an expression of sadness and patience.

"Betty, it's been twelve . . ."

"No, Jack. He really is alive!" She took an envelope from her purse and handed it to him.

He removed the heavily creased and stained pages from the envelope and began reading, his face expressionless until he saw the map that was enclosed with the letter. He reread the letter and studied the small, crudely drawn map. One landmark in particular held his attention.

"Jesus, Betty! I know this area. It's no more than ten or eleven miles from our old camp. We ran patrols and ambushes all through here." He held Betty's gaze for a long moment, stunned by what he had just read. "How long have you had this? Where did you get it?"

"Last week. A Canadian journalist came to see me in New Orleans. He had been in Vietnam with a group of journalists to whom the Vietnamese were giving a tour of war-ravaged areas, building their case for war reparations claims. One night in Hue, on the way back to his hotel, he was approached by a man who put this envelope in his hand, asked him to deliver it, and disappeared down an alley. That was seven months ago. The journalist just got back last week and brought it to me. Unopened. He refused any payment for what he had done, and only asked that if there was a story in it, I give him an exclusive." Betty squeezed his hand again and shook it. "Frank was alive and well seven months ago, Jack!"

"Have you told the Army?"

Betty nodded and lowered her eyes.

"What action are they taking?"

"None. The official position is that there is no verifiable evidence of American POWs being held in Vietnam."

"Who did you talk to?"

"Everyone who would listen. Including a three-star general at the Pentagon. He suggested the letter was merely a cruel hoax. He refused to give it any credibility."

A sobering thought crossed Jack's mind. "Are you certain it's from Frank?"

"Absolutely certain." She pointed to a sentence near the bottom of the second page.

Jack read it. " 'Say hello to *tiny'?* Who's tiny?"

Betty blushed and smiled. "It's Frank's way of authenticating the letter. I have one breast that is smaller than the other. He used to tease me about it—affectionately. He named it 'tiny.' "

"What did the general say when you told him that?"

"He said Frank could have told any number of people about it. Jack, I know Frank. I know him better than anyone does. He put that in the letter to assure me that he had written it. Believe me!"

"I do. Frank and I had a lot of long conversations: on patrol, on ambushes, in the team house. We spent the better part of three years together and he never mentioned it to me. It wasn't his nature to disclose strictly personal things like that."

"Thank you. That's the first positive thing anyone has said to me since this happened."

"He lists seven other POWs who are in that camp with him. Have you contacted any of their families?"

"The Defense Department wouldn't give me any information on them. They said they didn't want me raising false hopes in people who had suffered enough. Frank only gives their names. I don't have any idea where they are from. I contacted the civilian POW-MIA organizations, but the names weren't on any of their lists. They may be listed as 'killed in action.' I haven't had time to check further."

"Can the civilian organizations bring any pressure to bear on the Defense Department?"

"They've been trying for years. Regardless of the evidence they present, and there has been a great deal, everything from live sightings to reports from reliable sources, the government hasn't done much more than request further information from Hanoi. And Hanoi's answer is always the same—they are not holding any more American prisoners. The Defense Department has begun to investigate some of the reports, but there hasn't been any direct action.

"What about former POWs? You might get some support from them."

"No. I doubt it. When they were returned in 1973, the Defense Department ordered them not to discuss any of the men they knew were left behind. Most of them hold to that, at least the ones who are still in the service. Shortly after they were brought home I managed to contact a few of them who agreed to talk to me off the record. One gave me the only shred of hope, beyond my own intuitive belief, that has kept me going all these years. He remembered a man named Frank who was a Green Beret in the prison he was in. He wasn't sure of his last name. He never saw him, but did communicate with him through the prisoners' tap code. He was vague about it; he was being subjected to torture sessions at the time and his memory was hazy. But it was all the encouragement I needed."

"What's Frank's official status with the Defense Department now?"

"He was carried as MIA until 1978, then declared 'presumed dead.' They awarded him the Congressional Medal of Honor—posthumously."

"I didn't know that. He deserved it." Jack leaned back in his chair and tossed down what remained of his bourbon. Politics, he thought. The rotten sons of bitches were still playing politics with men's lives. He understood the mechanics of the situation. There were enough firsthand sightings from refugees and others to verify the fact of Americans still being held by the Vietnamese. But the price was too high. No one wanted to back up Nixon's war-reparations guarantee. We hand out billions every year to liars and sneaks who take our money and spit on our flag. And those who put their lives on the line, the believers, the dues payers, end up with the shitty end of the stick. So what else is new?

He stared thoughtfully at Betty and slowly shook his head. "What's your next step?"

"That's what brought me here. My father is a wealthy man, Jack. I'm his only child and he loves me dearly. He has suffered through this with me, and he wants Frank home. He believes there is only one thing we can do: hire professional soldiers, mercenaries, to go in and get Frank."

She studied Jack's face for his reaction. There was none. "He's prepared to provide the funds necessary to organize and equip a rescue team, and to pay each man fifty thousand dollars."

Jack nodded and sat quietly.

"I came here for your help and advice. I thought you might be able to put us in touch with the right people."

"There are a lot of people who will take your money, but not many who can do the job."

"I understand they have their own organization. Even their own magazine."

"They do. Unfortunately the men who run that magazine aren't for hire. If Bull Simons were still alive I'd know where to send you."

"Can you give me a name? Someone you would recommend?"

Jack signaled the waitress for two more drinks. "The problem is, there are too many reckless and incompetent clowns with one year of combat in 'Nam trying to pass themselves off as professionals. The top-notch mercenaries are seldom looking for work. They go from one war to another; they're usually in demand.''

Betty sat twisting her wedding ring, her hopes slowly diminishing. She fought back the tears that began to well in her eyes. ''Jack,'' she spoke softly, just above a whisper, ''if you would look into it for me I'd really appreciate it. I just don't know where to go from here.''

Jack nursed his drink, and sorted through the jumble of thoughts running through his mind. He glanced again at the map, then reread the portion of the letter where Frank described the camp, the location of a small army base ten miles away, and the number of guards.

He reached out to Betty and lightly brushed a single tear from her cheek. ''You leave this to me. I'll see what I can do.''

Betty removed a handkerchief from her purse and dried her eyes. ''Thank you, Jack. Frank really cared about you, you know.''

''I know. When are you going back to New Orleans?''

''I planned on leaving tomorrow morning.''

''Are you still at the same address?''

''No. We're living with my parents. My father believes in gathering the clan in times of crisis.'' She took out a note pad and wrote down the address and telephone number.

''Give me a week to see what I can come up with.''

Betty remembered something Frank had said about Callahan. How when he made up his mind that something had to be done, you could, if you looked closely, detect a cold spot in his eyes just beyond the surface. It stayed there until the task was completed. Frank had described it as a manifestation of superhuman determination and single-mindedness. Betty caught a glimpse of it now.

She asked, hesitantly, "Do you think it's possible . . . to get Frank out?"

"Yes. With the right men, proper planning, and a little luck." He picked up the papers from the table. "I'll need these. I'll take some notes from the letter and return it. I'll need to keep the map." He glanced at his watch. "It's almost six o'clock. Why don't I drop you off at the lodge and I'll go home and shower and change. We'll have dinner tonight. Talk over old times."

"That's the best offer I've had today, believe me." She told him about the man on the sundeck and Jack laughed, assuring her that she had met one of the more subtle ones.

The two men watching from across the street when Callahan and Betty Detimore came out of the Chart House restaurant waited until they had walked a short distance before following them to the Continental Inn where Callahan embraced Betty, kissed her on the cheek, and said good-night.

They waited by a corner of the lodge while she stood on the steps and waved to him as the Jeep Cherokee pulled away. She went partway up the steps, hesitated, and came back down, walking toward the center of town.

The shorter of the two men turned up the collar of his parka and shoved his hands deep in his pockets. "Jesus Christ. Where's she going now? It's too goddamn cold for this bullshit."

"I'll take it. You go into the lounge and warm up," his companion said. The sharp features of his angular, pockmarked face were pinched and drawn from the cold, dry air. "How long has it been since you called in to run the check on this Callahan?"

"Four . . . five hours."

"Call back. See what they have on him."

"Five bucks says he's a zero and she's here to get laid."

"We'll see. Check out her room while you're at it."

Luger shrugged deeper into his coat and started after Betty, his footsteps squeaking and crunching on the crusty snow. He wished he had drawn someone else as a partner. Thompson was beginning to get on his nerves.

The streets were still full of vacationing skiers, window-shopping and barhopping. Luger kept a casual pace, walking on the opposite side of the street, stopping when she stopped, observing her through the reflections in the shop-windows. After a slow tour of the malls, she headed back toward the lodge.

He found Thompson sitting where he had a view of the heated swimming pool, captivated by three attractive, well-proportioned girls in bikinis.

"What's up?" Thompson asked.

"Just an evening stroll. She's back in her room. You find anything?"

"Nothing."

"What about the call?"

Thompson grimaced. He removed some money from his pocket and counted out five one-dollar bills, handing them to Luger.

"What did they say?"

Thompson checked his notes. "Callahan is ex-Special Forces. Captain. Three years in 'Nam; four years Rhodesian Selous Scouts. Distinguished Service Cross, Bronze Star with two oak leaf clusters, three Purple Hearts."

"Some zero. Frank Detimore served with him?"

"He was Team Sergeant on Callahan's A-Team and they were both with MACV/SOG." He turned over the notepaper and added, "Oh, yeah. He was on the mission that got Detimore bagged."

Luger said, more to himself than Thompson, "Why do I have the feeling that I know where this is all going to lead?"

"Huh?"

"Nothing. Any instructions?"

Thompson nodded and began to speak.

Luger interrupted. "No, let me guess. When Betty Detimore heads back to New Orleans somebody down there will pick up the surveillance and we stay with Callahan, right?"

"You got it."

Boomer lay stretched across the king-size bed in Callahan's bedroom, his head and front paws hanging over the edge, watching with interest as Jack rummaged through the large storage closet on the far wall.

Callahan removed a heavy padded-leather training sleeve, a quick-release leash, and a thick leather collar from the top of the footlocker at the rear of the closet.

Boomer's head snapped up at the sight of the attack-training equipment. He leaped from the bed and sat obediently at Jack's side.

Callahan laughed. "No. No. You don't get to maul anybody tonight." He reached down and massaged the eager animal's thick neck. Boomer's off-leash attack work was his favorite recreation, but with the training completed, Jack only worked him once every two or three months. More frequent workouts made Boomer anticipatory and overly aggressive—a dangerous combination in a dog with the size and strength of a Rottweiler.

He pulled the footlocker out into the room and sat on the floor in front of it. He paused momentarily, recalling the combination of the lock, then opened the scarred and battered trunk. A memory-jolting musty odor greeted him as he raised the lid.

His dress uniform and beret lay on top, and beneath them two sets of faded and frayed tiger-striped camouflage fatigues. He took them out and placed them on the floor beside him. Allowing an urge, he put on the Green Beret and mashed it down on one side, then stood in front of the full-length mirror on the closet door and smiled when he noticed that he was standing with his weight on one hip in the self-confident stance that went with the territory.

"What do you think, Boomer?"

He returned to the trunk and sifted through the contents, taking out the low-slung western holster with the six-inch .357 magnum in it—a remnant from the days before the Army had disallowed personal weapons. He checked the pistol for rust and found it in good condition.

A Viet Cong flag reminded him of the ambush and the man he had killed to get it, and the painful arm wound he had suffered during the action. (He found himself rubbing the long fishbone scar on his left arm where a piece of metal now replaced the bone.) An assortment of brass bracelets from the Jeh tribe and a Sedang beaded necklace brought back the memory of the Montagnards and he shuddered at the thought of the god-awful concoction he had had to drink as part of the acceptance ceremony.

He pushed aside a layer of T-shirts and underwear and found what he was looking for at the bottom of the trunk: his old patrol maps. Taking them to the coffee table in the living room, he removed them from the plastic folders and spread them across the table. He got Frank's map from his coat pocket and placed it beside them. Putting another log on the fire, he sat down to study them. Boomer hopped onto the sofa and curled into a ball at his side.

He carefully checked the sketchy landmarks and terrain features on Frank's map against those on his patrol map. The river and the village were exactly where Frank had indicated. He searched his memory for the location of an area that was the hinge to what had been dominating his thoughts all through dinner. Folding the patrol map to the section in question, he traced his finger along a dotted line that indicated a jungle footpath. He paused and examined in detail the surrounding features of a plateau.

Yes. It was here, in this immediate area. He was certain of it—as certain as he could be after fourteen years, he reminded himself. If he could verify that what he remembered was where he remembered it to be, get some recent intelligence, the rudimentary plan that was beginning to crystallize in his mind would not only be conceivable, it would be a textbook infiltration, a classic Special Forces mission; what they had been trained for; what they did best—hit and run; hard and fast.

The telephone rang and retrieved him from the avalanche of thoughts he was rapidly sorting and arranging by priority. When he answered the phone and heard the irate female voice he remembered what earlier that evening he had reminded himself not to forget.

"Damn you, Jack. We were supposed to have dinner tonight. I waited until nine o'clock."

"I'm sorry, Cathy. Something important came up."

"You could have called."

"I know. I apologize. Forgive me?"

"What was so important?"

"An old friend."

"At least the first half of the description is honest."

"What is that supposed to mean?"

"I went out with my girl friends when you didn't show and I saw you at the Chart House with your 'old friend.' You don't take me to the Chart House."

Jack's temper flared. She had baited him. He despised insidiousness, and in the two months he had known Cathy he had seen signs of its being a basic part of her nature. "I'm busy now. I'll call you tomorrow."

"One of my girl friends saw you earlier today at the Tippler. How do you think that makes me look?"

"What the hell do I care how it looks? I'm telling you how it was. She's a friend who needed my help. Now this conversation is getting to the point where we're both going to say things we don't mean. I'll call you tomorrow."

"Bastard." There was a loud click as she slammed down the phone.

Jack had been considering breaking off with her. She was demanding and possessive, or maybe he was inattentive and inconsiderate and brought out the worst in her. Either way, it was only a matter of time. How the hell could he take someone seriously whose stated goal in life was a white Eldorado with white leather interior—and wire wheels, can't forget the wire wheels. There hadn't been anyone special since Paula, and at times he missed her more than he liked to admit. He had wanted to marry Paula. And they had lived together for a while until her need of the city and the love of her career as a journalist took her back to New York. He knew she was right. She was always right. It would never have lasted. He was content to live apart from a world he had learned to view

70

with a jaundiced eye, having seen and taken part in its hatreds and violence. He understood its inherent evils. She believed it redeemable, and wanted to be a part of it. Maybe some time away from each other might make a difference, she had said. But he knew it was over the day she left. He opened a drawer in a table beside the sofa, and shoved aside the unanswered letters that covered the photograph he had taken of her on a backpacking trip. The bold, inquisitive eyes looked up at him from a face of remarkable beauty set in a challenging and captivating half-smile.

He closed the drawer, shook off the distracting thoughts, and poured himself a glass of Jack Daniel's from the bottle he kept in a cabinet below the bookshelves. Slowly sipping the drink, he stared out the large plate-glass window that took up most of one wall of the living room. It had begun to snow; heavy, wet snow that clung to the naked aspens and rich green spruce in the grove of trees that separated his house from his neighbors'.

He turned to the cluster of framed citations, medals, and photographs on the wall beside the fireplace. A group of men he had fought beside in the Selous Scouts smiled out at him—all dead now. His old A-Team stood in front of the team house: eleven of the best men he had ever served with, six of them killed in action. And there was Frank: burly, steady, resourceful Frank. Special Forces Officer School had taught Jack a lot, but it had only scratched the surface compared to what he had learned from Frank Detimore. Frank had had all the right instincts and a wealth of knowledge on guerrilla warfare, plus years of combat experience.

Callahan studied the faces of the other living members of the team. Joe Galimore: a first-rate communications man and one tough trooper in combat. Rick Donatelli: an expert in light weapons and a master of hand-to-hand combat. Phil Houser: a medic's medic, brilliant, dedicated, and an expert knife fighter. And Stan Badowski—good old Smashy: the finest demolitions man he had ever seen or heard of. All senior sergeants in Vietnam. All hardened combat veterans—the best. They all had the training and experience necessary for what he had in mind. They could do it. Five highly trained men with the proper weapons and planning, with the element of surprise and quick, violent action, could decimate a company and disappear before the enemy knew what had hit them. Hell, they had done it before.

The location was isolated, and Frank's letter had said the guard detail was small. The army camp ten miles away could be a problem, but if the mission was planned and executed properly the team would be in and out before they knew the POW camp had been hit.

It had been twelve years since he had seen any of the men, but he was sure he could trace them through the Special Forces Association. He had no idea what paths they had chosen when they left the Forces, but he knew these men; he knew their sense of honor and loyalty. If it hadn't been for Frank, none of them would be alive—that would be their motivation. The fifty thousand dollars would make it possible for them to take a leave of absence from whatever they were doing. And then there were the primal elements; they all had loved adventure and danger and the opportunity to prove they were the best. The inner voices that had led them to the Forces when they were younger would still be a part of them now.

He would need a week to make the necessary contacts. Three weeks of conditioning and planning in Aspen. Two or three months would be better, but seven months had already passed since Frank had written the letter. They could do it in a month.

He poured another drink and sat on the sofa, his feet on the coffee table, and watched the fire. His life had meant little, he thought, since those days of commitment. But Vietnam and Rhodesia had stretched to the limits his ability to believe, to care. He had sickened of the thankless causes and the hypocrisy. Aspen was his refuge. The past seven years, if not rewarding and challenging, had at least been peaceful. Maybe part of the reason for the adrenaline rising in him now was a need to prove himself again, to deny the inexorable attrition on reflexes and skills perhaps left unused too long to be finely honed again. Some of the edge was gone, he knew, but he was equally certain that at thirty-six he was not yet ready for a pipe and slippers.

His experiences in Vietnam had cast a shadow over the rest of his life. They had taught him a great deal about himself, his strengths and his weaknesses. Probably more than he needed to know, more than most men ever knew about themselves. He had learned there were aspects of himself he didn't like, but being aware of them, he could now deal with them.

He had done his job well and so had the men he had fought with, but their contribution was never acknowledged by those in power. It had been a mistake, they finally said, and they rushed to get out; they ran for their political lives. Cheerleaders in the beginning, they hadn't the stomach or resolve to finish the fight. They seemed to be men to whom honor and integrity were abstractions to be used in campaign speeches. Point a finger. Fix the blame. Cut and run. And it ended in disgrace and dishonor. And now they didn't want to discuss it, and they didn't want to pick up the pieces, and they didn't give a damn about the Frank Detimores.

Well, he gave a damn. He understood and accepted the obligations and exigencies of friendship. He still believed in loyalty and honoring your word. It was his personal Bushido and he lived it and so had the other members of the team. They had had a Stygian bond, forged by what they had been through together. He had seen it in its purest form—valuing honor more than life—when they were together as an A-Team, and later on missions with SOG, when each of them had, with complete disregard for his personal safety, repeatedly done what was necessary to help his friends and comrades. That wasn't something you lost in twelve years, or twenty or fifty. It was always there at the core. It was what you were.

The snow was coming down more heavily now and had changed to a light, dry powder that swirled and drifted as the wind picked up. He heard a soft, high-pitched whine and glanced at Boomer who had moved from the sofa to a cool spot on the brick floor just off the edge of the area rug. He was hunting in his dreams, his legs twitching in pursuit of an elusive prey.

Jack filled his glass again. He was beginning to feel the effects of the warm, soothing liquid. How many had he had? Four? He usually limited himself to one a day, before turning in. And how many at dinner? Two . . . three? We can do it. We can pull it off; still have our stuff. Damn right.

Memories of Frank and the mission into Cambodia drifted in a dense, haunting fog through every corner of his mind, parting and lifting, revealing vestiges and vignettes, descending again, then parting. In his mind's eye he watched the events unfold, and sat motionless listening across a

dozen years to the sounds of battle and the cries of pain
. . . the hurried rush of footsteps and the rattle of death.

Cambodia—Parrot's Beak Region
April 1970

Callahan lay huddled on the ground. He stared blankly at
the bloodstained midsection of his camouflage fatigues.
Consciousness came and went and came again. The pain
grew more intense.

Houser, the team medic, had given him a shot of mor-
phine and as much blood expander as time allowed before
Donatelli opened up with the M60 machine gun on the
North Vietnamese point man who had closed on them.
Then they were up and running again.

"Come on, Jack," Frank Detimore said, lifting him to a
sitting position. "You can make it." He slung the weakened man's arm around his shoulder, gripping the wrist
tightly, placing his other arm around his waist, struggling
them both upright. For a moment they stood swaying, then
Detimore caught his balance and planted his feet, and they
began stumbling once more down the jungle trail.

Badowski lurched along behind them, grunting with the
effort. Houser had done what he could with the shattered
knee, but the makeshift bandage gave little support and
each step was agonizing.

Two Nungs carried an unconscious Cambodian in a
ground cloth strung between two poles, and Donatelli and
another Nung pulled the captured NVA officers along
behind them, tugging on the ends of the detonating cords
they had tied around their necks. The remainder of the
Nungs and Cambodians brought up the rear.

Joe Galimore led the column, talking on the radio to the

75

Forward Air Controller as he ran. His handsome black face was crusted with dried blood from a scalp wound, and a tourniquet stemmed the flow of blood from his left arm, riddled with shrapnel from a grenade blast.

The fourteen-man SOG recon team of six Green Berets and eight Nung and Cambodian mercenaries had been inserted into the dense jungle of the Cambodian valley four days ago. A classified unit, specializing in ambush and long-range reconnaissance operations, they were highly skilled at locating and engaging larger enemy units, inflicting damage far in excess of their numbers.

Headquarters had received reports of unusually heavy enemy activity in the remote valley, and Callahan's team was sent in on a reconnaissance mission. Things began to go wrong minutes after their insertion. Despite the decoy helicopters that preceded them—making diversionary passes and dropping in mechanical fire-fight simulators in areas away from the team's intended landing zone—the North Vietnamese LZ watchers had located them, finding the telltale debris scattered in a 360-degree radius by the helicopter's prop wash when it settled to insert the team.

Following the footprints leading away from the circle, the enemy patrol began tracking them, and the nerve-racking sound of clacking bamboo sticks carried through the mountainous jungle as the trackers communicated their position to other enemy troops in the area, calling them in from all directions.

Avoiding the trails, Callahan and his men moved cautiously through the dense underbrush, disturbing the jungle as little as possible. When one of the men got snagged on a vine, he would stop in his tracks and the man behind him would remove it, carefully placing it back in its natural position. Their progress was painstakingly slow, but they left no sign of their passing on the route they had taken. The bamboo clacking ceased two hours after it had begun and the team stopped, knowing they had eluded the men tracking them. They settled into their remain-overnight position, continuing their search the following day.

On the morning of the fourth day, they located their objective—an NVA training camp and staging area—and called in and controlled air strikes, destroying the base camp and food and munitions caches, capturing classified documents and taking two North Vietnamese army officers prisoner. Heading back to the predesignated coordinates for extraction, they ran into a reinforced regiment of seasoned NVA troops. Unable to reach the designated area, the team were running for their lives in search of a way out.

Galimore informed the Forward Operational Base of the situation and was in contact with the Forward Air Controller high above them in a single-engine Cessna Bird Dog. The FAC kept track of their progress, directing them to a suitable landing zone as the rescue helicopters rushed to the area.

"Stinger, this is Bird Dog," the Forward Air Controller called. "What is your position?"

Galimore hurriedly took the small signal mirror from his pocket and held it at an angle to catch the sunlight. A brilliant light flashed through an opening in the jungle canopy. "Do you see my shiny?" Galimore asked.

"Roger, Stinger," the FAC replied. "The LZ is a quarter mile due west your present position. Where are the bad guys?"

"A hundred meters behind; maybe less," came Galimore's breathless reply.

"Choppers are about ten klicks out. Three slicks, three gunships. Inform me when you reach the clearing."

"Roger."

A few minutes later the team entered the clearing and Frank Detimore led them to the best defensive position available—a depression in the ground, fifty yards into the knee-high grass.

Donatelli set up the M60 facing the trail, and the team deployed on both sides of him, giving them an excellent field of fire in the direction of the approaching enemy. Houser quickly hog-tied the NVA prisoners and rolled them into the lowest spot of the depression.

The surrounding jungle, dense and tangled with heavy underbrush, would be difficult to penetrate, slowing the North Vietnamese advance. Using the trail would be suicidal, not a deterrent to hysterical Viet Cong recruits, but enough to give pause to seasoned NVA regulars.

As the first enemy troops cautiously entered the clearing, a hail of automatic fire and a salvo from grenade launchers cut them down and scattered those behind them into the cover of the jungle.

Houser worked feverishly on the wounded team members. Callahan was unconscious and Badowski was racked with pain and weak from loss of blood. The Cambodian in the litter was dead, and three of the Nungs and Cambodians were seriously wounded.

A heavy volume of fire began to reach them from the edge of the jungle, and Galimore got on the radio to the Forward Air Controller.

"Bird Dog, this is Stinger," he said. "Do you have us in sight?"

"That's a roger, Stinger," the FAC replied. He had

watched them run into the clearing and set up their defensive position. "Where's Charlie?"

"Fifty meters due east our position. In the woods."

"Hug the ground, Stinger. We got a welcoming committee for him."

"Hawkeye, this is Bird Dog," the Forward Air Controller radioed to the leader of the F-4 Phantoms in position overhead. "Report position and ordnance."

"Roger, Bird Dog. On station at seventeen grand. We've got seven-hundred-fifties and five-hundred-pound snake eyes."

"Roger, Hawkeye. Come in on my marker and keep it tight. It's danger close."

"On your marker," answered the deep, heavily accented southern voice.

The Forward Air Controller banked into a steep turn and aligned his aircraft with the target, firing a phosphorus rocket that hit to the right of the trail thirty meters into the woods. A plume of white smoke rose from the jungle floor through the thick canopy of trees.

"Comin' in," the Phantom leader said.

The F-4s thundered down in a steep dive from the far end of the clearing. Streaking toward their target, they delivered their ordnance with pinpoint accuracy and roared out of sight with blurring speed.

The team lay facedown as the shock waves from the powerful explosions shook and rippled the ground beneath them, lifting their bodies and dropping them back down to be bounced again. A storm of dirt and leaves and twigs blew across the clearing, covering them with debris.

Galimore raised his head to see the jungle engulfed in flames and billowing black smoke. Cries of pain could be heard above the shouting of shrill commands.

"Stinger, this is Bird Dog. How'd we do?"

"Say again," Galimore said. The ringing in his ears caused by the explosions had momentarily impaired his hearing.

Bird Dog repeated the question.

"On target," Galimore replied. "Put the next batch on the other side of the trail."

"You got a bull's-eye," Bird Dog told the Phantom leader. "Do it again on the other side."

"Roger, Bird Dog," Hawkeye replied.

The F-4s returned on a reciprocal heading, barreling in low and lightning fast, mercilessly pounding the target. The deafening blasts again rocked the ground and showered the clearing with debris. A third pass by the big jets raked the jungle on both sides of the trail with a withering hailstorm of 20mm cannon fire that shredded everything in its path. Their ordnance expended, they pulled into a steep climb and within moments were gone from sight.

"That's it for the fast movers," Bird Dog said. "Lead chopper is one klick out. Talk him in. Nice doin' business with you, Stinger."

"Roger, Bird Dog. We owe you." Galimore saw the helicopters approaching above the horizon at the north end of the clearing. A call from the lead helicopter came an instant later.

"Stinger, this is Mud Hen. What is your position?"

"Southeast corner of the clearing; fifty meters into the grass."

"Roger, Stinger. East corner of clearing."

"Negative, Mud Hen. That's southeast. Southeast."

"Roger. Southeast."

Sporadic fire reached the team from both sides of the trail along the edge of the still-smoking jungle, and Galimore crawled in closer to the deepest part of the depression. A young Cambodian beside him rose to his knees to fire an M79 round and was immediately shot through the neck, drenching with blood the Buddhist prayer cloth he wore as a cravat. As he slumped over the crest of the grassy mound another round pierced the top of his head, blowing away a piece of his skull.

Badowski, having regained some of his strength, reached up to pull the man under cover, and let out a scream of pain. Withdrawing his left hand, he stared in disbelief at the bloody, ragged stump where his little finger had been.

"*Son of a bitch!*" he bellowed. "Son of a bitch! They shot my goddamn finger off!"

Houser crawled in beside him to treat the wound.

"Stinger, this is Mud Hen. We are inbound. Where's Charlie?"

"Charlie is to our east, in the woods," Galimore answered. "Do you have us in sight?"

"That's a negative, Stinger. Pop smoke. Pop smoke."

"Roger. Pop smoke. You identify." Galimore tossed a smoke grenade to the team's left flank, sending a cloud of yellow smoke billowing into the air.

"I see yellow smoke, yellow smoke," Mud Hen said.

"Roger. Yellow smoke," Galimore confirmed.

"Are you receiving fire?"

"Roger. We are receiving heavy ground fire."

"Are you on the yellow smoke?"

"Roger. On the yellow smoke. How about some rockets?"

"Roger, Stinger. We are in position for a rocket run. I'll be putting them to the east of the yellow smoke."

"Roger. To the east."

An NVA mortar team opened up and began to find their

range, walking the rounds to the team's position. Donatelli spotted them and Galimore radioed the gunship.

"We've got a mortar team spotted. Twenty meters off the south side of the trail, a few meters into the woods."

"Roger, Stinger. We'll put some rockets on them."

The gunship came in from the north end of the clearing, releasing three pairs of rockets that impacted with a brilliant flash, each pair extending the path of destruction by fifty yards. A steady stream of fire burst from the left doorgunner, the rounds tearing into the dense foliage to the right of the trail.

"Your fire is a little too far right," Galimore directed. "Shift a little left."

"Roger. Left."

The second gunship nosed down, cut back on the power and trimmed out, centering the turn and slip indicator ball, keeping the aircraft from slipping sideways. The rockets tracked true to the crucial area, splintering trees and gouging holes in the jungle floor.

The left doorgunner continued strafing the edge of the jungle as the gunship climbed out rolling hard to the right as enemy ground fire ricocheted off the armor-plated undercarriage.

"You're right in there," Galimore shouted. "Keep it comin'. Keep it comin'."

The third gunship followed with another attack, then climbed to join the others. With the gunships back in orbiting position, the North Vietnamese were up and moving, working their way through the undergrowth to the edge of the clearing on both sides of the trail. Again, a heavy volume of fire began reaching the team.

Frank Detimore crouched behind the grassy mound, his

attention focused on the distant figures moving just inside the jungle to the right of their position.

A platoon of NVA was moving to outflank them while the main body of the enemy probed the perimeter in front of the team.

Grabbing a bandolier of M79 rounds, Detimore signaled three of the Cambodians to follow him. They crawled through the grass to a point where the depression became more shallow and turned toward the south end of the clearing, thirty yards from the rest of the team.

Frank positioned the Cambodians, who waited until the enemy soldiers entered the clearing, then opened up with automatic fire from their M16s.

An enemy machine gun maneuvered into position at the edge of the jungle and tore into the ground around them. Detimore fired two of the 40mm grenades in the direction of the gunner. Both landed wide of their mark. As he reloaded for a third try, a bullet ripped into his side, shattering a rib and exiting through his back. The impact and the searing pain stunned him momentarily, and as he lay on the ground struggling to reload his weapon, he saw two of the Cambodians jam their Buddhist necklaces in their mouths and begin crawling toward the machine gun before he could stop them. The men had advanced no more than twenty yards when a grenade blast wounded them both, knocking them unconscious.

Frank kept the remaining Cambodian from crawling out after them, directing his fire at the machine gun as he reloaded the M79. His third round from the grenade launcher was a direct hit, knocking out the enemy gunner.

''Cover me,'' he told the Cambodian as he slithered on his stomach to the wounded men. The Cambodian laid down a barrage of fire along the jungle's edge while Frank brought the men, one at a time, back under cover.

"Stinger, this is Mud Hen. The slicks will be coming in from the north."

"Roger, Mud Hen," Galimore replied. "Stay clear of the south end. There's a heavy concentration on our right flank."

"Roger, Stinger. We'll bring the slicks in from the north and go out the same way."

"Mud Hen Three and Four," the lead helicopter called. "Keep protective fire to the east of Stinger when the slicks go in."

"Roger. We'll hose it down with rockets."

"Lead, this is Mud Hen Two. You want a two ship or you want me to hold?"

"Go in one at a time. One at a time."

"Roger. Slowing down to open my doors."

"Stinger, the slicks will be comin' in one at a time. Put some M79s and automatic fire into the woods when he comes in. He's about a klick and a half out now. Do you understand?"

"Roger," Galimore confirmed.

"Put out another smoke, Stinger."

"Roger. You identify." Galimore tossed another smoke grenade close in to the team.

"I see green smoke," Mud Hen said.

"Roger. Green smoke."

"We'll put the guns on them on a north-south run as the slick comes in, Stinger."

"Roger."

Mud Hen called to his doorgunner, "I'm gonna put you right over the smoke, Gunner. This will be a left gun.

Blast the shit out of it . . . about fifty meters out to the east . . . left gunner you are clear to fire.''

The edge of the jungle was inundated with the door-gunner's sustained bursts, and the volume of enemy fire decreased immediately. The rescue helicopter settled to the clearing and the doorgunner in the second gunship worked over the same area while the pilot fired rockets into the jungle at the south end of the landing zone.

Under cover of the gunship's rockets, Frank Detimore and the Cambodian, dragging the wounded men with them, crawled back to the team as the rescue helicopter touched down, flattening the grass around it and sending swirls of red dust into the air.

Frank took over the M60, laying down covering fire as Donatelli and Houser helped the wounded Nungs and Cambodians to the helicopter.

Callahan had regained consciousness and propped himself up at the crest of the mound, adding to the covering fire. He swung his M16 to his left flank as two enemy soldiers broke from cover and ran wildly toward him, Chinese stick grenades in their raised hands. With two quick, accurate bursts, he brought them down, the grenades exploding harmlessly away from the team. As he turned to fire at three men who darted from a thick tangle of underbrush near the trail, a round tore through his left arm, knocking him back into the trough of the depression. In the effort to get back into position, his head reeled and a curtain of darkness descended as he rolled onto his back.

Galimore froze for an instant when he caught a glimpse of an enemy soldier standing just inside the cover of the jungle. He recognized the weapon the man held on his shoulder—an RPG-7, a close-in, hand-held combat rocket. Weighing only twenty pounds, the highly accurate weapon was capable of penetrating twelve inches of armor plating, and could knock out a tank at five hundred yards.

Galimore's expression was one of horror. He frantically shouted a warning into the radio, realizing it was too late when he saw the trailing wisp of smoke as the deadly rocket streaked from the launcher and tracked toward its target.

"Get out! Get out!" he shouted. *"Get the chopper out!"*

The rescue helicopter took a direct hit, exploding into a fiery ball and rolling onto its side in a huge cloud of orange flame and black smoke. The second rescue ship, halfway across the clearing, immediately broke off its approach, taking evasive maneuvers as it hurried from the area.

"What the hell . . ." Mud Hen shouted. "Rockets . . . they have rockets! Son of a bitch!"

Houser and Donatelli were nearing the helicopter when the rocket struck. As they turned back to the team, a mortar round exploded off to their right, killing one of the Nungs they were carrying and severing the leg of the other.

Houser felt a burning, tearing pain as his right leg and back were laced with shrapnel. Staggering painfully to his feet, he helped Donatelli drag the wounded Nung back under cover.

The gunships made pass after pass as the remaining rescue helicopters got into position for another approach. The first ship moved quickly in and out with the severely wounded and the NVA prisoners and documents, and the second followed in close behind.

Out of ordnance and low on fuel, the gunships made dry

runs in hopes of keeping the enemy down, and watched anxiously as the rescue ship settled to the clearing.

"Let's go! Let's go!" Donatelli shouted, pulling the Nungs and Cambodians from their firing positions and directing them toward the helicopter.

The main thrust was coming directly at them, and the ground fire reached a new intensity as pockets of enemy soldiers broke from cover and rushed the team's position.

Frank Detimore stayed at the M60 covering the withdrawal, and a Nung stayed with him, firing and reloading an M79 at a frantic pace. Outgunned and outflanked, they fought desperately to hold back the surge of men about to overrun their position.

Donatelli and Houser helped the last of the wounded men on board the helicopter, then scrambled through the door.

"Where's Frank?" Houser shouted, then saw him still firing from the grassy mound.

The mortar team opened up again, the rounds landing dangerously close, throwing a shower of dirt and huge clumps of earth against the side of the helicopter.

"We're getting out of here now!" the copilot screamed at Donatelli as he saw him start out the door.

A burst from an AK-47 struck Donatelli in the arm and shoulder as he leaped to the ground. Houser went out after him, getting him back inside and diving in behind him after he glanced over his shoulder and saw Detimore and the Nung crouching low and running toward the helicopter as it shuddered and rocked, preparing to lift off.

Frank turned to fire a burst, killing two men who were closing on them, and out of the corner of his eye saw the NVA soldier with the portable rocket launcher step into the clearing.

"Go! Go!" he shouted to the Nung.

Dropping to one knee, he took careful aim and cut the man down before he could fire the fatal missile. Spinning and firing again, he dropped another man who had vaulted the grassy mound and was poised to throw a grenade at the helicopter. The grenade exploded inches from the man's head, forcefully spraying a mist of blood and pieces of gray matter across Frank's face and chest.

Getting to his feet, Frank gripped his blood-soaked side, and ran for the helicopter and the outstretched hands of Galimore and Houser.

A violent force picked him off his feet, throwing him into the air, as a mortar round exploded close behind him, gouging the side of the helicopter with large chunks of shrapnel. The enemy mortar team had their range; the next round would be on top of the rescue ship.

"Now! Now!" the copilot screamed above the roar of the engine.

"No!" Houser shouted. "I'll get him."

"He's dead, goddamnit! He's dead!" the copilot said, his voice hysterical with fear and tension.

Dazed and racked with pain, Frank Detimore stared at his pulpy, shattered leg as he rolled onto his stomach and tried to crawl to the rising ship. A series of blows fell heavily on his shoulders and back as the enemy soldiers who had reached him pounded him with their rifle butts.

"No, goddamnit! No!" Houser shouted as he fired from the door of the rising ship into the swarm of soldiers surrounding Detimore.

His shouts died in the pulsating rush of air as the pilot whirled the craft off the ground away from the surge of enemy soldiers, rising swiftly and banking steeply to the far side of the clearing, skimming the treetops as he sped from the area. . . .

Callahan awoke with a start, perspiring heavily and clutching his stomach. Boomer sprang to his feet and growled, his protective instincts aroused by the sudden, unexpected movement.

Jack glanced at the glowing embers in the fireplace, then out the window at the morning light along the ridges of the mountains. "Sorry, Boomer," he said, as the dog curled back up at his side. "Bad dream."

Boomer grumbled with contentment as Jack massaged the back of his massive neck. "I have to leave you for a few days, old buddy," Jack said. "Then we're going to have some company. You'll like that. More people to play tug of war with."

4

Phil Houser leaned forward in his chair, rested his arms on the edge of the table, and absently picked at his salad. The murmur of dinner conversations and the occasional soft laughter in the crowded restaurant went unheard as he reflected on the visit from Jack Callahan that afternoon.

Twelve years. And there he was. A specter from the past, standing in the doorway of the Retina Clinic as though he commanded everyone in his presence. The warrior, trim, fit, and self-confident as ever; the same deadly look in his eyes. Even the chief of surgery had nodded a respectful greeting—he had that effect on people. He had loved it. The jungle, the war, the constant reaffirmation. He believed in it. He would have stayed and fought with the Yards if they had let him. Frank's alive. Just like that; Frank's alive. Jesus. Okay. Okay. I'm in. Like a wide-eyed recruit; a dumb-assed emotional decision. But then there really wasn't a choice, was there? Damn, Frank, you tough old bird.

"Did you have a rough case in surgery today?" Angela Fisher asked, getting no response. She could feel the tension from his lean, wiry body as he stared at a fixed point across the room. He was a man of great physical contradictions. A fine-boned, sensitive face and the hands of a surgeon belied what emanated from within. The deep-set, penetrating steel blue eyes had seen more than an academic life, and she sensed that what he had been and what he was now would be mutually exclusive in anyone else. He was a private man, almost to the point of being abrasive, and she had never heard him give more than brief, cursory comments about his past.

"Phil?"

"What?"

"I've gotten two uh-huhs out of you in the last hour."

"Sorry, honey."

"Did you have a rough day in surgery?"

"No. Routine."

"Then what is it? Your body may be here with me, but your mind is somewhere else."

"Fort Bragg, North Carolina. In the Dog Lab."

"The Dog Lab?"

"The first surgery I ever did. In the Army, as a medic."

"You did veterinary surgery?"

"Sort of. They inflicted gunshot wounds on dogs and we patched them up."

"That's barbaric."

"I think they use goats now."

"Oh, well, that's different. We all know goats don't have a central nervous system."

Houser smiled sympathetically. "The experience we got there helped save a lot of lives."

"I'll bet that pleased the dogs."

"It's an imperfect world."

"What got you thinking about that?"

"A visit from an old friend. My commanding officer in Vietnam. He stopped by the hospital today."

"You've never mentioned him. He lives here, in Philadelphia?"

"No. Colorado."

Angela watched him draw back and his eyes grow distant again. "It wasn't just a social visit, was it? Did he need money?"

Houser held her questioning look for a long moment, then settled back in his chair. "He needs *me*. For a month, maybe a little longer?"

"Needs you for what?"

"To help a friend."

"Phil. You're being evasive. Do you want to tell me what this is all about?"

Houser watched her expression change and her soft green eyes widen as he explained about Frank Detimore and the proposed mission. When he had finished, she sat silently for a few moments, a stunned look turning to one of disbelief.

"You can't be serious. You're a surgeon. Why would he ask you?"

"We were all in the same outfit."

"But you were a medic."

"A Special Forces medic. It's different."

"Special forces? The Green Berets?"

Houser nodded. "Put silver wings on my son's chest . . . and all that."

"You never told me."

"It never came up."

"Why did you join them?"

92

"It probably has something to do with the five-foot-seven syndrome."

"You can't do this, Phil. It's insane. You'll get killed." She was frightened by the firm, committed look in his eyes. "We're getting married in June and suddenly I have the feeling I'm talking to a complete stranger. Phil Houser, the quintessential pragmatist, the eternal cynic, now an impassioned paladin. I don't know you at all."

Angela waited for a reply, but Houser remained silent.

"You've spent the last twelve years of your life working hard to get where you are," she said. "There isn't a doctor on the staff of Wills Eye Hospital who doesn't agree that you have a brilliant career ahead of you. I just can't believe you would consider doing something so irresponsible."

"It's not irresponsible. If anything it's the exact opposite. Besides, it's only a month. The Director of Medical Education will give me a leave of absence. It means finishing my surgical residency a month later, that's all."

"Or never finishing it."

"The man saved my life, Angie. I owe him. And we each get fifty thousand dollars. That'll cushion that first year in practice."

"Please, spare me that." The anger and disappointment were evident in her voice. "There isn't a bank in the country that wouldn't gladly lend you whatever you needed. You'll be making five times that by the end of your second year."

"I'm sorry, honey. It's something I have to do."

"Have to, or want to?"

Houser shrugged. "Have to . . . want to, maybe we all do what we're programmed to do. I just know I'd lose my self-respect if I didn't."

"You could lose your life, or be captured, or crippled. Just to satisfy some nebulous debt of honor and the urge to play soldier again. Don't you care how I feel about this?"

Houser saw in her eyes the frightened, little-girl-lost look he had seen the night her father died. He reached out and held her hand.

"I love you, Angie. I'm asking you to understand."

"I'm trying. I really am. But this isn't like you. In the two years I've known you, you've never done anything that could even remotely be considered rash or impulsive."

"I'm not playing soldier. I didn't like the war. I didn't like the patrols and the ambushes. I went because I was needed. I did four tours in Vietnam. Four years. Three of them alongside Frank Detimore. I can still see him, trying to reach the helicopter. And I couldn't do anything to help him. It tears at my guts every time I think about it; and I do think about it. Even now. And it will always be there if I turn my back on him again."

"Why can't you leave this to professionals? For that amount of money you could hire the best."

Houser smiled. "We were the best, Angie."

"Past tense. You're almost forty years old. And the others are the same age?"

"More or less. I'm a little slower, a little older. But I run three miles every morning. I do sit-ups, push-ups. The reflexes aren't the same, but the skills and experience are there. With a little reorientation and training . . . we were damn good."

"Phil, please rethink this. It's just not an intelligent, rational decision."

"Look around you, honey. We live in a world where indifference and selfish materialism are becoming the norm. Where people grab what they can and refuse to take responsibility for their actions. Doing something out of personal loyalty and a sense of honor isn't irrational or unintelligent; it only seems that way because it's become unfashionable."

Angela lowered her eyes and slowly shook her head. "I don't want to lose you, Phil. I lost my brother in Vietnam. He had just graduated from Penn State; he wanted to be a writer. The place he died didn't even have a name. It was a hill with a number. In his last letter he wrote about the brutality that tore at him until all sense of reality and reason was gone. About how he was stretched and twisted to the limit and didn't know if there was enough resiliency left in him to return to what he was. He quoted Matthew Arnold when he told me how he felt about our involvement there. He said it was the home of lost causes, and forsaken beliefs, and unpopular names, and impossible loyalties. Yours is an impossible loyalty, Phil. It could destroy you. And losing you will destroy me."

"Angie, I promise you, if it isn't a good plan with a high probability of success, I'll drop out. I don't have a death wish and I'm not fatalistic, but I've got to go to Aspen for the briefing. And if it looks good and there's a chance to get Frank out, I have to go. Just remember, we're not callow kids; we've all been there and back."

Angela nodded wearily, a look of sad resignation on her face. "The Greeks said, to do something once is to challenge the gods; to do it twice is to tempt them."

Houser smiled mischievously. "What the hell did they know? Pederasts, the whole damn lot of them."

"Oh, Phil."

"It'll be all right, honey."

Houser finished what remained of a warm, flat beer, and smiled inwardly as he remembered his last day in Viet-

95

nam. He and Callahan and Donatelli and Galimore, standing on the tarmac at Tan Son Nhut air base, waiting for Smashy. The plane was due to leave in ten minutes and he was nowhere in sight. Then Donatelli cocked his head and stared down a long row of hangars.

"Here he comes."

A jeep careened around a corner, balancing on two wheels, then bouncing back on all fours and racing toward them. It weaved among the parked aircraft, narrowly missing a few, and finally skidded to a screeching halt dangerously close to where the men waited to board the plane.

A ripple of laughter spread through the crowd as Smashy stepped from the jeep and staggered over to Callahan, snapping to a swaying attention.

Jack burst out laughing at the spectacle before him. With the exception of a beret perched on the back of his head, one jungle boot—on the wrong foot—and a Rolex watch strapped to his ankle, Smashy was stark naked.

5

Callahan drove past the phalanx of seedy massage parlors, adult bookstores, pawn shops, and used-car lots that lined both sides of Bragg Boulevard. Slowing to read the sign at an intersection, he continued, turning onto the next side street and driving to the end of the block where he pulled into the parking lot of a painted cinder block building. The sign over the door flickered in pink neon script: Sm s y's Bar.

The thumping beat of hard rock bounced off the walls, and a blaring jukebox greeted him as he entered the small room cluttered with tables and chairs, empty, with the exception of the young, sultry-looking girl in tight sweater and jeans behind the bar.

"What can I get ya?" she asked, moving sensually to the music.

"A draft Bud."

"No draft," she replied, grinding her hips to accent the movement.

"A bottle's fine."

"You got two choices. Miller or Schlitz."

"Miller."

"You got it."

Callahan scanned the array of military memorabilia on the walls, his attention drawn to a collection of Special Forces flashes and pictures of Smashy in Vietnam.

"Smashy around?"

"Nope. At the fights."

"Who's fighting?" he asked, noticing the can of mace within easy reach on the counter behind the bar.

"He is." She jerked her thumb to the beat of the music, indicating a poster tacked to the wall above the jukebox.

Jack took his beer and walked over to the poster.

HOW TOUGH ARE YOU
WE'RE LOOKING FOR THE TOUGHEST MAN IN
THE FAYETTEVILLE AREA. COULD IT BE YOU?
PROFESSIONAL BOXERS NOT WELCOME.

The poster went on to invite all barroom brawlers, bouncers, truck drivers, construction workers, and anyone who qualified as a heavyweight to register for an amateur boxing tournament.

Callahan had heard of the Toughman Contest. In the past few years it had become increasingly popular in small towns across the country. The only resemblance to boxing was that the men wore gloves and fought in a ring—a sanctioned brawl was really what it was. The winner was determined by a process of elimination and often fought three or four opponents in one night. The first-prize money of one thousand dollars, with five hundred for the runner-up, hardly compensated the men for the brutal beatings they took. But most of them weren't there for the money, rather for bragging rights and to feed dreams of provincial fame.

The music stopped when the record changed, but the girl behind the bar continued dancing until it began again, inspired to more animated undulations by a song she obviously liked better and knew the words to.

"How do I get to Joe's Roller Rama?" Jack asked.

"Back out to Bragg, hang a right, go six blocks to Sunset, hang a left. One block down, across the street from the 7-11," she said, without missing a step.

"Thanks . . . what's your name?"

"Candy."

Callahan smiled and nodded. "Of course it is. You'd better take a break; you'll end up in traction."

Candy winked and cracked her gum as she executed a perfectly timed bump and grind.

The air inside the huge roller-skating rink was thick with smoke that rose to the ceiling and drifted like a layer of clouds among the rafters. The heat was stifling and the smells of beer and perspiration permeated the crowded room. Callahan guessed there were at least two thousand people packed shoulder to shoulder in rows of flimsy wooden folding chairs that covered every inch of the floor.

As Jack made his way to his seat, a fight broke out between two men near one of the exits, swelling to a ten-man Donnybrook before the security guards got it under control.

"For twenty bucks more I can give you a seat down front where you'll hear the skin rip and smell the blood," the man at the door had told him. "Otherwise, it's standing room only."

Callahan squeezed into his second-row ringside seat between two sweaty behemoths swilling beer from large paper cups. The shouting and hooting rose to deafening proportions as one man in the ring mercilessly pounded his much smaller opponent. Both men were heavyweights, but they were mismatched—two hundred fifty pounds against one hundred ninety—and neither was in good physical condition, judging from their flabby midsections and overall lack of muscle tone.

"Kill the son of a bitch!" Jack heard someone yell close behind him. "Peel his head like a grape!"

Turning to the source of the shrill screams, he saw a stocky, middle-aged woman standing in the aisle, punching the air with fat, clublike arms.

"Kill 'im! Kill 'im!"

The larger of the two men was pummeling his defenseless opponent at will, bouncing his head off the ring post with each blow, splattering blood in all directions from the deep cuts over his eyes and on the bridge of his nose. He leaned into him to hold him in place, then backed off to throw a brief flurry of short, choppy punches before propping him up again.

Stepping back to deliver a looping right hand, he stopped in midswing as a stream of urine ran down the beaten man's leg onto the canvas and over the shoes of his assailant; his final act of retaliation before crumbling into the corner.

"Yeah! All right!" the man seated on Jack's left shouted. "Beat the piss out of him! Yeah!"

The crowd roared its approval as the next pair of combatants made their way to the ring from the back of the room. The cheering changed to a chorus of boos midway through the first round as the overweight, clumsy men wheeled and stumbled around the ring throwing wild haymakers that invariably missed their mark. A protest of paper cups took flight, dousing the ring and those nearby with a shower of beer.

The promoter of the fights sat at ringside, shouting into a microphone.

"Come on, you bums! My mother could do better than that."

"Knock him down and fuck him!" the glassy-eyed man on Jack's left bellowed.

The audience joined in the taunting, screaming obscenities and insults. The match ended in the second round when one of the men inadvertently landed a solid punch to his opponent's kidney, knocking him to his knees where he cried out in pain and waved his arms to indicate he had had enough. The crowd booed and shouted for more action.

Jack didn't see Smashy until he ducked under the ropes and entered the ring. His broad, square-jawed face was a little fuller than when he had last seen him, and he had gained twenty pounds, but he was solid and seemed to be in good physical condition as he prowled the ring, slapping his gloves together and rolling his head around on his thick neck.

Callahan studied Smashy's opponent. A trim, well-muscled kid, a few inches taller and probably half Smashy's age. He wore cutoff jeans and an orange tank top.

Jack smiled when he saw the Special Forces emblem on Smashy's T-shirt and trunks.

101

"Go get him, Smashy," he shouted, the encouragement lost in the roar of the crowd as the promoter announced the contestants.

"That old man won't do shit," the grossly overweight man on Jack's right said.

"I don't know. He's pretty tough."

"You want to put your money where your mouth is?"

"Why not?"

"Twenty bucks?"

"Make it fifty?"

"You're on," the fat man said.

Jack felt a nudge from the row behind him.

"You got twenty more you wanna lose?"

Jack took the bet.

At the sound of the bell Smashy charged across the ring, caught his opponent unprepared, and landed a hard right hand on the side of his head that sent him stumbling backward. He closed in, but the kid recovered quickly and spun away as Smashy fell against the ropes, off balance from throwing a wild left hook. The kid slammed two fast rabbit punches to the back of Smashy's head and followed up with a blow to the kidney.

The crowd roared with delight as Smashy grabbed his opponent and wrestled him into a corner, holding his head with one hand and pounding him in the face with the other, opening a cut on the kid's forehead that speckled Smashy's close-cropped blond hair with blood.

The round was a give and take, with both men inflicting damage. The kid's face was smeared with blood, and Smashy's left eye was almost swollen shut when the bell ended the round.

The second round began with another charge and flailing assault by Smashy. Arm-weary and breathing heavily, he chased him around the ring, missing with every punch.

The kid was up on his toes, moving gracefully, landing combinations and connecting with stiff jabs and hard right leads. Smashy's mouthpiece flew out in a spray of blood caused by a wicked left hook followed by a straight right hand that partially closed his other eye.

"See, asshole. I told you that old fart couldn't do nothin'."

Callahan glared at the man beside him, but said nothing.

"Kill the fucker!" the fat man screamed. "Tear his ugly head off!"

A solid combination landed with authority and Smashy dropped to his knees with the kid still raining blows on his head until he fell forward onto his face.

"See, asshole! See!"

Jack's temper flared, but more in response to Smashy's fate. "You call me asshole one more time, I'll rip your lips off."

The fat man's florid face paled. "Hey, nothin' personal, man. Nothin' personal."

Jack felt a revulsion at the sight of his friend, bleeding and battered, crawling on his stomach to loop his arm over the ropes in an attempt to get to his feet.

"Stay down! Stay down!" Jack shouted.

"Fuck that shit!" the man behind him yelled. "Get up and fight, you bum!"

Smashy pulled himself to his knees, only to be met by another series of brutal blows that left him hanging halfway out of the ring. Jack saw the glazed look in his swollen eyes as he tried to free himself from the ropes, falling into unconsciousness with the effort.

"He's no bum," Jack said, throwing the money at the

two men. Leaving his seat, he made his way to the small room where the seconds had taken Smashy after helping him from the ring.

Smashy sat slumped on a wooden bench in front of a row of lockers, a cold, wet towel held to his face.

"I hope you're not thinking of turning pro," Jack said, closing the door and shutting out the crowd noise.

"Another round I'd a had him," Smashy said without looking up.

Callahan laughed. "Sure. By then he'd have broken both hands on your head and passed out from exhaustion."

Smashy removed the towel from his face and turned toward the familiar voice. Staring through puffy eyes, he grinned, wincing from the pain of a split lip.

"Jack? Ah, shit. You didn't see that, did you?"

Callahan nodded. "What the hell were you doing in there?"

"Got a mortgage payment due. I thought I had a shot."

"You okay?"

"Yeah. I feel better than I look."

"I hope so. How are Marge and the kids?"

Smashy shook his head. "It *has* been a while, old buddy. I screwed that up when I got back from 'Nam the last time. She got tired of sending me out for a loaf of bread and having me stagger back three days later."

"Still up to your old tricks."

Smashy shrugged. "Yeah. I spent about a year as a kneewalkin' commode-huggin' drunk before I got over that. Missed the kids a lot. Married a real winner on the rebound. She took me to a double feature, left me with the clothes on my back. . . . How the hell are you?"

"Okay. I stopped by the bar. It looked a little lean."

"Yeah. The bank gets fifteen hundred by Monday or they padlock it."

"Is it always that slow?"

Smashy nodded. "I tried topless dancers. Too many fights, and the broads were macing a dozen guys a night in the parking lot. Goddamn animals."

"Come on, get dressed. I'll let you buy me a drink."

Smashy rose wearily to his feet and clapped Callahan on the shoulder. "Good to see you, Jack."

"And will you turn down that damn music!" Smashy yelled as he signaled Candy for two more drinks.

"You've got to be kidding, Jack. Am I in? A chance to help Frank, make fifty grand, and come out of there a winner? Give me five minutes to get my toothbrush and lock up the joint and I'm yours."

"How's the knee?"

"A little stiff, but no problem."

"Think you can drop twenty pounds in a month?"

"Fifty if I have to. Shit, Jack. I miss it. I mean I really miss it. Especially the old days before the legs took over."

Callahan nodded. "Me, too. Parts of it."

"You contact the other guys?"

"Houser said yes. Donatelli backed off, and I'll see Galimore in a few days."

"Rick said no? He and Frank were tight."

"He's running his father's restaurant in Ocean City, New Jersey. They're opening up a new one in Atlantic City, says he can't get away."

"That doesn't sound like him. Maybe it's because of that Vietnamese girl."

"What about her? I thought that ended when he came home with us."

"Hell, no. The next year, just after you went TDY down to Panama, he went back to 'Nam for another tour. Married her."

"I didn't know that."

"He didn't tell nobody. Not even his old man, and you know how close they are. I found out a couple years later from the guy who stood up for him."

"She isn't with him now."

"I hope not," Smashy said. "She was killed in a VC rocket attack on Saigon. Three days after they were married. The day before he was bringing her home."

"Jesus. I saw him just before I got out. He didn't say a word about it."

"You know what he's like. He never leaned on nobody. Always with the jokes. How's he look anyway? Still pumpin' iron?"

"Yeah. He looks good."

"Listen. I can round up as many guys as you need. Christ, the whole 5th Group would volunteer if we put the word out."

"No. We can't take anyone on active duty, and I want to keep it small and limited to people we know. We'll see how it goes. I've got a meeting in New Orleans with an arms dealer after I see Joe Galimore. We'll play it by ear until then."

"Where is Joe?"

"Cincinnati."

"I hope he can make it. Ain't many guys better in a fire fight than Joe."

Smashy grinned and chuckled to himself. "One hell of a weird sense of humor though. I can still see that cherry Kool-Aid comin' out of the shower and the faucets," he said, remembering the day Galimore had put ninety-six

106

packs of punch mix into the camp water tower at their Forward Operational Base.

Jack laughed. "He hated that junk. Said he'd rather drink paddy water."

"You got a plan worked out?" Smashy asked.

"Just the basics. We'll have a briefing in Aspen at the end of the week. I am going to need some help up front," Jack said. "Do you have any friends on active duty at Headquarters? An Intelligence sergeant?"

"Yeah. Bill Danby. He's a sergeant major in G-2."

"Can you trust him?"

"Oh, yeah. We worked a platoon of Hre Yards behind NVA lines when we were with the Mobile Guerrilla Force, before I joined up with your team. He's good people. Best man with an M60 I ever did see."

"I'd like to talk with him."

"Sure. I'll have him meet us for lunch at the NCO Club at the base tomorrow. Speaking of food, are you hungry?"

"A little."

"There's a Vietnamese restaurant a couple of blocks from here. They got a fifty-meter *nuoc mam* that'll cross your eyes."

Jack frowned at the thought of the fermented fish sauce he had never acquired a taste for.

Smashy smiled and winced again, gingerly touching his upper lip. "Then we'll top the evening off with a nostalgic ride on the Vomit Comet."

Jack laughed at Smashy's name for the last bus back to the base before reveille. "I'll settle for the dinner."

A few minutes before noon, small groups of trim, fit men dressed in camouflage fatigues and wearing 82nd Airborne or Special Forces patches on their sleeves, began sauntering into the dining room of the Fort Bragg NCO Club. Callahan and Smashy sat at a table by a window facing the Special Forces Headquarters building. Some of the older sergeants stopped at their table to kid Smashy about the fight he had lost, and Smashy took it good-naturedly. They had just ordered their lunch when Jack noticed a husky, thick-necked man with a hawkish nose and narrow penetrating eyes standing in the doorway looking about the room. Smashy signaled to him, and the man came toward them.

"Mean lookin' bastard, isn't he?"

Jack nodded as he watched him stomp across the room.

Sergeant Major Bill Danby stared at Smashy's bruised and battered face as he sat down at the table.

"What the hell happened to you?" he asked, casting a sidelong glance at Callahan and nodding.

"Don't ask. This is Jack Callahan. He's one of us."

Danby nodded again. "You did it, didn't you? You entered that tough guy contest. You damn fool."

Smashy shrugged. "Jack and I need some help."

"You need your head examined, that's what you need."

Danby munched on a carrot as he listened to Callahan explain what he wanted, his hard brown eyes betraying nothing of what he was thinking.

Jack removed from his coat pocket the pictomap he had brought with him, shielding it from the other tables, and showed the area in question to Danby.

"I need current intelligence on what's in this area now. Specifically this section," he said, keeping his voice low and pointing to a quadrant near the X that marked the location of the POW camp. "There used to be a clearing here, about five hundred meters by two hundred meters. I need to know if it's still there or if the jungle has re-claimed it.''

He folded the map over and pointed to another area he had circled with a grease pencil. ''There's a small army base here now. I'd like to know how small and what they have there. Particularly if they have any heliborne capabilities.''

Moving his finger along the line that designated a road between the army base and the POW camp, he said, ''It would also help if I knew what kind of shape this road is in.''

''Can you do it?'' Smashy asked.

Danby ran his hand through his bristly crew cut and gave Smashy an angry look. ''Goddamn you, Badowski. That's highly classified information. And I don't know your friend from shit. You've got your twenty in and a nice pension. I'd like to have the same, not spend my last two years in the brig as a private.''

''Come on, Bill. This is me, Smashy. This won't go any further.''

''I'll do you one favor. I'll forget this conversation ever happened.''

As Danby rose to leave, Smashy gripped his arm and pulled him back into the chair.

''Can you forget about it if it means leaving Frank Detimore hanging?''

''What's that supposed to mean? What's Frank got to do with this?''

''Can I tell him?'' Smashy asked Jack. ''He and Frank went through the course together.''

Callahan saw the light go on in Danby's eyes. ''I think you just did.''

Danby waited until a group of men dressed in fatigues

with berets stuffed in their pockets had passed the table. He leaned forward, speaking in a conspiratorial tone. "Frank's alive. You're goin' in after him."

Jack nodded.

"This official or unofficial?"

"Strictly unofficial. Paramilitary."

"Will you help?" Smashy asked.

Danby glanced from Jack to Smashy and back to Jack. "We don't have that stuff here. We're concentrating on Central America . . . but I know where I can get it."

"How soon?" Jack asked.

"A few days, if I can pull it off."

"Who's got it?"

"Directorate for Collection and Surveillance at DIA. It's on a need-to-know basis, but I might be able to get it through channels; they're used to getting off-beat requests from us. But if somebody along the line raises an eyebrow and questions why we need it . . ." He gave Callahan a direct look. "I'm going to check you out, and I may have to bring the colonel in on this. Which may get me a fast trip to the slammer as soon as I open my mouth."

"Colonel Britton?" Smashy asked.

"The same."

"He was with Project Delta," Smashy said to Jack. "Congressional Medal of Honor. He just might go for this."

"And he might not," Danby said. "I'll do what I can. No guarantees."

"Fair enough. What can you get from them?" Jack asked.

"You name it. Close inspection reconnaissance photographs from low-perigee satellites, SR-71 photo tracks, even Big Bird stuff."

"Detailed close-ups?"

"Hell, they can zero in on a pimple on a water buffalo's ass from ninety thousand feet. And that's from one frame that covers an area of a hundred and fifteen square miles."

"How current will they be?"

A week, maybe two. They got tracks covering every inch of that country on a regular schedule. They keep tabs on the Russian nuclear submarine base at Cam Ranh Bay and the supply base for long-range recon and antisub aircraft at Danang, and they're always watching for changes in Vietnamese military deployments."

Jack took a slip of paper from his pocket and handed it to Danby. "These are the coordinates of the places I need closeups of. It would also help if you could get me one shot, an overall view, of everything in a thirty-mile radius from the *X*." He handed him the map. "You can keep that. I have another one."

"That's it?" Danby asked.

Jack smiled. "Since you asked. I could use a long-range weather report for the area a few weeks from now and, if it's possible, some information on Vietnamese radar."

"Like which way it's pointed?"

"Exactly."

"I can answer that for you now. Ninety-nine percent of their air defense system is concentrated to the north, and the South China Sea. They're paranoid about the Chinese. Give me a call a couple days before you need the weather report. That's an easy one."

Jack extended his hand as they rose from the table. "If there's anything I can do for you . . ."

"One thing. If you pull this off, tell Frank he owes me a beer. I'll be in touch, Smashy."

As they reached the door to the dining room, Danby

stopped and turned to Jack. Speaking in a low voice, he asked, "You gonna make a night jump?"

Jack nodded.

"That's beautiful. Beautiful. Exactly what I'd do."

Before leaving the base, Smashy and Jack visited the Hall of Honor in the entrance to the John F. Kennedy Center. Glass-enclosed displays exhibited the equipment used by Special Forces, and in the center of the long corridor there were columns hung with portraits of the Green Berets who had won the Congressional Medal of Honor. Beneath each portrait a plaque told of the events that had led to the award. Jack stopped at the portrait of Frank Detimore and read with interest the description of the mission he had been part of. Outside he could hear the hollow pounding of the big guns on the artillery range, and for a brief moment he was back in Cambodia, and he could feel the terrible pain, and the wet, sticky mess as he clutched his stomach. He stood before the portrait, unable to move, feeling a film of perspiration soak the back of his shirt and bead on his forehead. Again he tried to move, but his muscles wouldn't respond. A sudden panic gripped him and then lifted as quickly as it had come.

"You all right, Jack?" Smashy asked.

"Sure. Must be the *nuoc mam* you talked me into last night."

"Yeah. That'll be with you for a week."

"I want you to take this," Jack said, handing him a check he had written out that morning.

"Ah, Jack . . ."

"You'll pay me back out of your money for the mission. That will keep the wolf from the door until we get back."

"I appreciate it."

"I know."

"Okay. When do you want me in Aspen?"

"I see Galimore tomorrow . . . then two days in New Orleans. Monday. Bring whatever Danby gets for us with you, and stay away from the beer and pizza."

6

Joe Galimore turned the clock on the nightstand toward him. It was 2:00 A.M. For the last two nights he had been jolted awake by the stark realism of his dreams. He propped his head up with a pillow and lit a cigarette, knowing that sleep wouldn't come again for a few hours.

Sarah Galimore rolled toward her husband and slowly opened her eyes. "You okay, Joe?"

"Yeah."

"What are you thinking about?"

"Frank Detimore."

"What was he like?"

Galimore exhaled a stream of smoke and rearranged the pillow to a more comfortable position. "He was all right. The only guy I ever knew who didn't see color."

"Come on, Joe."

"No. I mean it. With anyone else that's a joke. But not with him. I got along with the other guys okay. We respected each other. But Frank was different. I think we were friends."

Sarah laughed softly and squeezed his arm.

"What are you laughin' at?"

"You. I was thinking about that time at the airport. Before you left for your first tour."

"What about it?"

"That white lady who asked you if you were a Green Beret. And you pointed to your head and said, 'No lady, I'm a nigger. This is a green beret.' "

Joe laughed and put his arm around his wife.

"You having second thoughts, Joe?"

"No. I'd like to help Frank out. And fifty grand looks real good when you're laid off and workin' two part-time jobs."

"I don't know. It scares me."

"Hell, the money can do more for you than I can."

"Don't talk like that, Joe. Nothin's worth more to me than you."

He felt the top of the nightstand for the ashtray, and crushed out his cigarette. "We can pay off the house, clear up the bills, and put some in the bank for Natalie's education."

"She needs *you*, Joe. More than the money."

"I'm too mean to die, baby. You know that."

Sarah had seen a great change in her husband since Jack Callahan's visit. It was a rebirth. He had been moody and bitter since being laid off, and the stress was beginning to affect their relationship. He was proud of his skills as an electrician, and she saw how the menial jobs he had taken had stripped away his dignity and filled him with frustration and anger. She knew he hurt deep inside when he couldn't buy their five-year-old daughter a toy she wanted,

115

and how embarrassed he felt when he couldn't go to a ball game with his friends. And she cried, privately, when she saw the defeat and humiliation that haunted him for days after the monthly— now weekly—calls from creditors. He had always been a reticent and quiet man, literal when he spoke, though considerate and open with those close to him. But he had been withdrawing more each week, and avoiding their friends; and the time spent in front of the television set, alone, was increasing, and she was worried about him. And then came the visit from Callahan, and his mood changed overnight, and she felt that regardless of the dangers, she hadn't the right to ask him not to go.

"It was different over there," Joe said. "It wasn't what you had in the bank that mattered; it was what you had inside. Could your buddies depend on you when Charlie was screamin' and goin' crazy and comin' at you with everything he had? I was good, baby. I was *good*. And Frank, he had the killer instinct. Always did the right thing at the right time."

Sarah listened to her husband's reminiscences for a while, then drifted slowly back to sleep, dealing, as best she could, with the gnawing fear that had been with her for the past two days, and would remain with her, she knew, until he was safely back home.

7

Rick Donatelli sprinted the last one hundred yards of his daily run on the beach in front of his house. Checking his stopwatch, he smiled, pleased with the time. Not bad, he thought, two miles in eighteen minutes, in the sand, with boots on. He massaged the bulging triceps of his powerful arms, sore from the extra sets he had done.

He walked along the water's edge to cool down, feeling the tension and frustration drain from him. He searched his memory for the name of the hotel Callahan had said he would be staying at in New Orleans. The Saint Louis? Yeah, that was it . . . in case you change your mind. That Mick bastard. He knew.

As he crossed the beach and approached the house, he saw his father's Cadillac pull into the driveway, and knew what had prompted the visit.

The small, nattily dressed man turned up the collar of his vicuña overcoat against the cold wind coming in off the ocean, and waited by the steps leading up to the deck that extended out over the sand.

"What's the matter with you, Ricky? I don't have enough problems?"

"I'm sorry, Pop."

"Sorry. He's sorry. The chef says you told him his food was garbage. And Vinnie tells me when he asked you nicely not to drink any more you threw a glass at him. What kind of behavior is that? It took me all morning to make peace."

"I said I was sorry. It won't happen again."

"You tell them you're sorry."

"I'll take care of it."

"You have a problem, you come to me. You can't talk to your father anymore?"

Donatelli put his arm around his father's shoulder. "Yeah. Of course I can. It's something I had to work out for myself."

"Something to do with your friend from the Army?"

"Yeah."

"Trouble?"

"No. I owe a debt, Pop. To a friend."

"I asked you . . . stay away from the casinos. How much?"

"Not money. Honor."

Salvatore Donatelli listened quietly, his large, liquid brown eyes showing concern as his son told him of the mission and his decision to go.

"That's dangerous business, Ricky. But you do what your heart tells you."

"Can you get along without me for a few weeks?"

His father smiled. "Somehow I'll manage." He shook his finger at his son, then pointed to the house. "When

118

you come back, you marry that girl. I don't like you living together like that. It's not right. If your mother were here . . . God rest her soul. She's a good girl, a nice girl. She'll make you a good wife.''

"I don't need a wife, Pop. Not yet.''

"I've got a son who'd send me to my grave without grandchildren.''

"I'll work on it.''

"You get married first. Then you work on it.'' As he walked toward the car, he stopped and turned to his son. "You be careful. And go to confession before you leave. And put some clothes on. You'll catch pneumonia dressed like that.''

8

Pleased by Donatelli's call, Callahan left the hotel room in good spirits. He crossed the inner courtyard, through the miniature jungle of semitropical plants, to the lobby and on out to the quiet street in the heart of the French Quarter. The air smelled sweet and clean after the rain and the pavement glistened in the bright early-morning sun.

As he reached the end of the block and turned the corner, he looked back and caught a glimpse of a man crossing the street near the entrance to the hotel. Certain it was the same man he had seen last night after leaving the restaurant and touring Bourbon Street, he continued walking slowly, then stepped into a doorway where he could watch the corner through the reflections of the shopwindows across the street.

The tall dark-haired man in the tan raincoat stopped when he reached the intersection, quickly looking in the direction Callahan had gone, then crossed the street with a purposeful stride and walked in the opposite direction.

Jack saw him stop, look in a shopwindow, and glance back before continuing on.

Callahan left the doorway and walked to the end of the block where he turned onto the cross street and immediately ducked into an alleyway and waited. He heard footsteps approaching, the pace quickening, then slowing, then stopping at the corner.

The agent the Defense Intelligence Agency had assigned to tail Jack chose to go to his right. After a few more steps he was pulled off balance and dragged by the collar into a narrow, dimly lit alley and slammed against the wall. He was pinned there by one hand that gripped his hair and held his face against the rough, damp surface, and another that was clamped tightly on his throat.

"Move and I'll crush your windpipe," Callahan said, tightening his grip.

Luger coughed and gagged. "Easy," he said in a strained, raspy voice. Judging the odds to be heavily in Callahan's favor, he decided against any offensive moves and relaxed against the wall, dropping his arms to his sides, not wanting to challenge the power and ability that emanated from the man.

"What the hell do you want?" Callahan asked, loosening his hold.

"Just doing my job."

"For who? CIA, DIA, FBI, who?"

There was no answer.

"You do it somewhere else or you're going to get hurt."

"Can't do that."

Callahan shoved his face harder against the wall. "Stay out of my way."

"Can't do that either."

Jack spun him around and drove a fist deep into his

stomach, buckling his knees and knocking him to the ground, where he sat, stunned and gasping in the middle of a dark, oily puddle.

"I find you on my tail again, I'll break both your legs." With that he left the alleyway and moved quickly down the street.

Luger sat calmly until his breathing returned to normal, then struggled to his knees, and with the support of the wall, got to his feet.

" 'Let him know he's being followed,' " he mumbled to himself. "Damn idiots. You couldn't scare that hard-nose off with an M79."

Callahan checked the slip of paper with the address, then pressed the buzzer on the brass plate, swinging the gate open when the catch was released.

The paint on the front of the narrow two-story house was faded and peeling, and the windows were shuttered on the street side, but as he entered the walled walkway and approached the rear of the house, the atmosphere changed dramatically. The back of the house, freshly painted and neatly trimmed, faced an inner brick courtyard filled with the flavor of the Old South. High walls, covered with wisteria, sheltered a private and peaceful garden partially shaded by a large live oak tree draped with Spanish moss, and the scent of green olive trees and tulip trees filled the air.

Callahan stopped and enjoyed the scene before climbing the stairs leading to a wrought-iron balcony overlooking the garden. Knocking on the doorframe, he walked through the open French doors and entered a large room, tastefully decorated with antiques and Oriental rugs, and dominated by a large, highly polished mahogany desk set to one side.

The delicate silk draperies billowed, and a faint musty odor stirred with the breeze that swirled in from the courtyard.

"Not exactly what I expected from an arms dealer," Jack said, studying the oil paintings on the pale ivory walls.

"What did you expect?" asked the broad, heavyset man seated behind the desk.

"Steel file cabinets, a card table. A folding chair."

"I enjoy the finer things in life, Mr. Callahan."

Jack glanced at the Chinese porcelain displayed on an ornately carved table. "That stuff real?"

Justin Hanks raised an eyebrow and gave his most condescending look. "That *stuff* is priceless. I know men who would kill to have it."

"Nice. Aren't you afraid someone will steal it?"

Hanks smiled, his small, close-set eyes becoming mere slits in his fleshy face. "It's rather foolish to go to a great deal of trouble to possess something you will never live to enjoy."

"Words to live by," Jack said flatly. "Did you check my reference?" he asked, referring to the call he had made to Hanks the previous evening.

"Collins authenticated your background and vouched for your trustworthiness. He said to give you his best. You served with him in Angola?"

"Rhodesia," Jack answered, knowing that Hanks was testing him.

"May I see your left forearm, Mr. Callahan?"

Jack removed his jacket and rolled up his shirt sleeve.

"Excellent," Hanks said, seeing the long fishbone scar.

"Eddie said you could get me whatever I wanted: weap-

123

ons, equipment, even arrange the necessary contacts for transportation.''

"I can. What are your resources?''

"More than adequate for what I have planned.''

"I require payment in full in advance. In cash. I'm certain Collins told you that I too am trustworthy.''

"Oh, he did. Considering your clients, the fact that you're still alive confirms that.''

"Fine, Mr. Callahan. We understand each other. Now, what is it you need?''

Jack handed him the list he had worked on for the past two nights, and sat in a velvet-upholstered wing chair while Hanks scanned the pages, putting small check marks after some of the items.

"Do you want the Special Forces medical bag?'' Hanks asked.

"Two of them.''

"The M60 with the barrel cut back to the gas piston is not a problem, but the one-hundred-round box magazine may be. The rest I have in stock or have easy access to. When and where do you want to take delivery?''

"Bangkok, in three weeks.''

A mild look of surprise briefly appeared on Hanks' face. "I would have thought South America.''

"Is that a problem?''

"Nothing is a problem, Mr. Callahan, if the money is right. Actually it will cost you less. I have excellent contacts in Thailand. Most of my stock is there.''

Jack unfolded a map of Southeast Asia and placed it on the desk. Pointing to the northeast section of Thailand where the Mekong River followed the Laotian border, he said, "I'll need a staging area somewhere in here, a plane that can operate from a jungle strip and take five men to

124

thirty thousand feet, and a helicopter with a range of at least three hundred miles, depending on the departure point, and the capacity to carry thirteen men. A Huey would do it. I'll also need the crews.''

Hanks studied the map and made a circle north of Ubon with his pen. "I have some people working in this area. The men near Khemmarat would have what you require.''

Khemmarat was situated on the Laotian border where the Se' Bang Hieng flowed into the Mekong. Jack carefully measured the distance across Laos to a point in Quang Tri province. It was just under a hundred twenty miles. "That'll be fine.''

"I assume you'll need a parachute drop and a helicopter pickup in that area?'' Hanks said, scribbling some notations.

"Yes. What are the qualifications of the men you have there?''

"They are very well qualified, Mr. Callahan. They are mercenaries under contract to me, and quite familiar with your type of mission.'' Hanks checked his notes and handed his calculations to Jack. "When will I receive payment?''

"It will be delivered to you within forty-eight hours.''

Hanks shook his head and gave Jack a business card with the name of a bank and an account number on the back.

"Have the funds deposited in that account. If in forty-eight hours they have been credited, there is no need for further contact.'' He pointed to the card. "The address below the account number is where you will find your contact in Bangkok. His name is Marcel. He will take you to a small warehouse I will have rented to store the things you have ordered, and then lead you to the mercenary camp. Good luck, Mr. Callahan.''

*　　*　　*

Jack drove uptown to the Garden District, the exclusive residential area where Betty Detimore lived with her parents and found the Crawford residence with little difficulty.

The large antebellum-style mansion was surrounded by ten landscaped acres enclosed by a curving, ten-foot-high Jefferson-style brick wall. Through the front gate, the driveway wound past meticulously maintained formal gardens, ending in a circle before the towering white columns at the entrance to the house.

Betty Detimore greeted him at the door before he had time to ring. An anxious look disturbed her quiet beauty.

Jack smiled and nodded. "It looks like it's on."

Betty embraced him and held him tightly. "Daddy has been waiting all day to meet you. He's in the library."

"Little Bit," Harley Crawford called out. "Who was at the door?"

"Daddy, this is Jack Callahan," she said as they entered the large oak-paneled library.

Harley crossed the room and vigorously shook Jack's hand. "It's a pleasure to meet you, son. Little Bit, go get Mommy. I want her to meet this young man."

Jack glanced about the room, studying the World War II mementos on the walls. A large photograph of General Patton hung above a grouping of unit and personal citations, and a green-matted frame enclosed a Silver Star, a Bronze Star, and a Purple Heart with two clusters.

"You served with the 4th Armored?" Jack asked.

"Best damn fighting outfit there ever was; led by the finest American who ever lived."

Jack grinned. "Was there a question in there?"

Harley Crawford laughed heartily. "The subject isn't open to debate, son. Not in my library."

Amanda Crawford entered the room and stood next to

her husband. The attractive, elegant woman was the perfect foil for the rangy, rawboned man beside her.

"Mommy, this is Jack Callahan. Frank's commanding officer, and friend."

"How nice to meet you, Mr. Callahan. Betty has told us quite a lot about you."

Callahan smiled and gently shook Mrs. Crawford's hand.

"Will you be staying with us for a while?"

"I'm afraid not. I have a flight out tonight."

"You must stay for dinner."

"I believe I can."

"Wonderful. We appreciate what you're doing. I only wish our grandchildren were here to meet you."

"We'll join you later for drinks," Harley said. "Right now we have some business to discuss. So you two just scoot on out of here." Placing his arms around Betty and his wife, he escorted them to the hallway, closing the large, raised-panel doors as he came back in.

"What's your pleasure, Jack?" he asked, going to the built-in bar in a corner near the doors that opened onto the terrace.

"Bourbon, sir."

Harley's rough-hewn face showed grave concern as he handed Jack his drink. "Tell me, what are the chances of getting Frank out . . . the bottom line."

"Good. It's our kind of mission, Mr. Crawford."

"Harley. Call me Harley."

"Harley. The surviving members of the team have all agreed to go, and we have in-depth experience in this kind of operation."

"Damn," Harley said, taking a long drink. "I can't imagine what he's been through these past twelve years. I didn't approve of him at first, you know. Nobody was

127

good enough for my Little Bit. But when I got to know him . . . Tried to get him to leave the Army, come and work for my construction company. He didn't want any part of that. Said he wasn't going to be the boss' son-in-law.''

"He loved the Forces," Jack said. "He was what they were all about.''

Harley shook his head in disgust. "A man who won the Congressional Medal of Honor, and they won't lift a finger to help him. Just write him off.''

"It's not the military. If they had their way, they'd go in after them tomorrow. It's the politicians.''

"It always is," Harley said. "They wouldn't listen to Patton either. He told them they had better let him kick those Russian bastards back across their own border, but they didn't want to hear it.''

"Maybe we'll learn our lesson one of these days.''

"Let's hope not too late," Harley said. "Tell me about the mission. How many men are you taking in?''

"There will be five of us," Jack said, handing him the list he had compiled of the men's names and addresses, and the instructions and amount to be paid to Hanks.

Harley showed no reaction to the two hundred thousand dollars required for the mission's logistics. He went to his desk and brought Jack a checkbook.

"This account is set up for you to draw on for expenses during the training period: five hundred dollars a week for each man, transportation to and from your destination, whatever you need. Tomorrow I'll have fifty thousand dollars deposited in separate accounts for each man on the list. If you need anything else, any additional equipment, just call. You can hire more men if you like.''

128

"No. I prefer to go in lean, with men I have confidence in."

"It's your show."

"I'll call you when we're ready to leave. It should be in about three weeks."

Jack accepted the offer of another drink, and at Harley's urging, related the details of his plan for the mission. Two hours passed and Jack lost count of the drinks, caught up in Harley's enthusiasm and questions.

"Damn, if I were twenty years younger, Jack, I'd be right in there with you." He looked at his watch, and emptied his glass. "Time to join the ladies for dinner." He placed his hand on Callahan's shoulder as they walked down the hallway to the dining room.

"Bring him back to us, Jack."

"I'll do my best."

"I know you will, son."

That night, after Callahan left, Betty Detimore sat alone in her bedroom. She brought out the photograph albums filled with snapshots of her and Frank and the children. She thought about the first years of their marriage at Fort Bragg and the difficulty she had had in adjusting to the life-style. She had almost destroyed their marriage by urging him to leave the Army and accept her father's offer, before realizing how much Special Forces meant to him and how proud he was to be a part of them.

A photograph of their first home brought back the bitter-sweet memory of how he had refused the expensive house her father offered to buy them as a wedding present. "That's in officer's country," Frank had said, and bought a small ranch-style house in a subdivision where some of his friends lived. She had been heartbroken and began to believe the marriage had been a mistake until she saw the kindness and gentleness that lay beneath the rough, hardened exterior of the complex man. She smiled at the memory of him, two days after they had moved into the house, standing in the hallway with a meticulously dressed young man—an interior decorator he had hired. "You can have him do anything you like to the inside of the house, honey," he told her. "Just do me a favor and schedule him so he isn't around when the guys come over."

A happy face, beaming with pride, smiled at her from a photograph of Frank, clad in filthy fatigues, his chin covered with black stubble, as he held his newborn daughter, having rushed to the hospital from field maneuvers.

She turned the pages of the album, glancing at the rows of snapshots of camping and fishing trips. Fondly remembering how he had patiently taught her to fly-fish, and how she had come to enjoy it, and the first salmon she had caught—the largest one of the trip.

Tears came to her eyes when she came to the large portrait-photograph that Frank had given her for her last birthday before he was captured. He was wearing his dress uniform, and his beret; the children sat on his knees. The tears streamed down her face as she read the inscription: *What more could a man ask for—you and two beautiful daughters. I love you, honey.*

Betty closed the album and dried her tears. She thought about calling Lisa and Karen, but held to her resolution, despite her father's opposition, of waiting until the mission was under way before telling them that their father might be coming home.

As the girls grew older, they remained sympathetic to her belief that he was still alive, but she knew that they had long ago resigned themselves to the fact that they would never again see the man who was now only a warm, distant memory of their childhood. Betty had decided that the pain and anguish of knowing where he was, and his circumstances, would hurt her daughters too deeply if nothing was being done to bring him home. She would tell them when Callahan called and the team was ready to leave on the rescue mission.

She glanced in the full-length mirror as she changed into her nightgown, appalled at how thin she was, having lost ten pounds she could ill afford to spare. She had been tense, and nervous, and afraid: afraid that the mission would fail; afraid that if it was successful, the man who returned to her would not be the man she loved. Nonsense! she told herself. Not Frank. He was strong. They could never destroy him.

She turned the photograph of him on the nightstand toward her as she got into bed, and stared at it until she fell asleep.

9

Smashy Badowski and Phil Houser stood beside Callahan watching the passengers from the Rocky Mountain flight from Denver file into the baggage section of the Aspen airport. They had arrived a half hour earlier and were now waiting for Rick Donatelli.

"Hey, Rick," Smashy shouted. "Over here."

Impeccably dressed in a custom-tailored three-piece pin-stripe suit, Donatelli made his way through the obstacle course of ski bags and luggage, stopping to grab hold of an attractive young girl who had tripped over a pair of ski boots and nearly fallen. She flashed a flirtatious smile, and Donatelli winked and continued on his way, straightening his tie and rearranging the handkerchief in his coat pocket.

"I see they still fall all over you," Houser said, shaking his hand.

"What can I tell you." He glanced at Smashy and grinned, noticing the paperback novel in his hand. "Still chewing on the covers, huh, Smashy?"

"Nice guy," Smashy said. "Twelve years, and you start in on me first thing."

Donatelli embraced him in a bear hug. "But I missed you, you goddamn animal."

"Hey. It's not like that anymore."

Donatelli pointed to the dark bruises around Smashy's eyes. "Yeah. I can tell by your face. Where's Galimore?"

"He didn't give me his flight number," Jack said. "He'll call when he gets in."

"It's good to see you guys," Donatelli said, grabbing his two Gucci suitcases as they came off the cart.

"Cute," Smashy said. "Real cute. You got a matching purse, too?"

"Style, Badowski. You know what I mean?" He made an exaggerated slow appraisal of Smashy's clothes, and shook his head. "Pull up your socks or I won't let you stand next to me."

The four men walked outside to the parking lot and Jack's Jeep Cherokee.

"Don't you ever clean this thing?" Donatelli asked, carrying his luggage to the back of the mud-splattered vehicle.

"The rain takes care of it," Jack said, lowering the tailgate and putting the bags in with the others.

Donatelli looked inside. "Nice. Matching interior. It looks like raccoons live in here."

"You worried about a little dirt, or what?" Smashy said. "Hell, you can just sponge off that cheap double-knit polyester you're wearin'."

Houser sat in the front passenger seat and looked over at Jack. They both laughed, reminded of how the constant raillery between Donatelli and Smashy had, in Vietnam, been a welcome source of comic relief.

133

"This suit cost more than your house, clown."

Boomer heard the strange voices and stood back from the door as Jack had trained him to do, snarling and growling, waiting to lunge at the intruders.

Smashy looked through the large plate-glass window of the small stucco house. "What's that? Your pet bear?"

"That's Boomer," Jack said. "You'll like him when you get to know him."

"If he lets us live that long," Houser said, backing away as Jack opened the door.

"It's okay, Boomer," Jack called to the still-snarling dog. "It's okay. Come on out and say hello."

Boomer bounded outside and sat protectively before Jack, nuzzling him for a pat, his wary eyes on the strange men. Satisfied that they were no threat, he sauntered over to each of them, bumping them with his muzzle to get their scent, going on to the next man when someone reached to pet him.

"It's going to be a little cramped," Jack said as they entered the house, "but we've got to live, eat, and train together if we're going to leave here as a team."

Boomer rushed in and ran to the kitchen, flopping on the floor in front of his food dish, a paw on either side, grumbling and watching the men in the living room.

"Easy, big fellow," Donatelli said to the dog. "Smashy ate on the plane."

"There are twin beds and a cot in the guest room," Jack said, "and the sofa here pulls out to a double bed. Take your pick. The water heater isn't very big, so we're going to have to schedule showers."

Jack heard a car pull into the driveway, and looked

outside to see Joe Galimore getting out of a taxi. Boomer followed him as he went out to greet him.

"When did you get in?"

"A couple hours ago. I thought I'd look around a little." He paid the driver and tossed his duffel bag over his shoulder. "I just saw a guy pay eight grand for a gold belt buckle with a few diamond chips in it."

"Welcome to the Beverly Hills of the Rockies."

"I feel like a raisin in a bowl of rice."

Boomer sat beside Jack, his eyes riveted on Galimore. Ignoring Jack's assurances, he continued growling and showing his teeth. Callahan suddenly realized that Boomer had never seen a black person.

Galimore let the duffel bag slip from his shoulder, and crouched down to Boomer's level. He made eye contact with him, then looked away, repeating the procedure four more times.

Boomer stopped growling and walked hesitantly toward Galimore, who extended his hand palm down. Boomer sniffed the proffered hand, then sat and cocked his head to one side.

Galimore moved in a precise, confident manner and stroked the top of Boomer's head. "That's a good boy."

"Not bad," Jack said.

"I made friends with all the junkyard dogs when I was a kid."

"Hey, Joe," Smashy called from the doorway. "Nice tan. Where you been, down the Bahamas?"

"Uh huh," Galimore said, picking up his duffel bag. "I see things haven't changed much."

Callahan set up a large display board at one end of the living room and tacked a map of Southeast Asia, and his

135

old patrol map, onto the surface. He sorted through the manila envelope containing the satellite and SR-71 photographs Smashy had brought with him, and arranged them in the order he was going to use them. The enlargements were excellent. Danby had managed to get everything he had asked for.

The team sat around the living room facing the board. Boomer jumped onto the sofa and curled up next to Smashy.

"Ahhh . . ." Donatelli said. "Look at that. Just like prom night, huh, Smashy?"

"Hey, Jack," Smashy said, "I think he likes me."

"No. You're in his spot."

Callahan got a yardstick to use as a pointer, and stood to one side of the board.

"You've all had a chance to read Frank's letter and see the map. I don't suppose any of you missed the irony of the camp's location."

"Hell, no," Donatelli said. "We humped every inch of trail in that area for six months."

"Exactly." Jack pinned a photograph on the board. "This is a photo of the camp Frank is in. Unfortunately there are a lot of trees in the compound, so the camera only got what wasn't underneath them. And that's not much more than edges of roofs and sections of fencing. But it's enough when added to what Frank gave us in his letter. By using what I could see from the photo, I made a rough sketch of what the layout should look like, and by extrapolation, I figured out the interior dimensions—a hundred twenty-five meters by two hundred fifty meters. We can fill in the blanks with an on-site recon before we hit them."

"Frank said there are usually twenty guards," Houser said. "Any idea what weapons they have?"

"I don't know. But it can't be more than automatic rifles, probably AK-47s. This is a subcamp out in the middle of the jungle. There's no war going on there, so there's no reason for them to have anything else just to guard prisoners."

"Anything new in the surrounding area since we've been there?" Smashy asked.

Jack removed the close-up of the compound and put up the series of photographs that covered a thirty-mile radius of the camp, carefully aligning the edges as he tacked them to the board. The photographs showed a region of lush mountainous jungle, and a wide river that coursed through the narrow valleys to the Laotian border where it branched off into smaller streams and disappeared beneath the jungle canopy. There were sections of a road visible at intervals between the POW camp and the small army base to the northeast. But there were few signs of man's existence and no easy access to the area other than the narrow dirt road. Callahan smiled inwardly, reminded of how beautiful and captivating the region was.

He pointed to a barely visible patch of open ground a mile north of the camp.

"The summary that came with the photographs identifies this as a village. Probably Montagnard, but because of a rice shortage they've moved some Vietnamese into the area to do slash-and-burn farming, so it could be one of theirs. We'll give it a wide berth on the way in. They'll hear the attack on the camp, but it's highly unlikely that they have any modern means of communication with the outside world. So from our standpoint, they're inconsequential.

"This is our only potential problem," he continued,

137

pointing to the Vietnamese army base. "It's ten miles away."

"How many troops?" Houser asked.

"The best estimate is an understrength battalion. Some of the buildings are identified as barracks, but there are three or four that just look like large warehouses. There is no armor, no artillery, and no heliborne capability. They have an old American Cayuse chopper, and that's it. So, the only way they can get a reaction force to us is by truck, over this road." He ran the tip of the yardstick along the route to the camp. "As of last week, it was in poor condition, with sections partially washed out. And knowing the Vietnamese, and the low priority it has to have, it's not going to be repaired in a hurry."

"But it is passable?" Donatelli said.

"Yes. But at best, a deuce and a half carrying troops can make twenty miles an hour on it. And that's giving them some. So if we assume the worst possible scenario—that Charlie will get in the trucks and under way the moment we hit the camp—it will still take him at least thirty minutes to get there. By then we'll be long gone. But they aren't going to be able to hear our attack, so a more optimistic assessment of the probabilities is that they won't even know the camp was hit until we're back in Thailand celebrating."

"How long do you estimate it will take us to own the camp?" Galimore asked.

"Ten minutes. Tops. There are only twenty guards, they'll be sleeping when we hit them, and that's a small area to control."

Galimore studied the map of Southeast Asia for a few moments, then said, "How do you figure we're gonna be out of their reach in another twenty minutes?"

"I'll start with our insertion, then get to the extraction."
He pointed to Khemmarat on the border of Thailand and
Laos. "There's a mercenary base here, exactly one hundred seventeen miles from the POW camp. They are going
to fly us in—"

"Where the hell are they going to land?" Smashy asked.

"They're not."

"We're going to jump in?" Donatelli said. "In broad
daylight?"

"No. We're going in at night."

"You don't think an airplane at night might attract some
attention?" Smashy said. "There are two guard towers at
that camp. The guys on duty might get a little suspicious
when they see us floating down on top of them."

"The drop zone is four miles from the camp, and the
plane won't get any closer than seven miles. They'll never
hear it."

Houser instantly realized what Callahan was proposing:
a High Altitude–Low Opening jump. "You've got to be
kidding! A HALO at night? And a blind drop?"

"That's right. The blind drop is insignificant; there
won't be anyone down there waiting for us. And we all
have HALOs and night jumps under our belts. We'll go
out three miles from the drop zone at thirty thousand feet;
we'll deploy our chutes at one thousand. With a maximum
of twenty-nine thousand feet of track time, we can easily
cover the ground distance to the clearing."

Houser remembered the High Altitude–Low Opening
jumps—thirty-four of them—he had made during his
years with the Forces. Jumping from an airplane at thirty
thousand feet and free-falling twenty-nine thousand feet
before opening your parachute seemed, on the surface,
simple enough for men trained in the procedures. But there

were inherent risks, even for the most experienced men, let alone someone who hadn't done it in twelve years. The jumps required total concentration, and conditioned reflexes and thought processes achieved only through training and discipline. The tracking to the drop zone—the technique of holding your body in an airfoil configuration to attain horizontal movement during freefall—was a precision maneuver, requiring constant practice to master. The HALO jump was an excellent method of secretly inserting a team into hostile territory, but it was extremely dangerous when attempted by men as out of condition and as far removed from their training as they were.

"None of us have jumped in twelve years, Jack," Houser said.

"We have three weeks, and the Glenwood Springs Skydiving Club is only an hour away. I've made the arrangements."

"What if the weather doesn't cooperate?" Houser asked.

"We'll use the same drop zone but make a standard jump, or we'll wait until it clears. I'll have an advance weather forecast before we leave."

"How big is the DZ?" Donatelli asked.

Jack tacked up a blow-up of a clearing on a plateau above a narrow, steep-sided valley.

"I thought of this place when I first saw Frank's map. We were ambushed here one morning."

"Yeah," Galimore said. "I remember that. It's about five miles from our old camp."

"Right. I wasn't sure if it was an abandoned Yard field used for dry rice farming, which the jungle would have reclaimed by now, or a natural clearing. The photograph confirms the latter. It's probably decomposed granite-base soil where only grass will take root. And it's perfect. More

140

than we need. One hundred fifty meters by eighty meters. There are trails leading down into the valley and the camp is only four miles away. The trails are probably still used by the locals, so they should be in decent condition. If we're on the ground by oh-one hundred, that gives us plenty of time to make it to the camp, check it out, and hit them at first light.''

Jack picked out one of the photographs from the thirty-mile-radius series and put it on the board. He pointed to a small valley fifteen miles from the POW camp, just across the Laotian border.

''There are a number of places here where a chopper can put down. The mercenaries will have a Huey in position there by the time we hit the camp. As soon as we've secured the area, we get on the radio, and they'll be inside the compound within ten minutes. We load Frank and the others on board and we're gone. Ten minutes more and we're across the border, another forty-five minutes and we're in Thailand.''

''Remember Murphy's Law,'' Donatelli said.

''Fuck Murphy. We've defied him before, we'll do it again. Questions.''

''What about spending twenty-four hours on the ground,'' Houser said, ''to observe the routine of the camp?''

''Only if we run into any snags or surprises when we check it out. Otherwise the risk of discovery far exceeds any benefits we'd get from it. Our edge will be maximum surprise with maximum impact.''

''I keep thinking about the Son Tay raid,'' Galimore said, referring to the 1970 raid by an elite Special Forces team on a prison camp in North Vietnam, from which prisoners had been moved just prior to the mission. ''What if we come up empty?''

"The prisoners have been there for five years, and the intelligence summary says the camp was still occupied last week. And we know Frank was there seven months ago. They're not expecting any trouble, so there's no reason for them to be moved. Remember, Son Tay took place during the middle of the war and had its own special problems. But to answer your question: if they're not there, it's mission in–mission out. Nothing happens. We call in the chopper."

"What are the target assignments?" Smashy asked.

"I haven't decided yet. We'll sketch them in roughly during training, but we can't make them definite based on the photograph of the camp. We'll have to wait until we recon it and pinpoint the location of the prisoners."

"What about weapons?" Galimore asked.

"All the equipment will be waiting for us in Bangkok. The primary weapons will be two CAR-15s, one M60, and two M16s with M203 grenade launchers mounted below the barrel. There are better weapons on the market, but I think it's best we stay with the ones we know inside out.

"Each man will have fifteen thirty-round magazines, and those with the M203s will carry two bandoliers of grenades—some high-explosive, some antipersonnel. The rest of us will each take an extra bandolier. We'll also have fifteen pounds of C4 plastic explosive and six Claymores. Everything is covered: fatigues, boots, smoke grenades, sidearms, rucksacks, radio, medical kits, equipment for the drop, and some other goodies we'll get into as the training progresses."

"Why don't we just go in with a larger force and hit the place with a helicopter assault?" Smashy said.

"It would require too many men and choppers to ensure taking the camp without giving the guards a chance to kill the prisoners. We don't have access to the men and matériel the Son Tay raiders had. That was a government-sanctioned operation. We sure as hell aren't.

"Also, we would be working with people we don't know, and organizing a larger force would take time. Frank's letter was written seven months ago. I'm not concerned about them being moved, but I am worried about how fast they are dying off."

"What about taking a chopper from Thailand to the drop zone? Then walk in to the camp?"

"We don't want to draw any attention on the way in. From thirty thousand feet, nobody is going to know we're coming. Believe me, the success of this operation depends on speed, the element of complete surprise, and above all, the KISS principle—keep it simple, stupid."

"Three weeks isn't much time," Galimore said.

"Patton said it best, Joe. A good plan violently executed now is better than a perfect plan next week. We can do it."

"You haven't said much, Phil," Jack said. "Do you have any questions?"

"Not about the plan," Houser said. "It's good. What I question is our ability to carry it out."

Donatelli shrugged. "That's no problem. We're all more than capable."

"Are we? Let's not kid ourselves. How long has it been since any of us has fired a weapon?" Houser glanced about the room. "That's what I thought. With the exception of Jack, not since 'Nam, if we exclude hunting. How far and fast can we move with fifty pounds on our backs, and how often in the last twelve years have we had to rely on instinctive reflexes to stay alive? This isn't a jog around the park, or an hour of weight lifting, or a barroom brawl.

143

This is for real, fellows. Face it, we're in decent shape, but we're not what we used to be."

"Yeah, but our strength is the strength of ten because our hearts are pure," Donatelli quipped.

"We're still a hell of a lot better than anything they got," Smashy said.

"It's that attitude that gets people killed. In our prime we were better than anything anyone had, but none of us can claim to be in his prime. We're all ten years past it."

"You saying we shouldn't go?" Galimore said. "We leave Frank to rot?"

Houser slowly shook his head. "No. I'm saying that we have some damn hard work ahead of us. Every one of us has got to get into top physical condition, or as close to it as we can come in three weeks' time."

"You just got the job," Callahan said. "You're in charge of PT."

Houser grinned. "You may live to regret that. We're going to run at least ten miles a day, and that's no mean feat at this altitude. And we're going to climb the mountains behind this house with fifty-pound packs on our backs, and we'll do calisthenics and anything else I can work into the schedule. And there will be a ten o'clock curfew and six o'clock reveille. I'm also in charge of diet. When we eat in restaurants, I order for all of us."

"Any place I can pump iron?" Donatelli asked.

"The health club has weights and Nautilus equipment," Jack said. "I can get us guest memberships."

"Good," Houser said. "I'll schedule a workout for us every other day. When do you want to start jumping?"

"Beginning the second week," Jack said.

"Are we going to have any weapons to fire?" Smashy asked.

"I called a friend with a gun shop in Carbondale. He'll have five AR-15s and five 9mm automatic pistols for me the day after tomorrow. They're not automatic weapons, but they are as close as we're going to get and stay legal."

"Where are we going to shoot?" Galimore asked.

"There's a small canyon behind the house. I've set up a course."

"What about your neighbors?" Donatelli asked.

"I only have one close enough to be bothered by the shooting. Maggie Hill. You can see her house through the trees. She's a good friend. We're five miles from town and this is the last house on the road. I have four acres; everything in front, behind me, and on the other side is federal land. We won't have any problems."

"You don't think our training is going to draw any attention?" Smashy asked.

"In Aspen?" Jack said. "Not only will they not notice, but if they did, they wouldn't care. There is no strange behavior in Aspen—with the possible exception of voting Republican."

10

Maggie Hill's curiosity was getting the best of her. For the past week she had seen Callahan and his friends adhering to their training schedule. Muffin woke her with her barking at six o'clock each morning as the men left the house and ran toward Independence Pass, and the frightened dog hid under the bed late in the afternoon when they went back into the canyon to shoot. She had talked to Jack in town, and he had told her that he was taking a month off from the ski school, but he had been less then candid about his friends and what they were doing.

Maggie was intrigued. They all had the same look of self-confidence and purpose about them.

"And they're cute, Muffin. Not a one in costume. No gold chains, no blow-dried hair, no designer jeans. Wouldn't it be nice? A man who spends less time in front of the mirror than I do?"

The expertly clipped and groomed white standard poodle

146

sat attentively at Maggie's side, her eyes on the contents of the saucepan just removed from the stove.

"Ah, shoot!" Maggie said. The fettuccine sauce was curdled and lumpy, and the noodles clung tenaciously to the bottom of the pan.

"Eight hundred dollars to that damn hermaphrodite for a gourmet cooking course, and look at this mess." She emptied the pan into the garbage disposal and turned it on. "There goes our snack, Muffin."

Turning the disposal off, Maggie was treated to a loud, raucous gurgling that came from a myna bird in a large cage set among a forest of plants in front of the floor-to-ceiling windows.

"Oh, shut up, Edgar. You're brain-damaged."

Taking a sprig of grapes from the refrigerator, Maggie put them in the bird's food tray. "Now don't throw them all over the floor, you filthy little bugger."

A University of Texas graduate, Maggie had spent countless hours, to no avail, trying to teach the recalcitrant bird to say "Hook 'em horns." Discouraged, she had given up his education and left him to his own devices. In three years he had learned to imitate the garbage disposal and a flushing toilet.

Looking out the window toward town, Maggie caught sight of a distant, lone figure coming up the road. She moved to the powerful Questar telescope set on a sturdy tripod at the window, and focused on the slow-moving figure a half mile away.

The rambling glass-and-redwood house was situated on a rise with an unobstructed view down the valley to the edge of town, and she had purchased the telescope to watch the coyotes hunt and play in the large meadow

147

across the road, and to enjoy the sight of the elk when they came down from the mountains to graze.

She hurried through the house to the master bedroom suite and slid open the doors of a closet that took up the entire length of a thirty-foot wall. The dog trotted in and jumped onto the king-size bed, curling up against Maggie's pillow.

"I think I'll wear my Bognars. They do such a marvelous job of flattening the tummy and firming the backside."

She chose a richly hued green pair of the German-made slacks and slipped them on, pleased with the figure-flattering effect when she turned before the triple mirror. Her short, compact figure was firm and shapely, the result of limiting herself to only occasional self-indulgence in the rich foods she so dearly loved. Each lapse of willpower necessitated four days of near-starvation rations.

"It's mighty depressin', Muffin, when you can feel your buns against the back of your thighs."

"Let's see . . . the mink jacket? No. Too pretentious. Ahhh . . . this will do," she said, taking out a short-waisted downfilled ski parka. "This is more his type."

Maggie chuckled to herself. "Will you look at me, Muffin. Thirty-eight years old, three divorces, a fortune invested in self-awareness, self-actualization, consciousness-raising seminars, and all the rest of that crap, and I'm actin' like a schoolgirl."

The dog followed behind as she went back to the kitchen and looked briefly through the telescope. He was nearing the driveway to Callahan's house, moving slowly along the side of the road.

Maggie scraped the burnt edges from the coconut macaroons she had made the previous day, and placed them on

148

a plate, covering them with Saran wrap. She entered the attached garage through the kitchen door, and hesitated for a moment.

"What will it be, Muffin? Shall we take the Jeep? No. We'll walk over," she said, deciding to take the path through the woods. "More outdoorsy."

Smashy's breathing was labored and shallow. His lungs burned and his thighs ached as he plodded heavily up the driveway barely able to lift his legs. He had finished early at the health club and had decided to run the four miles back to the house while the others completed their workouts. Painfully aware that the others were in better condition, he was determined to trim down and close the gap by working harder.

Entering the house, he sat on the floor and petted Boomer before stripping off his clothes and going to the shower.

Maggie knocked on the door, and receiving no answer, stepped partway inside and called, "Anyone home? Jack? It's me, Maggie."

Boomer bounded forward and jumped up to greet her. Spotting Muffin outside, he darted through the door to play with his friend.

"Don't beat up on her, Boomer," Maggie called after him. "I wish the hell you'd learn how to play."

Boomer crashed into the reluctant animal, sending her tumbling into a snowbank where he straddled her and happily licked her face.

Maggie closed the door behind her and called out again. "Anyone home?" The large cork display board at one end of the living room caught her eye and she approached it, looking over the maps and photographs tacked to its surface.

"Who the hell are you?" a voice boomed from behind her.

She started and gasped loudly, turning to look into the massive blond-haired chest of the man she had seen running along the road. He towered over her, dripping wet, clasping a towel to his waist.

"Who the hell are you?" he repeated.

"Maggie Hill . . . I'm Jack's neighbor."

"What do you want?"

"I just stopped by to say hello. I'll . . . I'll just leave and come back later."

"No you won't," Smashy said angrily.

"I won't?"

"No. You sit down over there," he said, pointing to the sofa. "Jack'll be here in a little while."

"You mean I'm being held captive?" Maggie asked, regaining her composure and smiling disarmingly.

"I just want you here when Jack gets back."

"What's that all about?" Maggie asked, indicating the display board.

"That's none of your damn business. How come the dog let you in?"

"Boomer and I are old friends," Maggie said.

Smashy stared at the large expressive eyes and pleasant smile of the attractive woman across from him. "You always walk right into people's houses?"

"Jack doesn't mind. What are you and the other men doing here?"

"You ask too many questions," Smashy said, his tone softening.

"Will you tell me your name?" Maggie asked.

Smashy shrugged. "Yeah. Smashy."

Maggie smiled. "Smashy?"

"It's really Stanley. But my friends call me Smashy."

"Then Smashy it is. Would you like a cookie?" she asked, offering him the plate she had brought with her.

Smashy reached out, then pulled his hand back. "No. I'd better not. I'm on a diet."

"Aren't we all?"

Smashy heard Callahan's car pull into the driveway and went to the door, opening it as the men reached it.

Jack glanced at Smashy clad in the towel, and at Maggie sitting on the sofa.

"She just walked in when I was in the shower," Smashy said. "She saw all the stuff on the board. I made her stay until you got here."

Jack nodded. "I'll talk to her. It'll be okay."

Donatelli took in the scene and put his arm around Smashy's shoulder. "Now I know why you left early. This isn't like you, ole buddy. A fine-looking lady like that. We always counted on you to take the two baggers and the coyote uglies."

"What's a coyote ugly?" Galimore asked.

"When you wake up next to a girl who's curled up beside you, asleep on your arm, and you look at her, and she's so bad that you'd rather chew off your arm than wake her up—that's coyote ugly."

"Give me a break," Smashy said.

Jack sat on the sofa beside Maggie. "We've got a problem, Maggie. You walked in on something you're not supposed to know anything about."

"I gather it has something to do with that," she said, glancing at the display board.

"It has everything to do with that," Jack said.

"You're not mixed up in smuggling narcotics, are you?"

Jack smiled. "You know me better than that."

151

Maggie nodded. "I've heard the shooting back in the canyon, and I've seen you climbing the mountains with packs on your backs, and running every day. At first I thought maybe you were going back into the army." She looked again at the display board and fixed on the map of Southeast Asia. "There's not going to be another war in Vietnam, is there?"

"Sort of," Jack said. "A private one. We're training for a mission into Vietnam, to rescue a friend of ours. He's being held in a POW camp."

Maggie's eyes widened as she stared at Callahan, then at the other men who were standing in the kitchen talking among themselves. "I want to help, Jack. What can I do?"

"The most important thing you can do is not to say a word about this to *anyone*."

"Of course I won't. But I want to help. I want to contribute something."

"You can keep an eye on the place when you're home and we're not."

"And I can cook some meals for you," Maggie said enthusiastically.

"Sure," Jack said, against his better judgment. "I'll introduce you to the others, and you can work something out with Phil Houser. He's in charge of our diet during training."

Before leaving, Maggie had offered the use of her Jacuzzi to anyone who might need it, and arranged to cook dinner for them three days a week. Houser had accepted her offer of cooking every day, but yielded to Jack's insistence that they would need a few nights out, to get away from the rigors of training and planning.

"Can she be trusted?" Galimore asked when Maggie had left.

"Not to tell anyone what she knows? Yes," Jack said. "To cook an edible meal? No."

"She married or anything?" Smashy asked.

"No," Jack said. "Just your basic Aspen woman. She came here about two years ago and got a divorce, a dog, and a Jeep."

"She owns that big house?" Smashy asked.

"Yeah. Her last husband was Hill Oil. Hill Development Corporation. Hill Construction Equipment Corporation, and I don't know what else. The local paper said she got the largest divorce settlement in the history of the state of Texas. And that's saying something."

"I like her," Smashy said. "Pretty, too, you know."

"For what it's worth," Jack said, "she's a lot more sensitive than she lets on. She's been hurt. More than once."

"I was just askin'," Smashy said.

Donatelli grinned. "Ahhh . . . Smashy find woman. Fall in love. Go off feed."

"Come on," Smashy said, giving Donatelli a playful shove.

Houser sat in a chair in a corner of the living room, looking at the team. The high-altitude tans, the alert look in their eyes, and their relaxed expressions all gave evidence of the effects of the week's training. He knew that a goal of peak conditioning in the time remaining was unrealistic, but he was beginning to believe that they could, by strict adherence to the training program, attain a level of conditioning sufficient to do what they had planned. He had avoided calling Angela, not ready to tell her, yet not wanting to drag it out. His decision firm, he would call tonight. He was in it to the end.

11

Frank Detimore awoke with the first hint of pale light on the horizon. He had heard Donahue cry out in anguish twice during the night from his troubled sleep. This had happened only occasionally after the three days of torture he had been subjected to for his attempt on Latrine Lips' life following the Montagnards' escape. But in the past eight months it had become more frequent, until now it was a nightly occurrence.

Donahue had no memory of it when he woke, and Frank no longer brought it to his attention. He knew what was happening—Donahue was near the breaking point. The bold facade was still there during his waking hours, but it was crumbling; no longer a show of unconquerable spirit, but a desperate struggle to hold on to what remained of his dignity and sanity.

Latrine Lips was not satisfied with torture after Donahue's attack. He was determined to destroy him. His harassment of the young Marine was not random and whimsical as before, but carefully designed and coldly calculated. He had instructed Donahue to bow deeply in his presence, and scheduled frequent appearances arranged to deny his victim any respite—appearing at the lean-to during meals, and at the dock when they were washing, and making daily trips to the work area. Any act of disrespect or sign of rebellion brought instant and prolonged retaliation. He was obsessed with reducing Donahue to a groveling shell of what he had been.

The beatings were no longer merely meant to punish, but to injure and maim. Bones were broken and cracked, limbs dislocated, and Frank had repeatedly set his jaw, often to have it broken again before healing properly. Donahue's face was constantly swollen and discolored, and the few teeth that remained were splintered to jagged pieces.

Frank listened for the guard who would come and open the cage. He was thankful that Donahue had been put in with him where he could tend to his injuries as best he could. It was ostensibly meant as a punishment, making him share the early-morning duties, but Frank suspected it was also an insidious ploy by Latrine Lips to ensure that Donahue was kept alive and in repair. And Bad Eye was now less reluctant to give him the medical supplies he requested, forgoing the usual lecture and delivering everything on his list.

Frank heard the guard stirring in the hut, and gently shook Donahue's shoulder.

"Lock-up time, Mike."

Donahue rolled onto his back and extended his legs, placing his feet in the iron clamps. He moved his right arm back and forth from the elbow joint, finding that it would still extend only partway.

"How does it feel?" Detimore asked.

"Okay. It's getting there."

Frank had set the broken joint two months ago, removing the makeshift splint last week. "Don't force it. It'll straighten out in time."

"If that slope son of a bitch doesn't break it again." Donahue shuddered, remembering that it had been three days since he had been beaten, and knowing that his antagonist would not let a fourth go by without finding some excuse to hurt him. "He'll probably dump on me today," he said, watching the guard approach the cage. "I'll be a motherfucker if I'll bow to that asshole anymore. I've had it, Top. He's gonna have to kill me first."

Detimore knew he meant it. He had seen the hatred in his eyes whenever Latrine Lips stood before him. And he had seen him fight back the tears and rage when his instincts for self-preservation won out over his courage and pride. But he also knew that Latrine Lips wouldn't let him die, not the way Donahue wanted to.

"He ain't gonna break me, Top," he had told Frank countless times, but Frank knew that, given enough time, any man could be broken. He had made his decision. He couldn't stand by and watch Donahue being destroyed. It had been eight months since the letter had left with the Montagnards, and he had given up hope of its having gotten through. And even if it had, there was no guarantee that anything would be done. His only chance, the only hope for any of them, was for someone to escape and bring help.

"He won't get the opportunity," Frank said. "We're going. First chance."

Donahue's head snapped toward him. "Straight skinny, Top?"

"Today, tomorrow, the first chance we get, we're gone."

"Off the work detail?"

"Yeah. They pulled us into the woods three times yesterday when the rains hit. They can't see ten feet in front of them when it's really comin' down."

Donahue sat quietly when the guard reached the cage, but his thoughts swirled and his eyes came alive.

"Di! Di!" the guard commanded as he opened the door.

Donahue climbed out after Frank, nodding and smiling to the scowling guard. "Fuck you, rodent," he muttered under his breath as he walked toward the latrine.

Frank swung his machete in a wide arc, hacking at a tangle of vines and heavy brush at the edge of the small field they had cut from the jungle. Keeping one eye on the guards, he edged his way over to where Hendricks was flailing away at a thick vine and chanting a litany of invocations to his friend Jesus.

"I know you hear me, Lord. I can feel your presence. This ain't right. You came to see Maffey last night, and he won't tell me what you said. Now this is serious business, Lord. We gotta talk."

"Pete," Frank whispered.

Hendricks, startled, abruptly stopped working. His eyes darted about, coming to rest on Frank.

"Was that you, Frank?"

"Yeah."

"Wow! You had me goin' there for a minute. I thought you was the Lord."

"I want you to do something for me."

"Sure."

"I want your word that you'll do it."

"Yeah."

157

"If anything happens to me, I want you to take care of Dan Lucere."

"You sick or somethin'?"

"Somethin'. Make sure he eats, and walk him around the compound in the evening before lock-up. And take him to the latrine."

"Okay, Frank. I'll pray for him, too."

"You do that."

Detimore worked his way back to his assigned area. He caught Donahue's eye and jerked his head to the right. Donahue looked in the direction he had indicated and nodded.

A dark wall of rain covered the horizon above the mountains to the east. In a few minutes it would reach them and the guards would herd them from the edge of the jungle to the protective canopy of the trees.

Harry Cambell was working beside Detimore and had seen him talking to Hendricks.

"Hey, Frank," he whispered. "What's up?"

"Nothin'."

"What were you talking to Hendricks about? Anything I should know?"

"No. Just bullshit."

"Don't cause any trouble, Frank. We'll all end up like your friend Donahue."

"Get back to work, Harry. You're gonna draw heat."

The rain came in solid sheets. One moment the sun was shining brightly, and the next the sky was black and the ground became a red sucking mire. A few minutes later, and a shallow stream bed, where only a trickle of water had been, became a swirling torrent, swelling to crest its banks.

The prisoners sat in a loosely formed semicircle beneath the trees, a few yards into the jungle, while the guards, a short distance away, huddled together, giggling and smoking under a small tarp, protecting themselves from the rain that fell through the trees.

Detimore and Donahue sat on the left flank of their group, watching the guards closely, and inching their way backward into a dense clump of undergrowth. The noise of the torrential downpour smothered the sounds of their movements, and they were soon hidden from view less than ten feet into the brush.

Reaching the field, they ran along the edge to the far end where a small stream cut across and reentered the jungle. They followed the stream, running along the narrow, grassy strip on the bank, swatting at the branches that extended out into their path.

Donahue led the way, swinging wildly at the overhanging limbs, covering ground quickly with his long, even strides, occasionally losing his balance on the slippery footing. Frank tried to keep up, but his damaged leg was shot with needles of pain, and he fell twice, the second time nearly tumbling into the fast-moving water before grabbing hold of the clump of ankle-deep vines that had caused his fall.

Donahue slowed to a dogtrot after the first mile, and Frank managed to stay close until they were both forced to a slow, arduous walk when the stream narrowed and cut through a dense, swampy section of the jungle.

The soggy ground grabbed at their feet, doubling the effort of each step. Donahue twisted an ankle on a submerged root, and ignoring the throbbing pain, pressed on. The stream disappeared underground and they soon had to claw and scramble along the fetid, sulfurous ground, through prickly thickets and up steep, slippery banks. The jungle thickened until it was impossible to see more than a few feet ahead, forcing them to crawl on their stomachs. The unaccustomed exertion took its toll on the nearly depleted men.

"Gotta rest, Top."

"No. Keep moving. As far as we can before the rain quits and they miss us."

"What direction we headed?"

"Laos. I hope. Won't know until we get out of this stuff onto some high ground."

An hour later, when Frank was beginning to believe that the tangled underbrush would never end, they crawled into a stand of bamboo, enabling them to struggle to their feet and walk again. Another hundred yards and the jungle opened up to a small clearing of elephant grass as tall as a man. As though it had been turned off at its source, the rain stopped and the sun streamed through the trailing wisps of clouds.

Donahue shielded his eyes from the bright slanting rays and turned to Detimore. "Well, the shit is about to hit the fan."

The two men sprinted across the clearing and into the jungle on the other side.

Frank dropped to his knees, holding his side. "We'll rest for a few minutes," he said, "then climb to the top of that hill, see if we can get our bearings."

Donahue sat beside him, breathing heavily. "I ain't been this tired since boot camp."

"It's going to be a long haul, Mike. Fifteen miles to the border, then a hundred more across Laos. If we're lucky, we'll find some friendlies. If not . . ."

"We ain't prisoners no more, Top. That's somethin'."

Frank nodded. "Yeah." He kept his thoughts to himself. Dying in the attempt worried him least. Being recaptured held a terror all its own.

Gaining the top of the hill, they stood at the border of an abandoned Montagnard field, partially reclaimed by the jungle. A longhouse was visible through the trees at the other end, and the two men made their way cautiously toward it. A second longhouse came into view as they drew closer, but the absence of any activity confirmed Frank's suspicions that they were deserted, the inhabitants gone to another area in the custom of the seminomadic mountain tribes.

A thorough search of the bamboo and thatch houses set on stilts, and of the once-cultivated areas behind them where vegetables had been grown, provided nothing. There were no rice caches left behind in the granaries, and nothing remained in the garden plots.

A short distance through the woods behind the village, the ground dropped steeply away, and standing on a rocky ledge, Frank could see the terrain for miles around. A broad, muddy river snaked through the valley below, surrounded by a horizon that rippled with layers of jungle-covered hills extending to the Laotian border and beyond.

"Hey, Top!" Donahue called from behind him. "Look at this."

Donahue stood beside a large circular hole with a dome-shaped mound of earth eight feet high rising from it.

"It's a Montagnard grave," Frank said, having seen them before.

"What's all that shit?" Donahue asked, referring to the artifacts scattered about the site.

Frank pointed to the ten-foot-high pole topped with a small platform and a miniature longhouse. "That's where his spirit dwells. Temporarily, I think. The other things are

161

his personal possessions: clothing, farming tools, bracelets, whatever he owned. By the looks of it, he was probably the village chief.''

Recalling more of the tribal rites, Frank walked around the burial mound and found what he hoped would be there—a small thatch-roofed hut, two feet square, a few feet off the ground on stilts. Lifting the roof from the structure, he removed a cloth sack from inside.

"What's that?" Donahue asked.

"Rice. For his journey." Frank estimated, if properly rationed, there was enough to keep them alive for a week or more. With one of their problems temporarily solved, he felt some relief from the constant tension caused by the enormous weight of the difficulties he knew lay ahead of them.

He picked up from the mound a crudely fashioned shorthandled hoe and another similar tool, giving one to Donahue.

"It isn't much, but it'll have to do."

Donahue shrugged. "Hell, this is modern weaponry in the Corps."

Near the bottom of the mound, Frank saw a small earthen bowl he could use for cooking the rice, and stuffed it in the sack.

He led the way on the steep footpath that switchbacked down the hillside to the valley floor. The open woods at the top soon became thick jungle, all but impenetrable once off the path. With the rain ended, the jungle steamed and the heat became an oppressive burden, making breathing difficult. The mosquitoes, driven to the ground by the rain, rose from the undergrowth and swarmed in a prickly mist before their faces and over their hands.

The trail followed the course of the river through the

long, winding valley, taking them a few yards into the jungle away from the open area on the banks. They alternated periods of running with bouts of fast walking, taking advantage of the opportunity to move quickly that the trail provided. Frank knew the dangers of staying on the trail, but acknowledged the greater necessity of putting distance between them and the troops that must now be searching for them. The sooner they reached the Laotian border, the better the chance, regardless of how remote, of finding help. They ran and walked without pause for over three hours, until something ahead of them sent Frank diving off the trail and into the jungle, with Donahue on his heels.

Frank crawled on his stomach to the edge of the riverbank and looked across the smoothly flowing water. Less than fifty yards downstream, he saw the origin of the sounds that had alarmed him.

A group of children were playing along the far bank, and off in a clearing, twenty yards into the woods, he saw the outlines of a small village. Noticing the individual huts and the dress of the children, he determined that these were not Montagnards, but Vietnamese.

Signaling Donahue to stay low, they crawled back to the trail, crossed to the other side, and continued on their way, paralleling the river, but skirting the village, moving cautiously and not returning to the trail until they were well past it.

Both men were nearly dehydrated from their efforts. Frank was light-headed and feverish, and his leg hurt and began to swell below the knee, sending pulses of stinging pain up into his hip.

They stopped to rest and drink at a small mountain stream that flowed beneath a log footbridge on the trail, concealing themselves behind a dense thicket a few yards back from the path. Frank felt certain that they were within easy reach of the border, if not over it by now. A few hours of daylight remained, but neither of them had the strength to continue without resting.

Frank found a relatively dry and secluded area on a rise overlooking the trail where they could watch for approaching danger. Over Donahue's protests, he took first watch, letting the young Marine sleep soundly for the first time in months.

It was six hours into the silent, moonless night, the velvet blackness pressing against his face, when he could no longer concentrate on his duty. He woke Donahue and took his place on the bed of leaves, and instantly fell asleep.

The rains came again just after dawn, falling through the trees in large heavy drops, striking Frank's upturned face like lead pellets and jolting him awake. A heavy fog rolled off the river and spread through the jungle, gliding silently among the trees and chilling everything it touched with its cold, lacy tendrils.

Donahue crouched beside Frank, his shirt pulled up over his head, shivering and watching what little he could see of the muddy trail.

"How long has it been light?" Frank asked.

" 'Bout an hour."

Frank got to his feet and steadied himself against a tree until the numbness left his leg. He was cold and hungry, but the hours of sleep had renewed some of his strength.

"We'll try and get a fire going and cook some rice when the rain lets up," he said. "But let's cover some ground for now."

"How far you figure to the border?"

"Can't be far," Frank said, picking up the rice sack and the hoe.

Donahue took the sack from him. "My turn," he said, walking haltingly toward the trail, working the stiffness from his joints and favoring his swollen ankle.

The trail began a gradual ascent and cut deeper into the jungle, away from the river. They were slowed considerably on a steep section where the runoff had turned the trail to a slick, oozing mire, and they had to cling to rocks and vines to keep from sliding backward. Reaching an even steeper rocky incline near the crest of the hill, they climbed hand over hand on treacherous footing to reach the narrow, grassy plateau on top. The rain slowed and then stopped, and they sat and rested briefly before crossing to the drop-off on the other side.

A grim smile crossed Frank's face as he looked down into the next valley. He could see sections of a wide dirt road he knew was Highway 9 that crossed Quang Tri province from Dong Ha to the Laotian border and continued on across Laos to Thailand. He saw the edge of the village of Lang Vei, and off to the right, the rocky red-clay hill where shattered ruins of concrete bunkers were all that remained of the Special Forces camp where one of the bloodiest battles of the war had been fought, and where more decorations for valor were awarded than for any other single action of that war. A field of elephant grass now covered the camp, but still visible were the jagged edges of the reinforced-concrete and steel plate that had been the command bunker where he had lain trapped and wounded with seven other Green Berets in the Tactical Operations Center, watching some of them die, and all of them suffer, because of the indecision and stupidity of career-obsessed men in air-conditioned offices in Saigon who refused to believe hard intelligence reports and acknowledge pleas for help. They had insisted that the North Vietnamese had no tanks as the Russian-made tanks rumbled across the camp blowing doors off bunkers and chewing up everything in their path.

He remembered how they had called artillery and air strikes down on top of themselves in a desperate attempt to repel the attack. But the North Vietnamese were determined to take the camp, and nothing was going to stop them. They had tossed satchel charges and grenades and tear gas down the stairwell and ventilation shafts of the command bunker, and to this day he was unable to understand how he and the others had managed to survive and escape to the aid station at Khe Sanh.

The battle had raged for two days, and when it was over 480 South Vietnamese, and Bru and Hre Montagnards were dead, and half of the Green Berets had died with them. Of those that survived some were taken prisoner and some had escaped. He had been among the lucky ones, at least on that day. But the NVA had paid dearly, losing most of a crack regiment and thirteen tanks. The camp was never rebuilt, but replaced with a new one at Mai Loc, twenty miles northeast of Lang Vei.

Donahue spoke, disturbing his reverie. "What do you think, Top? We near the border?"

"At the end of this valley. About a mile."

Donahue smiled broadly and raised a clenched fist. He knew that crossing the border into Laos would be only a psychological victory and held no assurance of their freedom, but the thought of being out of Vietnam raised his spirits.

Frank had done saturation patrolling throughout the area, running search and destroy missions and ambush and reconnaissance patrols into Laos and the NVA sanctuaries. He ransacked his memory for a mental image of the quickest route that would circumvent the village and provide the least possibility of running into any of the villagers.

He stood quietly for a few minutes, choosing the way they would cross the valley, deciding finally to stay just inside the jungle along a large rice field south of the village where he recalled having traveled a network of footpaths that branched out and crossed the border at various points.

They began picking their way down the steep slope, digging their heels firmly into the soft ground with each step and grabbing hold of vines and branches until the grade became less severe and the trail more defined as it cut across the breadth of the hill in long slashes before dropping to the next level.

As they neared the bottom where the ground sloped gently into the valley, Frank stopped suddenly, and his mouth went dry and his stomach soured and tightened. Through a stand of widely spaced trees, he could see across the rice field to an open stretch of land leading to Highway 9. A convoy of mudstreaked troop transports raced along the roadbed toward the village of Lang Vei.

Donahue saw them, too, and Frank saw a mask of tension grip his face and terror flash in his eyes.

"They don't have us yet," Frank said calmly, watching the trucks enter the village and disappear from sight.

Donahue stared toward the village and remained silent.

"You didn't think this was going to be a cakewalk, did you?"

"They ain't takin' me back, Top. No way. I'm goin' home or I'm dyin'. And if I can pick off one of them dink bastards and get me a weapon, I'll take a bunch of them with me.''

Detimore clapped him on the back. "Let's get the hell out of here.''

They moved as quickly as they could down to the valley, but their progress was slowed because they were careful to stay well inside the jungle, keeping off the heavily traveled footpaths, but following the southern edge of the field in the direction of the border.

They dropped to the ground when they heard the approaching sounds of voices and the short, shuffling footsteps as troops moved along the trail off on their flank. They lay motionless in the underbrush until the patrol had passed, and then moved deeper into the jungle, farther from the trail.

Frank heard more voices and caught a flicker of movement through the trees ahead of them where two trails intersected. Crouching low, they waited until the soldiers were well out of sight before crossing the trail and scrambling down a bank to a small stream at the bottom. Moving along the edge of the stream, they paralleled the trail, now thirty feet above them, staying close to the heavy brush that covered the steep bank. The stream was in a deep gulley, and the ground on the opposite side rose straight up, making it impossible for them to move in that direction.

The shallow stream wound into a long S-curve, and now both banks were perpendicular to the bottom of the gulley. Frank's worst fears were realized a moment later.

"Dung lai! Dung lai!" a shrill voice shouted, followed by a chorus of urgent commands in the distance.

The report from a burst of automatic fire shattered the silence, the rounds impacting in the stream, raising short spurts of water.

The two men stopped in their tracks, obeying the command of the Vietnamese soldier standing on the bank above them. Frank saw two more soldiers approaching from behind, and another appear upstream, directly in their path.

Frank slumped wearily, feeling what remained of his strength drain slowly away.

Donahue turned to him and spoke softly. His tone was abject, but his words told of release, not defeat.

"This is it, Top. This is where it all ends."

Holding the primitive hoe at his side, he walked slowly, purposefully, toward the soldier standing at the bend in the stream twenty yards ahead.

The young soldier grinned and chattered to his sergeant on the bank as his captive advanced, his expression changing to one of confusion as he read the intent in Donahue's eyes. He backed up a few steps, then as if remembering that he was armed, stood his ground and shouted at Donahue to stop. His command unheeded, the frightened man fired a warning burst into the bank.

Donahue kept coming. "You're gonna have to do better than that, asshole." He raised the hoe, gripping the handle like a bat, and continued toward the soldier who looked to his sergeant for help.

The man on the trail above instructed him not to shoot, and slid down the bank, landing on his knees a few feet in front of Donahue where he was met with a stunning blow from the sharp edge of the hoe that sliced a long gash in the side of his head, knocking him onto his back.

Frank came to his senses, finally realizing that Donahue's purpose was not to surrender. He saw the young soldier panic and raise his weapon.

"Don't shoot! Don't shoot!" he shouted in Vietnamese as he ran toward him.

He grabbed the hoe from Donahue's raised hands just as he was about to deliver another blow, shoving him to the ground and covering him with his body. Donahue screamed and cursed and struggled to reach the rifle that had dropped from the dazed soldier's hands.

The two soldiers who had been upstream were now standing over him, and Frank saw a blurred image of a butt plate before being knocked unconscious.

Pete Hendricks sat on his heels, his hands gripping the bamboo bars of his cage as he pressed his face into the narrow opening, watching through the dusk of late evening as the canvas-covered truck rumbled into the compound and stopped just inside the gate. He flinched when he saw the two men thrown from the tailgate and land sprawling on the muddy ground.

Bad Eye stood at the entrance to his hut, his short, bowed legs more pronounced when backlighted by the lantern in his office. At his command, the guards prodded the tottering men toward him, shoving them through the doorway.

"Oh, Lord," Hendricks said. "You gotta help them. Deliver them from this, Lord. Or you could strike them heathen, evil bastards dead."

Detimore and Donahue, exhausted from their efforts and weakened from two days without food, barely managed to stay on their feet.

Bad Eye rested his elbows on his desk, and pressing the tips of his fingers together stared coldly at the gaunt, filthy men before him.

"You have caused me much embarrassment," he said

in a flat, impassive voice. "My superiors are angry. I am angry." He pointed to two stools placed behind them and gestured for them to sit.

"*Motherfuckers, sit!*" Latrine Lips shrieked from a corner of the office where he stood glowering in the shadows, his face set in a psychotic grin.

Neither man had been aware of his presence until now, and Donahue turned slowly to face his nemesis before being pulled off his feet and onto the stool. The young Marine startled Frank and the others in the hut with the volume and length of the dreadful sound he made.

The jungle fell silent as the hollow, plaintive wail filled the chill night air, touching the very souls of the other prisoners. Dan Lucere sat huddled in a corner of his cage. His eyes twitched in a prolonged spasm, until wrapping himself tighter in his own arms, he whimpered softly and retreated still farther from the reach of the horror and suffering that surrounded him.

12

The late-afternoon sun heightened the color of the cloud-less cobalt blue sky and glistened off the snowcapped peaks that lined both sides of the narrow valley. Along the winding black ribbon of road that led from Aspen toward Independence Pass, a column of deeply tanned bare-chested men in shorts moved in unison with fluid, powerful strides.

"Keep an eye on Badowski," Donatelli called from the head of the column. "We don't want to lose him again."

Smashy smiled and kept a steady pace, holding ten yards behind the rest of the men. He felt fresh and strong, and his knee hadn't bothered him all week. The bulge in his midsection had gone with the fifteen pounds he had lost, and the spring in his step had returned.

He had been a bit embarrassed when early that morning, on their tenth and final parachute jump—after free-falling and flawlessly tracking two miles to the airport—a miscal-culation had landed him wide of the drop zone and he had disappeared into a twenty-foot snowbank off the end of the runway. Donatelli had howled with laughter as he and the others dug him out, and had kidded him mercilessly throughout the day.

The team was nearing the final mile of the run as they rounded a curve at the top of the hill where the road leveled off and then gradually descended to a long flat stretch that led to Callahan's driveway.

Smashy watched for a small pile of rocks by the side of the road, his marker, put there to tell him when to make his move. He had been planning this for weeks, waiting until the final day of training to put it into action. The others had run ten miles each day, but he had put in another five on his own, building his stamina and improving his time. And now he was ready. By carefully pacing himself, he knew just how fast he could run the final stretch without fading before reaching the driveway, having practiced his kick on his solo runs.

Spotting the pile of rocks, he stepped out of line and increased his pace. His feet pounded the pavement as his treetrunk legs pumped like huge blond-haired pistons. He first passed Houser, then Galimore and Callahan, and drew abreast of Donatelli.

"What's this?" Donatelli said, grinning. "The little engine that could?"

"Twenty bucks says I can take you," Smashy said, seeing that Donatelli was breathing heavily through an open mouth.

"Let's go."

With that, Donatelli shot ahead with a burst of speed that Smashy knew he could never sustain to the finish. Staying a few yards back, he kept close to him, watching for his second marker that would tell him there were exactly two hundred yards remaining.

He saw the change in Donatelli's rhythm and stride, and knew he had him. Upon reaching the marker, he closed the distance between them and pulled steadily away from his fast-fading opponent.

At the third marker, a hundred yards from the driveway, he glanced back to see Donatelli ten yards behind, and out of the corner of his eye saw the dark brown skin and rippling muscles of Galimore as he closed on Donatelli, passing him with ease, and came on strong toward the finish line.

"Oh, shit!" Smashy said, pushing himself to his limit as he sprinted for the driveway, now forty yards ahead.

There was nothing more to reach for, and his legs were on the verge of giving out as he entered the driveway with only a split second to spare before Galimore streaked past him shouting, "Way to go, Smashy."

"Nice," Donatelli said, gasping for breath as he put his arm around Smashy's shoulder. "You earned that."

"Yeah, and I get to use the shower first tonight."

"You could give me a chance to get back my twenty bucks on the shooting range."

"You're on."

Callahan had placed targets at numerous points in the brush along the path leading through the canyon, and each man went through the course twice—once with an AR-15 rifle, and again with a 9mm automatic pistol. The object was to cover the course as quickly as possible while placing two shots in vital areas of each of the man-size silhouetted targets, using a variety of shooting positions.

The time and accuracy of the men had vastly improved during the past three weeks to the point where none of them missed a shot, and only thirty seconds separated first and last place. Smashy won another twenty dollars by a scant four seconds to the exhortations of everyone including Donatelli.

A strained silence fell among the men as they walked through the snow-covered woods back to the house. This would be their last night in Aspen. It was over—the training and preparation completed. And they were once again a team.

A brief altercation at a restaurant a few nights earlier had brought that realization to Callahan when a group of rowdy ersatz cowboys with their dates attempted to jump the waiting list for tables. Galimore had called them on it and became infuriated by the stream of stage-whispered racial slurs that followed. The suggestion that he might not be comfortable in a restaurant without watermelon on the dessert list was the final straw.

There had not been a moment's hesitation on anyone's part. The reaction was instantaneous and in concert, and six men of poor judgment and limited abilities soon found themselves outside in the snow, prostrate and dazed, surrounded by their indignant, hysterical dates. The last of Jack's doubts concerning the effect of the intervening years on their teamwork were gone.

Smashy headed for the shower upon entering the house, claiming his hard-won right. Jack laughed when he heard him talking to Boomer.

"Goddamnit, Boomer! Get outta there. I gotta get a shower. Come on, move it.

"Hey, Jack! This clown's sleeping in the bathtub again."

Boomer responded to Jack's call, picking up his large rawhide bone on the way in hopes of interesting—intimidating if necessary—someone in a tug-of-war. Galimore obliged him.

Callahan took two cans of beer from the refrigerator and

went outside to where Phil Houser was sitting on the edge of the woodpile, watching the sun drop slowly behind the mountains.

"It's beautiful out here, Jack. I can see why you live here."

"Yeah. Once you've been here for a while it's hard to leave."

"You go up into the mountains much?"

"As often as I can. In the summer."

"I was thinking of practicing out west. Wyoming or Utah. Close to the mountains. I don't think Angie will go for it though. She's a city girl."

Jack handed him a can of beer. "Are we ready?"

"Physically? Yes. We're doing ten miles a day at eight thousand feet above sea level. We've scrambled up these canyons with fifty-pound packs on our backs in knee-deep snow, the practice jumps went well, and Smashy's knee is holding up. We're in good condition, and the skills are still there."

"Then what is it? Something's been eating at you all week."

"Do you remember the conversations we used to have . . . about the road to life . . . the road to death?"

"Yeah."

"Well, that's it. None of us, Jack, not a goddamn one of us can make that choice again."

Callahan nodded, his face expressionless.

"Are you sure you want to hear this?"

"Get it off your chest."

"We were in our twenties, Jack. Loose, believers. We were the Green Berets, lords of the jungle, fabled in song and legend. And we were young enough that that meant more to us than life. Most of us accepted the probability that we were going to get killed. So we took the road to death. It gave us the edge. We fought offensively. If we got greased, we got greased.''

Houser hesitated and took a long drink before continuing. ''But Charlie took the road to life. He didn't give a damn about the *cause*. For the most part he was threatened and forced into the fight. All the poor bastard wanted to do was grow his rice, play his flute, and live in peace for the first time in twenty years. His family, his girl friend, kids, his village, meant everything to him. So he fought defensively, and he paid for it when he was up against us.

''We had a commitment. We believed in ourselves and what we were doing, and that made us stronger. And I believe to this day that that is why every one of us here walked away in one piece. But we're not the same people now. None of us are. And we're going over there for all the wrong reasons. We're telling ourselves it's Frank, but that's only part of it, and you know it. Every goddamn one of us found something over there that's been lost to us ever since. And don't kid yourself, Jack. We're not going to get it back. And it's best not to try.''

''We owe Frank.''

''Yes. We owe Frank. And we're going to try and get him out. But this time we aren't prepared to take the road to death, and I hope to God this all doesn't fall apart when we have to deal with that.''

''You want out?''

''No. I *don't* want out. That's what has me so goddamn worried. I spent twelve long years becoming a surgeon, and I haven't given a moment's thought to that part of my life for days. I'm really into this thing.''

''Do you have any doubts about the mission?''

177

Houser shook his head. "No. I remember something Bull Simons said—the more improbable something is, the more likely it is that you can pull it off. What about you? What do your gut instincts tell you?"

"It looks good. I got a weather report this morning from Smashy's buddy at Bragg. We'll have a full moon and CAVU weather if we get this off the ground within the next four days."

"What's our schedule?"

"We have a noon flight out of Los Angeles tomorrow that puts us in Bangkok at twenty-three hundred hours the next day. I figure we can make our contact that night, pick up our gear, and get to the mercenary camp the next day. We'll run an equipment check, rest up, and go in the following night."

"Yeah. We'll need a day of rest after that flight."

"Hey, Jack!" Donatelli shouted from the doorway. "You've got to see this. Smashy's got on an almost new T-shirt. Only three rings under the arms. It must be love."

Houser laughed. "One of these days Smashy is going to deck him."

"He loves it."

"Is he going with us tonight?"

"No. He pulled a muscle during that hundred-yard dash he ran this afternoon. Maggie has offered to let him use her Jacuzzi. She's going to cook him some dinner."

"Christ, I hope he lives through it. Did you taste that casserole she brought over yesterday? Even Boomer wouldn't eat it, and he'll eat anything."

Jack laughed. "That's one of the advantages of leaving him with Maggie when I go away. He never gains any weight."

*　　*　　*

178

The two DIA agents sat watching the highway from a side road, repeatedly clearing a small circular area on the frosted windshield of their rented car.

"The damn temperature must have dropped forty degrees since this afternoon," Thompson said, stomping his cold feet on the floor.

"You checked the house for an alarm system, right?" Luger asked.

"Yeah. Nothin'. The place is clean."

A Jeep Cherokee passed by in the direction of town, and Thompson started the engine. "That's them," he said, pulling out onto the highway and heading in the opposite direction.

Patches of ice had formed on the road where the sun had melted the snow, and twice Thompson almost lost control on the curves.

"Slow down!" Luger ordered. "We have plenty of time." Thompson turned off the headlights as he entered Callahan's driveway, continuing on to the top of the hill where he backed around and faced out before pulling in close to the side of the house.

"Who lives over there?" Luger asked, pointing to Maggie Hill's house.

"Some broad. She can't see much through the trees."

Luger walked around to the front of the house and tried the door. "He doesn't even lock the door."

Boomer had been awakened by the sound of the car pulling into the driveway, and sat in the bathtub, his head cocked and his ears forward—listening.

Emitting a low grumble, he stepped from the tub and stalked slowly to the door where he peered down the hallway to the living room. Cocking his head from side to side, he remained quiet as he heard the front door open and the whispered voices of the intruders.

Leaving the bathroom, he moved warily down the hall to where he could see the two men standing, flashlights in hand, partway in the living room.

The beam of light illuminating two glaring red eyes, the bloodcurdling snarl, and the leap toward Thompson, all happened in the same instant.

Thompson screamed and raised his arms to cover his face, howling in pain as the powerful animal sunk his teeth deeply into his upper arm.

"Get him off! Get him the fuck off!"

Boomer shook his thick muscular neck and pulled Thompson off balance, tossing him to the floor like a rag doll.

Luger removed his parka and swatted at the snarling animal who released his grip on Thompson and lunged toward him, grabbing a mouthful of the heavy down jacket.

Holding on to a sleeve, Luger ran down the hall into the guest room, pulling Boomer along after him. Mustering all his strength, he swung the raging animal in a wide arc, throwing him against the side of a bed just as a piece of the parka tore away. Running from the room, he slammed the door behind him a second before the dog roared and thudded against it from inside.

"Now I know why he doesn't bother to lock his doors," Luger muttered.

Thompson knelt on the floor, holding his arm. "Why didn't you shoot that crazy son of a bitch?"

"I don't shoot dogs. You were supposed to have checked this place out."

"I didn't see the goddamn dog."

"How much damage did he do?"

180

"It hurts like hell, but it doesn't look too bad. A few puncture wounds and a little blood, that's all."

"Let's get what we came for and get out of here."

Maggie and Smashy sat in the conversation pit before the living room fireplace. A warming fire crackled and glowed in the dimly lit room.

"Is your leg feeling better?" Maggie asked.

"Yeah. That whirlpool helped. It's not stiff anymore."

"I'm sorry about the dinner," Maggie said. "I don't know what happened to the sauerbraten. Maybe too much vinegar . . . or sugar."

"No. It was good," Smashy lied. "A little spicy, but good." He could still feel the dumplings stacked like cannon balls in his stomach.

Maggie lit a cigarette and stared thoughtfully at the fire. "Are you afraid?"

"Of what?" Smashy asked.

"The mission. And what you have to do."

Smashy shrugged. "No. We've all been there before. We'll come out of it all right."

Smashy started to say something, then hesitated, choosing his words carefully. "Listen . . . ah. I didn't get to talk to you much over the past few weeks. With the training and everything, we've been busy, you know."

"I noticed."

"Well, I was thinking. Maybe when this is over, and we get back, I could give you a call. We could go out on a date or something."

"That would be nice."

"Yeah?"

"Yeah," Maggie said with a warm smile. "I'd like that."

Smashy grinned and nodded. "I was afraid you'd turn me down. I'm pretty much a bum, you know."

"You may have been that at times, but that's not what you are."

"I was a good soldier," Smashy said. "As good as anybody; better than most. But I'm not much good at anything else."

Muffin ran in from the kitchen, nearly toppling a huge potted palm set at the edge of the conversation pit. She barked and growled and ran back out of the room, repeating the demonstration twice.

"Muffin, hush!" Maggie scolded, but the dog continued barking excitedly.

"Jack and the others must be back," she said. "Muffin probably saw them pull in."

Smashy glanced at his watch. "I don't think so. They were going to a movie after dinner and then to that cowboy bar for a few beers."

Muffin dashed in again, still barking.

"I'd better take a look," Smashy said, getting up and going to the floor-to-ceiling plate-glass windows along the front wall of the living room.

He could see little through the trees between the houses, and stepped out onto the sundeck and stood quietly. He heard the muffled sounds of Boomer's barking and snarling, and through an open section in the woods, saw a brief flash of light appear at the living room window. Rushing back inside, he grabbed his parka and headed for the door.

Smashy ran through the knee-deep snow, stopping behind a large spruce tree at the edge of the driveway, watching a narrow beam of light move from the living room to the hallway and into Jack's bedroom. Boomer redoubled his snarling protests.

Following the tree line to the back of the house, Smashy darted across the driveway and moved in a low crouch along the back wall toward the door leading off Jack's bedroom onto a small patio. Looking through the window, he saw in the glow from the flashlight a man with his back toward him taking Jack's map case and folder of aerial photographs from the closet shelf, stuffing them in the open front of his tightly belted parka.

As Thompson sorted through the other papers on the shelf, Smashy used the noise to his advantage. He edged the door open and burst into the room, grabbing Thompson by the neck and pulling him backward while simultaneously kicking him behind the kneecap, sending him crashing to the floor.

Thompson rolled to his right and quickly got to his feet, but Smashy was waiting for him and slammed a fist into his face, knocking him through the open doorway and out onto the snow-covered patio.

Smashy rushed out after him, but stopped abruptly as Thompson pulled a snub-nosed .357 magnum pistol from his shoulder holster and cocked the hammer.

A loud voice from the doorway startled them both. "No shooting!" Luger commanded.

Thompson released the pressure on the trigger, but kept the pistol pointed at Smashy's head.

"Back off, Thompson!" Luger said.

A deafening blast from a shotgun tore through the trees above the three men, sending a flurry of twigs and snow across the patio.

"Both of you back off," a rock-steady feminine voice said, followed by a rapid metallic clank as Maggie pumped another shell into the chamber.

Thompson turned to face her, his weapon still raised.

Maggie stood at the corner of the house, one foot forward, leaning into the 12-gauge shotgun held to her shoulder, her cheek pressed firmly against the stock.

"Drop it! Or the next one won't be over your head," she said confidently.

Thompson lowered the pistol, and Smashy took it from him, relieving Luger of his before going to Maggie's side.

"Jesus," Smashy said. "Where'd you learn to handle that?"

"Daddy taught me. I've been known to go a hundred straight on the skeet range."

"You made a believer out of me. We gotta do something with these guys until Jack gets back."

"I called the police before I left the house. They're on the way."

"Oh, shit."

"What?"

"I've got a feeling these guys are cops. Feds."

Callahan and the other team members entered the Aspen police station accompanied by the patrolman who had found them in the movie theater a few blocks away. The patrolman told Jack that he didn't know why the chief wanted to see him; he was acting on instructions from a radio call.

Entering the chief's office, Jack's apprehension increased as he glanced about and surmised what had happened. His eyes flashed with anger when he saw Luger and then, on the desk, his map case and the folder in which he kept the aerial photographs.

Chief Struther Nelson sat on the edge of his desk, his cowboy hat pushed back on his head. Luger and Thompson sat in chairs against the wall, and Smashy stood in a corner, his arms folded across his chest.

"Evenin', Jack," Nelson said, in his slow southern drawl, shaking Callahan's hand and nodding to the others.

"Struther." Jack had met Nelson when he first came to Aspen, recruited by the city council to head the police department. Never having skied before, he had enrolled in a clinic Jack was teaching, and later took a few private lessons from him. Close acquaintances, bordering on friends, they had lunch together on the mountain on the days Nelson skied.

Nelson shoved his hat farther back on his head and spoke in a friendly, easy manner.

"It seems we have a problem here, Jack. Your friend," he indicated Smashy, "wants these two gentlemen arrested for breaking and entering, and assault with a deadly weapon. They want him, and all of you, arrested for possession of stolen top-secret government documents."

"Who are they?" Jack asked.

"Mr. Luger and Mr. Thompson have identified themselves as employees of the Defense Intelligence Agency."

"That's right," Thompson said. "And I want these over-the-hill green beanies locked up and held to be taken into federal custody. Now."

Nelson stared hard at Thompson before speaking. "You don't mind if I make the determination as to what action, if any, is going to be taken here, do you, Mr. Thompson?"

"Yes. I mind." Getting to his feet, he reached for the map case and folder on the desk. "And if *you* don't mind, I'll take possession of these things right now."

Nelson rose to his full six feet four inches and clamped a fim grip on Thompson's wrist, moving his hand away from the desk.

"Sit down, Mr. Thompson. I'm not even sure what authority you people have; you're not a law enforcement agency to my knowledge."

"You listen to me, cowboy," Thompson snapped. "You're dealing with the United States government here, not some—"

"What I'm dealing with," Nelson interrupted, "is a couple of arrogant freebooters who don't know diddley squat about common courtesy and proper procedure. You came into my town without telling me you were here, or why you were here. You broke into a house in my town without a search warrant, and you threatened the life of a resident in my town with a concealed weapon you didn't bother to tell me you were carrying in my town. Now that, gentlemen, pisses me off."

"Excuse me, Chief," Luger said. "I'd like some medical attention for my partner."

"What's wrong with him?"

Luger pointed to the rip in the upper arm of Thompson's parka. "The dog got him."

"Tried to bluff ole Boomer, did you?" He noticed Luger's torn coat. "Get you, too?"

"Just missed."

Jack started for Luger, a menacing expression on his face. "What did you do to the dog?"

Luger gestured with his hands, palms outward. "He's fine. Just shut him in a room."

"My arm's okay," Thompson said.

"We'll have it checked at the hospital." Nelson called the patrolman in from the outer office.

When Thompson had left, Nelson turned to Luger. "Why did you want your partner out of here?"

"I thought we might be able to work something out."

186

"What do you have in mind?"

"I'd like to talk to Callahan alone."

Nelson agreed and motioned everyone out of the room, closing the door as he left.

Luger offered Callahan a cigarette, lighting one for himself. Jack shook his head.

"You'll never pull this off; you know that, don't you?"

"We'll see."

"My assignment is to discourage or prevent you from attempting this mission—within limits. It looks like I've reached my limit,- considering that you're leaving tomorrow."

Callahan said nothing.

"Tonight's outcome puts me in a unique position. If Thompson and I are detained overnight, and you leave on your scheduled flight tomorrow morning, I've done my job. I've screwed up, but I've followed my orders."

"What are you trying to say?"

"I'm saying that I think the whole damn lot of you are going to get greased, and possibly cause this country a great deal of embarrassment, but somebody has to do something. There's still a part of me over in 'Nam, Callahan. The part that all of us left with our friends—the ones who just disappeared one day on patrol, and the ones they couldn't find enough of to put in a body bag."

Luger ground out his cigarette. "I'm saying that my heart isn't in this goddamn assignment, but I've got a good job, and a family to support. So I needed a way out, and now I've got one. Sort of 'peace with honor,' to coin a phrase."

"What outfit were you with?"

"Third Marine Amphibious Force. We did some work with Project Delta."

"Yeah. I remember."

Luger opened the office door and asked Struther Nelson to come back in.

"Chief, you'd make my life a lot simpler if you locked me up for the night and kept Thompson in the hospital for observation until tomorrow morning."

Nelson looked at Jack. "Are you pressing any charges?"

"If I can drop them tomorrow morning."

Nelson nodded and picked up the map case and folder, handing them to Jack. Turning to Luger he said, "You've got one phone call."

"I thought my partner made it for us before he went to the hospital."

Nelson smiled. "Could be. I'll check in the morning." Gesturing toward the door, he said, "If you'll come with me, Mr. Luger, I'll give you the best room in the house. Might just leave the door unlocked in case you want some coffee during the night."

Before leaving the office, Luger unzipped the inner pocket of his parka, and walked over to Callahan. "Almost forgot. You might need these," he said, handing him the five passports he had taken from the house. "You did order me to return these, didn't you, Chief?"

Nelson returned to the office a few minutes later and called Jack away from his conversation with the rest of the team.

"My mother didn't raise any fools, Jack. I had a peek inside the map case and the folder, and I've had some reports on the shooting back in the canyon and the training over the past few weeks. Now if I put all that together with what I know of your background, nobody has to draw me a picture."

188

"You're a credit to your profession, Struther. A mind like a steel trap."

Nelson laughed and grasped Jack's hand firmly. "You get your butt back here in one piece, you hear?"

Betty Detimore felt a conflict of emotions rising within her as she hung up the telephone. She was elated by Callahan's call telling her the team was leaving in the morning, and frightened by the possibility of their failing, or of Frank being killed in the attempt. The rescue mission was no longer a comforting abstraction, but a perilous reality, and she would have to live with constant tension and uncertainty until it was completed.

"They're good men," her father said, comforting her in his arms. "You pray for them, Little Bit. We'll all pray for them."

"I want to talk to the girls alone," Betty said.

Harley nodded. "They're downstairs in the game room."

Lisa and Karen had been puzzled by their mother's request that they come home from college for their spring break. They both had made vacation plans with friends, but had complied with her wishes, detecting a note of urgency in her voice.

The carefree, happy laughter accompanying the sound of the Ping-Pong game the girls were playing filled the room.

"Come on, Mom," Lisa said, her bright blue eyes flashing mischievously. "I'll spot you eighteen points."

Betty sat on the overstuffed sofa near the fireplace and watched her daughters before calling them to her side. Lisa was her father's daughter: bold, confident, and her own person. Karen's quiet reflectiveness and sensitivity mirrored her mother's personality. The girls came and sat on either side of her, curious about her somber mood.

"I do believe we are about to have the unraveling of the mystery of the summons home," Lisa said.

Karen sensed that her mother was deeply troubled. "What is it, Mom?" she asked.

"I want you both to go to church with me tonight and pray for your father's safe return."

Karen had not heard her mother talk of their father coming home for a long time, and thought she was going through another difficult period similar to ones years before when they would often find her sitting alone in her bedroom going through the photograph albums.

"Mom, I love you," Lisa said. "And I loved Daddy. But he's never—"

Karen interrupted, casting an angry glance at her sister. "If it's important to you, Mom, we'll go."

"It's important to you also," Betty said. "In a few short hours, a group of your father's friends are leaving on a mission to rescue him from a Vietnamese prison camp."

Lisa and Karen sat stunned and incredulous as their mother told them of the letter from their father and the subsequent events. When she had finished, Lisa was the first to speak.

"Oh, my God, Mom! He really is alive? Daddy's alive?" Karen began crying and embraced her mother. "Oh, Mom. All these years . . . I never believed. I feel so guilty."

"There's no reason for that," Betty said, stroking her daughter's head. "I just want you to come with me and ask God to give your father and those men his blessing."

"When will we know if they have . . . when they have rescued him?" Lisa asked.

190

"Within a week. Perhaps a few days."

Harley Crawford entered the room, his wife at his side. "Monsignor Roche has agreed to meet us at the church and conduct a private prayer service for us," Amanda Crawford said. "It's in God's hands now."

"God's and Frank's friends'," Harley added.

13

Callahan felt a strange sense of homecoming looking down on the peaceful Thai countryside as the plane made its final approach to Don Muang airport. Clumps of puffy white clouds drifted slowly across the sky above the rich, fertile paddies, and the rising sun sparkled off the dark canals that striped the lush, green land.

A problem with the plane's hydraulic system had delayed their flight in Tokyo and again in Hong Kong, adding seven hours to their journey. But the team had managed occasional catnaps and a few hours of sound sleep on the last leg of the flight, and were now rested and eager to get on with the mission.

After the crisp, dry air of the Rockies, the tropical heat and humidity felt like an added weight, enveloping them in a moist, leaden blanket. They removed their jackets, stuffing them in their overnight bags, and rolled up their shirt sleeves as they boarded the minibus that took them the short distance into the heart of Bangkok.

Leaving the bus at the Oriental Hotel, they squeezed into a taxi and Callahan gave the driver the address on Patpong Road—Bangkok's "street of a thousand pleasures."

"You want girls?" the driver asked in heavily accented English.

"No," Jack said.

"I know where young boys, massage, movies, all kinds sex."

Jack repeated the address.

"Okay," the driver said, grinning affably.

The air streaming through the open windows brought the familiar odors of the Orient, stirring memories in each of the men. The palm-lined streets were beginning to fill with traffic, and the driver recklessly weaved among the samlors and pedicabs that increased in number as the wakening city came to life. He slammed on the brakes to avoid hitting a cluster of barefoot monks in saffron robes, returning to their wat with their daily offering of food from the local people. The silent monks continued in their unhurried way without acknowledging the incident.

The traffic on Patpong Road was even more congested. Even at this early hour the narrow, crowded streets teemed with people and taxis; the bars and massage parlors were busy day and night with a steady flow of European and Japanese tourists and businessmen intent on enjoying the pleasures of the flesh.

"Hey, Smashy," Donatelli said, leaning forward to unstick his shirt from the plastic seat covers. "This is your old R and R stomping ground, isn't it?"

"Yeah," Smashy said. "I wish I had half the money I left on the bars in these joints."

The driver pulled to the curb in front of a small building squeezed between two bars advertising topless dancers, their loud music drifting out into the noisy street. A sign in the curtained window proclaimed in three languages: Jasmine's Delight. Massage and Bath.

Standing aside as two short, fat Germans walked out of the door—mistaking some of the team for countrymen and greeting them in their native tongue—they entered the massage parlor to the cheerful greeting and warm smile of an Oriental woman with sharp features and a hard beauty that belied her age by twenty years.

"You would like a massage and a bath?" she said in a soft, atonal voice. "Perhaps a private party for all of you with some of our beautiful Eurasian girls?"

"No, thank you," Jack said, approaching the counter. "I'm looking for Marcel."

"He is expecting you?"

"Yes, he is."

The woman frowned. "He does not like to be disturbed."

Jack handed her a twenty-dollar bill.

"He is in room number six," she said smiling. "Perhaps we could entertain your friends while they wait?"

"I'll only be a few minutes."

Parting the beaded curtain to the right of the counter, Jack walked along the dimly lit corridor noting the numbers on the doors, knocking on number six.

"Entrez," a voice answered.

Jack entered to see a slightly built middle-aged man reclining in a bathtub. He was attended by a young, bare-breasted Oriental girl of remarkable beauty. Callahan guessed her to be more Chinese than Thai. She scooped steaming bowls of water from the tub, pouring them over the man's shoulders, then sensuously rubbed a washcloth over his body, lingering on a full erection before moving up to his chest. She gave Callahan a brief insouciant glance, then

194

with the Frenchman's guidance, returned to the erection.

"The only way to start the day," Jack said.

"Or end an evening," the Frenchman replied, reaching to fondle the young girl's breasts. He stared thoughtfully at Jack and said, "You should be Callahan."

"I am," Jack said. "I'd like to pick up our gear as soon as possible."

"If you will meet me at the Three Sisters' Bar at . . . let us say . . . two o'clock, I will take you to where your equipment is stored."

"We're already seven hours behind schedule," Jack said. "I paid for your services as a guide, not to wait around while you indulge your fantasies." He took a towel from the massage table, tossed it onto the edge of the bathtub, and told the girl to leave. She looked to the Frenchman who waved his hand in dismissal, wistfully caressing her breasts as she got to her feet.

"This is a great sacrifice," Marcel said, wrapping himself in the towel. "And I have not slept."

"You'll sleep when we get to Khemmarat."

"Americans," Marcel grumbled. "Always in a great hurry."

Callahan got the others from the entrance lounge and they followed Marcel to a door that opened onto an alleyway behind the building. They got into his Mercedes sedan and sped through the narrow back streets toward the Chao Phraya River and a motor launch he kept near the boat pier for the floating market tours.

Entering the choppy water of the fast-flowing river, Marcel navigated the boat in the same manner in which he drove his Mercedes—with reckless abandon. Weaving among the water taxis and barges, he headed south toward the floating market.

The banks of the broad river were lined with warehouses and sawmills, and in the background the spires and peaked roofs of Buddhist temples and pagodas dotted the skyline.

Shortly after passing beneath the Bangkok Bridge, Marcel swung sharply into the Daw Kanaung Klong, nearly swamping a small sampan with his wake before slowing to maneuver his way through the busy canal. Children swam and played while their parents bathed and washed their clothes in front of the tiny houses set on stilts in the muddy water near the shore.

The floating market was a navigational nightmare of foodladen sampans and rice barges and speedboats, and launches filled with shoppers and tourists. Without warning or care, they cut across each other's paths as the traffic police waved from atop their launches and blew their shrill whistles in a futile effort to bring order to the chaotic scene.

Straw-hatted farmers paddled their small boats among the houseboats and waterfront shops, their strident high-pitched voices rising above the deep-throated sputtering of the water traffic as they bargained and haggled with frenzied animated gestures, selling the fresh fruits and vegetables they had brought in from the countryside that morning.

The odors of dried fish and onions and sugar cane blended with those of the endless variety of spices and the sweet-scented delicacies being cooked on small charcoal burners. The indescribable, singularly Oriental redolence overwhelmed the senses.

Marcel approached the shoreline and turned into another canal leading away from the floating market into a quiet residential area where small wooden houses were nestled in a lush jungle setting. The delicate scents of orchids, hibiscus, and orange flowers permeated the damp, heavy air, and the bright hues of countless wild flowers filled the peaceful gardens. The occasional scream of a pet monkey, tethered to the railing of a balcony, shattered the stillness, eliciting a chorus of warning cries from the innumerable birds.

After traveling a mile or so down the winding canal, the Frenchman slowed the launch, then cut the engine and deftly manuevered alongside a small bamboo pier where he climbed out and tied the craft to a log piling.

He led the team through the jungle along a footpath that opened onto a quiet side street of shacks with rusted metal roofs and, near the end of the street, a row of newly constructed warehouses. Locating the proper key on his ring, he stopped at the last building, undid the lock, and slid open the long wooden door.

Two Toyota Land Cruisers were parked side by side at the front of the bay. Behind them, stacked on wooden pallets, were crates and shipping cartons neatly arranged and clearly marked as to their contents.

"The automobiles will of course be returned to me when you are finished with them," Marcel said. "They will not attract as much attention as a truck, and are better suited for the roads we must travel."

Callahan took his inventory list from his overnight bag and began taking stock of the gear. Getting a tire iron from one of the Land Cruisers, he pried open the crates, carefully checking the contents.

Beneath the printed labels the stenciling on the crates had been painted out, but Jack had no doubt that most of the equipment, if not all, was United States military aid intended for the Thai Army.

The weapons were new and meticulously clean, and the parachutes were sealed in mildew-free packages. Every-

197

thing he had specified was there and in excellent condition.

"The medical kits are complete," Houser said. "Nothing is out of date."

"Hey, Jack," Donatelli said, "they got the hundred-round box magazine for the M60."

"Good," Callahan said, impressed with the arms dealer's thoroughness and attention to detail. "Let's get this stuff loaded."

"How long will it take us to get to the mercenary camp?" Jack asked the Frenchman.

"Approximately nine hours," he said. "It is only three hundred and ninety kilometers, but some of the roads are not so good."

A car skidded to a halt at the open door. Two men in light-colored suits stepped from a white Datsun sedan and stood at the entrance to the bay.

Callahan walked toward them, immediately identifying them as Americans and suspecting they meant more trouble from the Defense Intelligence Agency. His anger mounted as he stood before the taller of the two—a heavily built square-jawed man with auburn hair and hard blue eyes.

"What do you want?"

"We'd like to see what you have in those crates."

"That's none of your goddamn business."

His wiry companion drew a wallet from his inside coat pocket and flipped it open.

Jack recognized the seal of the Central Intelligence Agency and struggled to control his temper. "It's still none of your goddamn business."

"The name is Stevens," the taller man said. "And anything that goes down around here is my business."

"The crates belong to me," Jack retorted.

"Look, pal. I don't know who you are or why you're

here, and I don't much care. But you cause any trouble in my territory and I'll come down on you with both feet. Now take a hike!''

"The contents of those crates are military surplus and I bought it legally,'' Jack said, realizing the foolishness of his words as he spoke them.

"Bullshit. That's stolen government property and it stays here.''

"It goes with me.''

Stevens grinned confidently. "We can do this the easy way or the hard way. Your choice.''

The sound of a magazine being slapped in place and a round going into a chamber drew all eyes to the side of the warehouse where Galimore stood beside one of the Land Cruisers, a CAR-15 at his shoulder, pointed at the two men in the doorway.

"Why don't we try the hard way,'' Galimore said.

Stevens looked at Callahan, the grin fading from his face, and gestured outside to a van blocking the street a short distance away.

"You really want to go to war over this?'' he asked.

"We need this gear,'' Jack said. "And one way or another it's going with us.''

Donatelli appeared from behind the other Land Cruiser, the M60 at his hip, followed by Smashy armed with an M16.

For the first time the CIA agents showed concern. Stevens read no signs of a bluff in the faces of the men confronting him.

"Jesus Christ, Jack!'' Houser said. "What the hell is wrong with you?'' He walked over to Callahan and grabbed his arm. "Have you lost your goddamn mind? We can't take these people on.''

"Why the hell not?" Jack snapped, pulling his arm from Houser's grip.

Houser stared at him in disbelief. "Count me out of this, Jack. I don't want any part of murder."

"You're splitting hairs, Phil. We've got a job to do."

"Listen to me, Jack. Goddamnit, listen to me!" He stepped in front of him and out of the corner of his eye saw Galimore and Donatelli lower their weapons. Smashy stood his ground. "If we kill them or any of their people it's cold-blooded murder. I could justify that DIA business because they had put themselves in the wrong by breaking into your house and stealing our stuff. Besides, the government's position is blind. Frank's more important than any moron political considerations. But this! Jesus Christ! Think it through."

"Listen to your friend," Stevens warned, his expression now showing his uncertainty of the situation. "There are ten men with automatic weapons in that van."

"Your ten men are shit," Jack said, turning away in disgust. "Put the weapons down," he said, spitting out the words.

The Frenchman appeared from behind a stack of crates, his eyes wide with fear. "We are free to go then?" he said to Stevens.

"I want to talk to you, Froggy," Stevens said.

"He goes with us," Jack said. "Or do you want to go to war over that, too?"

Stevens decided not to press the issue. "We know where to find him."

The six men sat around a table in a noisy, crowded bar on Patpong Road. The Frenchman's eyes wandered to the sultry dancer, clad only in a G-string, performing on a platform behind the bar. Her face was set in a mask of boredom and her tawny silken skin glistened with perspiration as she endlessly repeated the few awkwardly executed movements that constituted her entire repertoire: rubbing her crotch against a pole in the center of the platform, and massaging her breasts while grinding her hips from a full squat, sometimes accompanied by a fully extended tongue licking her upper lip.

Jack grabbed the Frenchman by his shirt and pulled him halfway across the table. "I want some answers from you," he said, releasing him after gaining his attention. "How the hell did they know about our deal?"

"I have not deceived you," Marcel replied. "They must have seen us unloading the truck when we delivered your equipment. Then they watch to see who comes for it. It has happened before. It will happen again. Stevens has many informants. Those are the risks."

"I want what I paid for," Jack said.

"I will contact my people and we will replace your equipment."

"When?"

"Two . . . maybe three weeks."

"Jesus Christ! Why didn't you just deliver our gear to Khemmarat if you knew you had these kinds of problems?"

"I do what they tell me, Callahan. We do not make deliveries to Khemmarat. It is a different operation."

"We have two choices," Houser said. "We can sit around here for two or three weeks and hope the CIA doesn't send us packing and lock up our friend here, or we can call it off. Try a different approach."

"What about the mercs?" Donatelli asked. "They might have the weapons and gear we need. Or some of it."

"They're not going to have the HALO equipment or

201

most of the gear we planned this mission around," Galimore said.

"Then we go there and sit tight until they get it to us," Smashy suggested.

Jack sat quietly, his eyes darting about the room. Finishing his beer, he leaned across the table and spoke to Marcel.

"Where will the CIA take our gear?"

"The military will come and get it."

"When?"

"Tomorrow. Perhaps the next day." Marcel grasped the implication of the questions. "But they will post guards at the warehouse until it is picked up. They have before."

"We'll get it tonight," Jack said.

"No. I want no trouble with that man Stevens. He is a dangerous man," Marcel said, shaking his head emphatically. "It is not how the game is played. He questions me, I tell him what I know, which is nothing, and he lets me go. He is only interested in who is operating in his domain. But if I cross him, he will kill me."

"That makes two of us," Jack said. "We're going back to that warehouse and get our gear and leave for Khemmarat tonight. And you'll be there."

"We're not killing any guards," Houser said.

"We can take them out without hurting them," Jack said. "Where does he get the guards?" he asked the Frenchman.

"They are nationals," Marcel replied. "He and his Thai counterpart have control of a special unit for their operations."

"Can you get us some weapons that will fire tranquilizer darts?"

"It is possible. But on such short notice?"

202

"Do you have contacts with access to hospital supplies?" Houser asked. "Drugs?"

"I can get any drug you wish," Marcel said.

"Ketamine," Houser told him. "Get us five surgical masks and some Ketamine. And some gauze pads."

Marcel wrote down the name of the drug as Houser spelled it.

"That I can do," he said, rising from his chair. "I should be not more than a few hours."

As Marcel headed for the door, Jack tapped Smashy on the shoulder. "Go with him."

Smashy caught up with Marcel outside. Putting his arm around the small-boned man, dwarfing him, he pulled him roughly against his side and whispered in his ear.

"I don't like Frenchmen. I've never liked Frenchmen. So don't you even think about turnin' rabbit on me, you needledicked little maggot, 'cause I'll chase you down and cut your goddamn heart out."

Callahan moved silently through the darkness, back into the brush where the team waited, watching the street and talking in whispers as Houser prepared the surgical masks, packing small squares of gauze on the inside of each one.

"Three guards," Jack said. "That's it. One on the street side and two on the other end. Their weapons are slung."

He pointed to Smashy and Donatelli. "You stay here with him," he said, glancing at the Frenchman who seemed ready to bolt at the first opportunity. "Joe, you take the guy on the street and Houser and I will get the other two."

One at a time, crouching low and moving quickly, the three men broke from the cover of the brush and crossed the open area behind the warehouse, grouping against the back wall.

Houser liberally doused the gauze on the inside of the surgical masks with the Ketamine and gave one each to Callahan and Galimore.

"Remember, you have to cover the nose and the mouth, and hold it in place for at least fifteen seconds."

Callahan and Houser disappeared around a corner and made their way along the far side to the opposite end of the warehouse, while Galimore crept on his stomach to a stack of empty crates ten yards from where his man leaned against the door, facing away from him.

Getting to his feet, he stayed in the shadows of the crates, approaching to within ten feet of the guard. With two quick strides, he was on him, cupping the surgical mask over the frantic soldier's face, effectively muffling his cries.

With his other arm around the man's chest, pinning his arms to his sides, he lifted him off the ground and held him, kicking and struggling until his body hung loosely in his grasp.

As Callahan and Houser appeared from around a corner, each carrying a guard over his shoulder, Donatelli and Smashy left their positions, pulling the Frenchman along with them.

Donatelli used bolt cutters to snap off the lock, and slid open the door just enough for the team to get through, then went inside and closed the door behind him.

"Tie them up and gag them," Jack said as he and Houser dumped the guards onto the floor beside the one Galimore had dragged in.

Smashy and Donatelli took the wide rolls of adhesive tape the Frenchman had carried and quickly bound and gagged the unconscious men, propping them in a sitting position against the wall.

Ten minutes after entering the warehouse, Donatelli slid open the door and jumped into the lead Land Cruiser as Callahan started the engine. Galimore and the Frenchman sat in the back seat while Smashy and Houser took the second vehicle crammed with most of the gear.

14

Four hours out of Bangkok, the two Land Cruisers left the well-maintained hard surface of the northbound Friendship Highway and headed east on a narrow dusty road that Donatelli likened to a tank proving ground when he took his turn at the wheel.

It was a demanding and tiring drive. Any lack of attention or sudden swerve on the part of the driver would bring them dangerously close to the soft shoulders and steep embankments along both sides.

With the headlights on high beam, Donatelli managed to spot and avoid the larger sinkholes and gullies caused by the torrential rains at the height of the monsoon season. But the stiff suspension of the vehicle did little to cushion the bone-jarring jolts and vibrations on the unavoidable washboard sections of the road.

Smashy and Houser followed a hundred yards behind, giving the night wind a chance to carry the swirling dust off to the side.

A few miles north of Ubon, a pinkish-gray light glowed on the horizon, slowly growing in intensity until the sun rose in a brilliant orange ball, bathing the mist-shrouded landscape in a pure white light that glistened off the rolling glades of dew-laden elephant grass and penetrated in bright slanting shafts through the stands of rubber trees and towering palms, dappling the lush undergrowth beneath the jungle canopy.

Nothing had changed in hundreds of years in this sparsely populated area of isolated farms and small secluded villages. It was a remote region of primitive rain forests and open savannahs, swampy and malarial during the rainy season, arid and dusty the rest of the year; and the terms of existence were harsh.

Marcel sat upright, leaning forward and straining to see through the dust-covered windshield.

"A hundred meters or so," he said to Donatelli, "you will see a road going off to your right. Take it."

The road the Frenchman referred to was little more than a deeply rutted cart path with a sign in Thai announcing that it was closed to vehicles.

The Land Cruiser listed precariously as it moved in and out of the ruts and potholes. The jungle closed in and branches scraped across the roof and along both sides of the vehicle. Donatelli stopped and waited until he was certain Smashy and Houser had seen him make the turn, then moved slowly on.

The road bordered a river, and after a few hundred yards the jungle gave way on one side to a grassy slope with a gentle declension to the water's edge. A fisherman stood in the bow of a small boat, tossing his net in the smooth-flowing water as he drifted with the current.

To the right of the road, visible through the trees, were

bamboo houses with roofs of teak leaves, built on stilts to keep out the snakes and animals. Chickens roamed freely, scratching and strutting about the brush, and pigs rolled in the dirt in pens behind the houses.

Donatelli made a sudden stop as a group of naked children with bright smiles and cheerful laughter darted across the road, running down the grassy slope and diving into the water.

A pretty young girl with smooth mahogany-tinted skin, dressed in a colorful blouse and long black skirt that reached to her bare, dust-caked feet, appeared at the side of the road. She balanced two large earthen jugs on her shoulders, and nodded and smiled shyly, waiting until they passed before crossing and continuing on her way to the well.

Their progress was further slowed by a buffalo-drawn cart on the road ahead. An old man, puffing on a black cheroot, walked beside the lumbering animal coaxing him along by tapping on his flanks with a cane pole. A toothless old woman with a raisin face rode in the cart, chewing a betel nut and staring with lifeless eyes at the sweaty, impatient faces looking down on her from the Land Cruiser.

An hour passed before the old man had guided the water buffalo off the road and into a thinly wooded area where another small village was secluded in the trees.

They reached their destination shortly before nine o'clock. The road ended in a large meadow dotted with scattered stands of trees. To their right, a half-dozen tents were set on wooden platforms beneath a canopy of palm trees. In front of the tents a wide swath of red earth, cleared of all trees and underbrush, bordered both sides of a steel-matted runway that Callahan estimated to be twenty-five hundred feet in length.

At the edge of the woods on the opposite side of the runway long rows of wooden crates covered with tarps were piled high beneath the trees.

Jack spotted an aircraft at the end of the strip—a vintage C-123 in sun-bleached camouflage paint—and an old Huey helicopter with Vietnamese markings sitting on a steel-matted pad just off the runway.

A short, muscular man with a ruddy complexion left a conversation with three other men and walked toward the team as they got out of the Land Cruisers. He wore a faded green T-shirt that stretched tightly across his thick chest and twenty-inch arms, and tiger-striped camouflage pants, bloused paratrooper fashion at the tops of his jungle boots.

"Ah, Frenchy," he said with a broad Australian accent. "You're lookin' as dissolute as ever. Still livin' the good life, are you?"

He slapped Marcel on the back, rocking him forward, and glanced at Jack and the others.

"Tommy Murdock," he said, extending his hand to Callahan who shook it and introduced him to the rest of the team.

Murdock's cheery voice and permanent lopsided grin were disarming until one saw the total lack of humor and animation in his pale green eyes.

Jack noticed a long ugly scar on the side of the Australian's neck, and the puckered scar tissue where half of his right ear was missing. The emblem of the British Special Air Service tattooed on his upper right arm answered one of the questions that had entered his mind.

"You lads look like you could stand a beer. Put your gear in the tent over by the fuel dump," he said to Jack, "then you and your mates can join us for a bite to eat if you like."

209

Jack saw a jerry-built camp shower over near the fuel dump. "I think we'll wash up first. It's been a while."

"Suit yourself," Murdock said. "What's your schedule?"

"We're a little behind," Jack said. "I'd like to take advantage of the weather. I figured we'd get six or seven hours of sleep, check out our gear, and go in tonight."

"Whenever you're ready. My pilots are off on a run in the Chinook. They'll be back before dark. We'll hold a briefing then."

After taking their gear from the Land Cruisers and stacking it alongside the tent, the team showered and changed into camouflage fatigues and joined Murdock and three of his men for a hot meal of freeze-dried rations. The two other Australians had done tours in Vietnam, and the Englishman had served with the Rhodesian Army. After a half hour of casual conversation about mutual exploits, the team returned to the tent and slept soundly.

Callahan awoke at four o'clock to the pulsating sound of whooshing air that fluttered and billowed the sides of the tent. Looking out the mesh window, he saw a huge Chinook helicopter settling to the ground near the mess tent. As the rotor blades slowed and the dust settled, the tailgate dropped and five men dressed in green fatigues exited the craft. At first glance, Jack thought they were Thais, but on closer inspection they had the distinctive look of the Nungs he had trained and led in Vietnam.

He saw Donatelli and Houser crossing the runway, stopping to inspect the Chinook and study the crew before moving on. They had been up for an hour, walking about the camp.

"Hey, Jack," Donatelli said as he and Houser entered the tent. "These guys aren't mercenaries. This is a black market operation. They're running guns." He jerked his head toward the runway. "They got crates of Chinese Type 56 assault rifles, stick grenades, mortars, hell, I counted six 75mm recoilless rifles and enough ammo and lurp rations to supply a division for six months."

"They also have a few hundred cartons of medical supplies from the International Red Cross and Catholic Relief Services," Houser said. "And some from the United Nations."

'What did you think they were doing stuck out here in the boonies," Jack said, "running sightseeing tours? It's none of our business."

"It's our business to know how reliable they are," Houser said. "They're our ticket out."

"It's been my experience that the pay-as-you-go boys are more reliable than the do-gooders," Jack said. "They're not subject to changes of policy and political considerations."

"They're also not responsible to anyone but themselves," Houser said.

"Haven't you ever heard of honor among thieves?" Smashy said, sitting up on the edge of his bunk.

"Sure," Houser replied. "The same time Nixon heard about it from John Dean."

Callahan shook Galimore's shoulder, waking him from a deep sleep. "Come on, Joe. Time to check out the gear."

"It might be a good idea to repack the chutes," Smashy said.

Jack agreed. "We'll fire a few rounds through our weapons and give them a light cleaning. And, Joe, check out the radio and get together with the camp operator and set up the frequency and call signals. We're Wolfpack and make them . . . Koala Bear."

"Very original," Murdock said, entering the tent.

A tall, thin man with a long handsome face came in behind him and introduced himself as Colin Harris. "I'll be your pilot," he said with a crisp British accent.

"Do you have any experience working in depressurized conditions at high altitudes?" Jack asked.

"A bit."

"What's a bit?"

"You can rest easy, Mr. Callahan. I've logged over fifteen thousand hours, most of it in and out of jungle strips like this, and I've unloaded my share of paratroops."

"I have the computed release point worked out," Jack said. "We'll sit down with the map later and go over the mission."

"What time would you like to get under way?"

"Twenty-three hundred hours."

"My copilot will join us for the briefing," Harris said, and left the tent.

"Who are you selling weapons to?" Houser asked Murdock.

"I don't sell to anyone," he said. "I deliver. Anything, anywhere. For a price."

"To which side?"

Murdock laughed. "Does it really matter?"

"Somewhere down the line it does."

"Ahhh . . . do I detect a note of moral judgment?" Murdock's eyes fixed hard on Houser. "We try to do things evenhandedly around here. Not leave anyone in the lurch, if you get my meaning."

Houser inferred what Murdock intended. "We fulfilled our obligations."

"Did you now. And here all along I've been thinkin' that the South Vietnamese had lost the war. Imagine that."

"That's a little simplistic," Houser said.

"And so are your superficial judgments, lad. I'd reserve them until I had some grasp of the reality of the situation here."

"Whose reality?"

"The hard reality," Murdock said. "The reality of a hundred thousand Vietnamese troops within a few miles of the Thai border. It wasn't too long ago, under contract to your government, that we delivered American weapons to the Vietnamese when they were fighting the Khmer Rouge of the Pol Pot regime. Now we supply the Khmer Rouge with Chinese weapons to fight those same Vietnamese. And then there's the rest of the bloody lot: the Khmer Serei and Khmer Angkor who sometimes fight the Vietnamese, sometimes the Thai Army, and occasionally each other. The alliances change with the months."

"That doesn't make any sense," Houser said.

"When did it ever, mate? You'd go mad tryin' to make sense of it."

"Who's winning?" Galimore asked.

"Who knows?" Murdock replied. "Who cares? It never makes any difference in the end, does it? The same bloody fools pull the strings and the puppets dance.

"Now to the matter of what you're selling then," Murdock said. "All I know is that we'll be dropping you into Vietnam and bringing you out by chopper. I assume you'll be bringing someone out with you."

"Eight men," Callahan said.

"Vietnamese?"

"American POWs."

Murdock's expression changed as he stared at Jack. A rare trace of emotion showed in his eyes. "God bless ya then. I thought it was a kidnapping you had in mind."

213

"What kind of shape is that Huey in?" Jack asked.

"A lot better than it appears. But my men won't take it into a hot LZ."

"I want it in position in Laos, just over the Vietnamese border. We'll call it in when we've secured the camp."

"Do you have this all spec'd out?"

Jack nodded. "We'll go over it at the briefing."

"I want a time frame. My men will not sit on that border indefinitely."

"You have them in position at first light. You'll hear from us within a half hour."

"I'll grant you an hour."

"Fair enough," Jack said. "There's a possibility we'll have to spend twenty-four hours on the ground. If that's necessary I'll radio your men and we'll repeat the procedure the next day."

"Someone will be on duty until you get back," Murdock said. "But you would be well advised to keep your transmissions brief and to a minimum. The Viets have a signal intelligence antennae field a hundred miles north of your destination."

"In all probability there will be only one call," Jack told him. "When we've taken the camp."

"Their radar may pick you up on the way in."

"Our intelligence tells us it's pointed north and east."

"They change their coverage occasionally," Murdock said.

"If your pilot is any good, he won't be around long enough for them to react."

"You needn't worry about Harris. Of the four I have, he's the best."

Callahan distributed the parachutes to the team. All five

main chutes were as specified—Para-Commander Mark Ones. He preferred the PC-class canopy over the new wing and ram-air types favored by the sport jumpers, having made most of his jumps with it. He had never been comfortable with the way the others deployed and handled.

The reserve chutes were the midair modification type, with more steerability than the standard reserve. Each man checked to see that the seals were intact and noted the date on the packing data card, then put them aside.

Placing the main parachute on the ground cloth Murdock had provided, Jack pulled the rip cord and opened the pack, removing the black nylon canopy from its sleeve, extending it its full length to the pin he had placed in the ground to hold the apex.

He checked for short-lining, finding the suspension lines unaltered, and made certain no lines were crossed through the panels. Carefully flaking each panel, looking for any that were blown or burned, he pressed them by hand, smoothing away any curls or folds.

Sliding the sleeve back over the canopy and down to the suspension lines, he sat on the ground on top of the sleeve, pulling the lines toward him, S-rolling them inside the skirt. Completing that, he S-folded the canopy into the pack tray, placing the pilot chute on top, closed the pack and replaced the pins.

He checked the filler gauge on the bail-out bottle—the small cylinder of oxygen that attached to the retainer bands on the bottom of the reserve parachute. The indicator was in the green, giving him a full ten minutes of oxygen—far more than he would require for his descent. He examined the feeder hose which led from the cylinder to the bracket on the webbing at the front of the harness, checking for damage, and looked for foreign matter in the fitting where he would plug in his oxygen mask.

By late evening, the briefing over, their equipment check completed, their weapons fired and cleaned, and their rucksacks packed, they had only to wait for the hour of departure.

Harris had asked all the right questions at the briefing, and seemed more than familiar with the procedures for the drop, and the two men who would bring the Huey into position for the extraction were experienced in special operations and evasive tactics.

The planning completed, the details meticulously attended to, they would now rely on their skills, and hope that the magic they had had eleven years ago would still be with them.

Callahan was satisfied with the apparent competence of Murdock's men, but aware that unforeseeable problems and snags, unless eluded by the intangible element of luck, could unravel the most tightly woven plan.

He sat on his heels, his back against a sago palm, staring out across the runway to the woods beyond. A light breeze moved the heavy air, bringing with it the fetid, decaying smell of the jungle, and his thoughts went back to his last mission in Vietnam and to Frank Detimore. The other men sat nearby, loading magazines, adjusting straps, and rearranging rucksacks for the second and third times, each deep in his private thoughts.

At ten-thirty they returned to the tent and dressed for the mission. They put on the thermal underwear necessary to protect them from the freezing temperatures at thirty thousand feet, and over their fatigues they zipped up a black herringbone twill jump suit. Proceeding to the aircraft, they strapped on their gear, securing their weapons, muzzle down, on their left sides, and conducted a thorough prejump inspection.

They checked the straps on the World War II Bunny hats—the leather flying helmet the men preferred for snug fit and convenience—and the hose leading from the oxygen mask to the bail-out bottle. Moving down, they checked the Capewell canopy releases, the chest strap, the D-ring installation, the reserve chute, and the leg straps.

An equally thorough inspection was made of the main chute, and the rucksacks were attached to the H-harness at the base of the pack tray. The portable oxygen console they would use before activating the bail-out bottle for the jump was checked and put on board.

Callahan insisted on double-checking for bent pins in the cones on the pack flaps. His only malfunction in 115 jumps had been the result of a bent pin that had locked his rip cord, necessitating the use of his reserve chute.

He rechecked the terrain map of the drop zone area, and made certain that each man's illuminated altimeter, attached to the front of the harness, was set to compensate for the elevation difference between ground level and the plateau where they would land. And finally, before boarding the aircraft, they affixed broad strips of luminous tape to each other's pack trays and rucksacks as a visual aid to assembly during free-fall.

The engines of the C-123 shuddered and coughed, blowing puffs of blue-tinted smoke through the exhausts as they came to life. The 2300 horsepower in each of the two main propeller engines was augmented by two J-85 jet engines attached to the wings, inboard of the auxiliary fuel tanks. The jet engines made it possible for the huge aircraft to take off with a minimum of two thousand feet of runway.

Harris decided to go out as light as possible to facilitate the climb to altitude, and had put only enough fuel on board for the mission and the reserve.

With the throttles fire-walled for maximum power, the old plane shook and rattled noisily, threatening to come apart at the seams as the engines whined and roared. Lunging forward, it rumbled down the textured-steel strip, building up speed and pulling into a steep angle of climb as it lifted into the air with only a few hundred feet of runway remaining.

Harris cut back from maximum power four minutes into the climb-out, and maintained the maximum rate of climb for twenty minutes before reaching thirty thousand feet where he cut off the jet engines and brought the plane to cruise speed.

The team sat strapped into the webbed bench seat in the rear of the aircraft. They had plugged into the portable oxygen console at twelve thousand feet, and would remain on the system until just prior to the drop.

Callahan felt the tension he always felt before a jump, but knew it would disappear the instant he left the plane. His desultory thoughts flashed from Boomer to Paula to a sapper attack on the Special Forces camp at Mai Loc, and back to Paula and her whiskey-baritone laugh.

The copilot appeared from the cockpit and made his way to the back of the plane. "Five minutes to the release point," he told Jack. "Only a ten-knot tail wind."

Callahan nodded.

Crossing to the other side of the aircraft, the copilot plugged into the oxygen console. Glancing at his stopwatch, he waited for the pilot to activate the hydraulic controls for the tailgate.

The huge doors rumbled open—the upper portion retracting into the overhead fuselage, the lower portion dropping down to a ramp—leaving a gaping black moonlit hole below the tail section of the plane.

The sky was bright and clear, and the trailing sound of the hardworking engines filled the rear of the plane to the accompaniment of a steady vibrating drone.

The copilot raised his hand in a quick upward motion, directing the team to stand.

The men disconnected from the portable oxygen console and activated their bail-out bottles; the rhythmic flow from the demand regulator was replaced with a steady, gushing stream of oxygen. They assisted each other in tightening their rucksacks, and with Callahan at the point, grouped before the open tailgate.

The green light flashed and the copilot pointed to the door.

Callahan exited the plane in a graceful swan dive, his back arched and his head high; his arms and legs pulled upward into a spread-stable position. The others followed a split second later.

Caught in the slipstream of the aircraft, they were pulled along for three hundred meters before falling free and reaching terminal velocity— 120 miles an hour—twelve seconds into the jump.

The sound of the aircraft's engines faded in the distance, and the rush of freezing air roared in their ears, tearing at their jump suits and stinging the exposed skin on their necks and foreheads.

Jack quickly assumed a ''spider'' position, reversing the arch in his back while stretching his arms and legs as wide as possible. He positioned himself for a slow turn, bringing his hands back slightly, lowering his left hand and shoulder, and looking into the turn. Once headed toward the drop zone, he stopped the turn and pulled himself into the tracking position.

Bending slightly at the waist, he rolled his shoulders forward and placed his arms back along his sides with the contour of his body, and cupped his hands, palms downward, while bringing his head back and stretching his legs out, holding them shoulder-width apart.

He felt the lift developing as his speed increased. The airfoil configuration gave forward motion to his fall as he tracked thirty-five degrees horizontal to the ground, the force of the rushing air increasing as he reached 135 miles an hour.

He scanned the ground twenty-five thousand feet below, searching for his visual reference point which would give him his bearing on the drop zone. His eyes moved quickly over the silhouetted mountainous jungle terrain until he spotted the broad, winding river he had seen in the satellite photograph. The murky water, luminous in the bright moonlight, cut a distinct swath through the valley, in clear contrast to the dark, shadowy jungle canopy.

His eyes followed the river upstream to a sharp bend he knew lay a few hundred feet directly below the plateau where the drop zone was located.

Looking to his right, he found his predesignated opening point—a horseshoe-shaped ridgeline west of the bend in the river—and tracked steadily toward it.

Smashy was the last man in the staggered line of rapidly descending figures. Holding twenty feet above Houser, he fixed his eyes on the luminous strips of tape below him. He glanced at his altimeter as he passed through fifteen thousand feet, and smiled inwardly, feeling alive and vital, caught up in the adventure of doing what he did best.

Suddenly, a loud *snap!* drew his attention, and a moment later he was pulled sideways and whipped into a violent left turn. At the edge of his peripheral vision he saw that his rucksack had broken loose from one of the quick releases on the H-harness, and was hanging off to his left side.

He immediately lowered his head in an attempt to stop the turn, but the centrifugal force had increased to the point where he was now in a radical flat spin horizontal to the ground. The proper procedures instantly came into play as instinctive reflexes as he plummeted toward the earth.

Struggling against the powerful force of the spin, he brought his left arm forward and lowered his right leg, building counteracting resistance. As his rate of rotation slowed, he adjusted his position, increasing the bend in the elbow of his right arm to cup more air, and managed to stop the spin entirely, stabilizing his free-fall.

Checking his altimeter, he saw that he had dropped five thousand vertical feet during the time it had taken to counter the spin. Needing to continue to hold his body in its present configuration to compensate for the loose ruck-sack, he could no longer track, and was now falling in a straight descent. In a momentary upward glance, he saw the rest of the team gliding effortlessly away from him as they tracked steadily toward the target.

A quick mental calculation told him that he would land at least a mile and a half short of the drop zone. By deploying his chute now, at ten thousand feet, he had no doubt that by running with the ten-knot wind, considering his angle of glide, he could make it to the clearing. But there were other considerations. Descending under canopy for ten thousand feet could, if sighted by someone on the ground, compromise the mission and endanger the lives of his teammates.

In Smashy's mind there was no option. He would, as planned, deploy at one thousand feet and hope for the best.

The terrain below him was dark and hostile. Jagged ridges surrounded narrow steep-sided valleys, with no sign of an open area. He could see nothing but the interwoven tops of trees, and prepared himself for what was to come.

Callahan read his rapidly moving altimeter needle as he came abreast of the horseshoe-shaped ridgeline. He was twenty-five hundred feet from the ground when to the east of the ridgeline he spotted the plateau and the fast-approaching drop zone.

Pulling his arms forward against strong resistance, and arching his back, he flared from the track position into a spread-eagle, and effectively stopped his forward motion and slowed his vertical rate of descent.

Within six seconds he dropped twelve hundred feet to the opening point that would put him under canopy at the altitude he wanted. Reaching up with his right hand, he grabbed the D-ring and pulled his rip cord.

The pilot chute streamed out, followed by the rustle and snap of nylon as it drew the sleeved canopy after it. The suspension lines unraveled and the sleeve slid off. The canopy inflated with a loud *pop!* pulling Callahan upright with a sudden jolt.

The roar of rushing air ceased, and Jack swung gently beneath the risers in the silence of the night sky. He looked up to check his canopy, and then to his right to see the others stacked above him. Removing his oxygen mask and pushing his goggles up onto his helmet, he looked again. He couldn't locate the fourth man, and thought one

of the team might be out of position directly above him, although he couldn't see him through the cutaway sections of his canopy. He turned his attention to the approach to the drop zone and concentrated on his landing.

Experience told him that on his present course he would overshoot the clearing. Reaching up, he pulled all the way down on the right steering toggle, taking air out of the canopy. He spiraled down in a small circle, releasing the toggle when the correction had been made.

Halfway across the clearing he turned into the wind and pulled both steering toggles down to a quarter brake, a half, then a three-quarter brake position, and almost to a stall. The canopy buffeted in the wind as he settled to touchdown and released both toggles, then surged, filling with air as he landed firmly on both feet in a standing position.

As he gathered his chute, the other men dropped silently in, landing within a twenty-yard radius of where he stood. A quick glance told him someone was missing. He searched the sky, finding no trace of another canopy.

"It's Smashy," Houser said. "He left the aircraft at the same time I did. I thought he was stacked above me. I don't know what the hell happened."

"Did anyone see him deploy?" Jack asked.

Galimore and Donatelli had seen nothing.

"We're going to have to backtrack through three miles of jungle to find him," Donatelli said.

"No," Jack said. "We don't know where he is, but he knows where we are. We'll sit tight. If he's not injured, he'll find us."

"And if he doesn't?" Houser asked.

"We'll give him an hour and a half. Then we'll look for him."

After stripping off their jump suits and insulated underwear, hiding them in the underbrush with the helmets and parachutes, they sat closely grouped at the edge of the clearing.

Galimore removed his grenades from his rucksack and attached them to his patrol harness. Leaning close to Callahan he whispered, "Welcome back to 'Nam."

15

"Goddamn son of a bitch!" Smashy muttered as he dangled forty feet off the ground in the branches of a mahogany tree.

He had missed a small rice field behind the Montagnard village by only ten yards, drifting into the trees near one of the longhouses. A family of pigs squealed frantically and raced about their pen as he crashed through the upper branches, waking a young man who came out to check on the disturbance and walked around the pigpen twice, then stood and listened, never looking up.

Smashy hung motionless, suspended from his harness, waiting until the man went back inside. When he was assured that he wouldn't be seen, he began to swing himself toward a thick limb, hooking his leg over it and pulling himself into a position where he could sit securely.

Bright moonlight filtered through the thinly wooded village, allowing him to see his surroundings. During his free-fall and descent under canopy, he had kept his eyes on the bend in the river, and estimated that he had come down two miles west of the drop zone. He had noted the terrain features in the vicinity of the village and saw that the river flowed through the valley directly below it. He knew that the Montagnards would have trails leading down to the valley and he could find his way to the drop zone by following the river upstream until he came to the sharp bend.

His immediate problem was getting to the ground without waking any more of the villagers. He had no idea what tribe they belonged to and could not risk confronting them. The chances of their being friendly were fair, but if they were from the Bahnar tribe, they might just as soon lop his head off as offer him food. In either case, contact with them could compromise the mission and he had to avoid them at all costs.

The mahogany-tree limbs were widely spaced and some not strong enough to support his weight; he would have to climb down his reserve parachute. Opening the chute pack, he placed his rucksack inside the canopy and slowly lowered it through the branches, stopping every few feet to listen for sounds of anyone alerted by the rustling of leaves and snapping of twigs.

He worked his way out of his parachute harness, slung his weapon across his back, and began his hand-over-hand descent down the outside of the canopy, thankful he was wearing gloves as he felt the suspension lines bite into the heavy leather.

Hanging on to the crown of the canopy, eight feet above the ground, he wrapped his legs around a limb to steady himself, and used his knife to cut through the rip-stop nylon and retrieve his rucksack. As he attempted to put his arm through one of the straps, the rucksack slipped from his grasp and fell to the ground, crashing noisily through the underbrush.

The pigs squealed again, and Smashy heard excited voices coming from inside the longhouse ten feet away. He instantly dropped to the ground, wrenching his knee in an effort to move quickly away from the tree. His leg buckled under his weight and he fell forward. Grabbing his rucksack, he rolled to his right into a heavy thicket.

An older man appeared this time, wearing a loincloth and carrying a bush ax. He walked slowly around the pigsty and stopped at the edge of the jungle, staring into the shadows.

Smashy lay hidden, almost at his feet. He was so close he could see the features of the man's face. Tightening the grip on his knife, he tensed his muscles, ready to spring, hoping he wouldn't have to kill the man, and considering the consequences if he did.

The Montagnard turned, now facing away from him but still standing in the same spot.

Smashy's leg began to cramp above the knee, and it was all he could do to keep from stretching it out to relieve the pain. He looked up into the tree and saw the pilot chute hanging from a limb, swaying with the light breeze, no more than seven feet off the ground. Fortunately, the Montagnard's attention was on the underbrush, believing that a tiger was after his pigs and foolishly prepared to defend them with his bush ax.

If the Montagnard looked up and discovered the parachute, Smashy would reach out, grab his ankles, and pull him off his feet, hoping to silence him before he could cry out. But the Montagnard didn't look up, and Smashy breathed a silent sigh of relief as he watched him walk toward the longhouse, hesitating and casting another long look at the pigpen before going inside.

Smashy waited a few minutes before moving deeper into the woods and getting to his feet. He knew the parachute would be discovered in the morning, but there was nothing he could do about it. If the raid went off on schedule, they would be on their way out of the country by then anyway.

Drenched with perspiration, he was sweltering in the insulated underwear and heavy jump suit, but only after he was away from the village did he dare to remove them—taking time to cut fabric from a leg of the suit and wrap it around his knee for support.

He dogtrotted through the woods, coming to a crude split-rail fence enclosing a small meadow. Climbing over the fence, he started across the open area, favoring his left knee—relieved that the injury wasn't as bad as he had thought at first. As he neared the fence on the other side, a sudden chill went through him as he heard what sounded like footsteps behind him, increasing in speed and closing quickly. He stopped running and turned to face his pursuers, dropping into a prone position, ready to fire.

"Oh, shit!" he said, seeing his attackers. Jumping to his feet and running for the fence, he tumbled over the top rail only seconds away from three snorting water buffalo disturbed from their grazing.

He picked up a trail leading from the meadow, and after a few hundred yards, began his descent into the valley.

The valley floor was an open field of saw grass with occasional stands of bamboo, and he followed a mountain stream toward the river at the far side. As he approached the river, he saw a small thatched hut on the bank of the stream and hesitated briefly before he realized it was no real danger to him.

It was a leper's shack. The Montagnards allowed a leprous member of the tribe to live in the village as long as he could work and take care of himself, but once he became incapacitated and the disease reached a highly contagious state, he was banished from the community to an isolated hut where a relative would take care of him until he died.

Smashy gave the hut a wide berth and continued on to the river, following it to the end of the valley where it twisted through a deep gorge. He had to scramble along the steep rocky banks until the river entered a large circular valley, from which it flowed into the rolling hills beyond.

From the top of a knoll he saw the sharp bend in the river, and to the north, the plateau where the drop zone was located. After resting briefly and drinking from his canteen, he started out for the plateau where he hoped the others would be waiting for him.

Galimore heard the snapping of twigs and the crackle of underbrush, and silently alerted the others. The team quickly dropped into a defensive position in the direction of the sound, their weapons at the ready.

Smashy stepped from the edge of the jungle into the clearing, kneeling as he looked about, not seeing Donatelli in the grass only a few feet away.

"You're a real silent mover, you know that?" Donatelli said, causing Smashy to instinctively dive flat on the ground before realizing who it was. "You could blow out the transmitter on a trail sensor."

"Jesus! You almost gave me a heart attack."

"You okay?" Callahan asked.

"Yeah. I landed in the trees. Twisted my knee climbin'

down, but it's okay. I couldn't get the chute down, Jack. The Yards are gonna find it in the morning.''

"Forget it," Callahan told him. "They'll keep it to themselves.''

Houser examined Smashy's knee, wrapping it properly with an elastic bandage. "You may have done some ligament damage. I can't be sure.''

"It doesn't hurt. Just throbs a little.''

"Favor it as much as you can," Houser told him.

Callahan checked the time. It was almost two o'clock. Still enough time to reach the camp and reconnoiter it while it was dark.

As they stood and adjusted their rucksacks and patrol harnesses, a shrill scream pierced the air, startling Galimore to such an extent that he drew down in the direction of the sound.

A frightened monkey leaped from a branch high above them, onto another tree, scampering into the upper reaches.

Donatelli chuckled softly. "She must have thought Smashy was going to ask her for a date.''

16

The team moved slowly and cautiously, staying just inside the protective cover along the fringe of the jungle. Skirting the perimeter of the clearing, they began a steep ascent up the side of a mountain to a vantage point overlooking the prison camp.

Callahan estimated they had less than two hours before morning light. Without the dangers of VC patrols and ambushes, they had double-timed on the open sections of the trails, but it had taken longer than he had anticipated to cover the distance from the drop zone to the camp. The last mile of jungle trail had been the most difficult. Heavy underbrush and thick, prickly wait-a-minute vines had slowed their progress considerably.

He raised his hand to halt the men behind him as he reached a rock ledge overlooking the small, sheltered moonlit valley. From here he had a clear view of the prison camp 150 feet below and 80 yards out in the center of the clearing surrounded by high, steep-walled mountains blanketed with dense jungle.

The team removed their rucksacks and unbuckled their patrol harnesses so they hung comfortably from their shoulders, and sat closely grouped on the ledge, within arm's reach of each other to enable them to signal silently. They were breathing heavily after the difficult climb. The musty smell and the night sounds of the jungle engulfed them; a light breeze rustled the leaves, sending a chill through their damp clothing.

Callahan smeared an oily mosquito repellent on his exposed skin as the voracious insects began to find their mark.

"How's the knee?" he asked Smashy.

"No problem."

"What do you think, Jack?" Donatelli asked, propping his back against a tree near the edge of the drop-off. "We stay on the ground for twenty-four hours, or hit them at first light?"

Callahan swatted at a mouse that scurried out from behind him and ran across his legs. "Let's see what we're up against first. Give me the goggles."

Galimore reached inside his rucksack and handed him the passive night-vision goggles. The near-infrared optics were designed to gather all available light, illuminating the target area.

Jack trained them on the valley below and scanned. The details were greatly enhanced. The cleared area from the camp fence to the jungle was no more than eighty yards wide at any point. A small mountain stream flowed from the jungle and wound its way along the perimeter before turning and cutting across the clearing, passing near the entrance gate to the compound where a narrow bamboo dock extended out a short distance from the bank. The stream then turned again and entered the jungle on the side where it originated, to flow on and empty into the river they had crossed near the road leading to the camp.

Callahan studied the layout of the camp, but much of it was concealed from his view. Trees scattered throughout the compound hid the details of the structures beneath them. He caught glimpses of corners of huts, and thatched roofs, and here and there a section of a bamboo cage, but no comprehensive picture—nothing more than he had been able to determine from the satellite photographs.

He focused his attention on the two guard towers at cross corners inside the compound—small thatch-roofed cubicles with bamboo sides, supported by cross-braced poles rising a few feet above the top of the eight-foot fence, providing the occupant with an overall view of the compound and the clearing. There was mosquito netting hanging on all four sides of the open area between the sides and the roof.

Jack recognized the shape of a light machine gun mounted in both towers, but saw no one on duty. Either they were unoccupied or the guards were sleeping—he suspected the latter.

"I'm going down and take a closer look," he said. "I want to know exactly where the guard shacks and prisoner cages are."

"I'm going with you," Donatelli said.

"No. You guys sit tight."

"I gotta know how thick the fence is," Smashy said, "and where you want it blown."

"We'll spec it out when I get back."

"Hey, Jack," Houser said. "We can't just sit up here.

If you're spotted we have to be in position to move on them."

"Follow me down to the edge of the clearing and stay in the bushes."

The team put on their rucksacks and secured their patrol harnesses, taking a few minutes to blacken their faces and hands with greasepaint.

Jack taped his camouflage fatigues snugly around his forearms and thighs and checked the blouse in his pants. There was nothing to snag and no shiny equipment to reflect, and everything that might rattle was padded and secure. After a final equipment check they began descending to the valley floor.

A soft wash of pale moonlight filtered through the jungle canopy as Callahan stood at the edge of the clearing watching the waist-high grass sway gently in a light breeze. He removed his rucksack and left it with the team, taking only his CAR-15, his knife in its sheath attached to his patrol harness, and the .22 Walther automatic pistol and silencer secured in the custom-fitted shoulder holster.

He tugged at the short brim of his jungle hat, crouched low, and entered the clearing. Moving slowly and carefully, he altered his course, back and forth, in an attempt to imitate the natural movement of the swaying grass. He had considered the possibility of the area being mined, but dismissed it because the camp had been built after the war.

As he drew nearer the compound, he heard the sound of water, and raised his head momentarily to check his position. He was only a few yards from the point in the stream where the dock jutted out from the opposite bank. The stream was wider and flowed more smoothly than where it came down out of the mountains. He lay still for a moment to identify the sound of fish splashing as they took insects off the surface of the water.

Moving forward, he stopped at the edge of the stream bank and peered across at the dock—constructed, he guessed, as a place for the guards and prisoners to wash. Before leaving the cover of the grass, he watched and listened for any movement and sound from the compound and the towers.

Crawling on his stomach, he slithered down the bank into the water. Although his clothing was soaked through from the heavy dew on the grass, he wasn't prepared for the galvanic shock of the icy water, and barely managed to hold in what would have been an audible gasp.

The stream was deceptively deep, the water chest-high. He held his weapon at his shoulders as he walked across the gravel bottom. At one point, a depression in the stream bed brought the water to his chin, nearly causing him to lose his footing. But the current was light and he regained his balance, reaching the other side and the relative safety of the grass in only a few minutes. Crawling quickly to the compound fence, he lay flat against it, out of the normal sight range of the guard towers.

After a few moments, he got to his feet and stood motionless, his chest against the fence.

The bamboo logs used to construct the fence had narrow spaces between them, allowing him to see into the compound. As he made his way along the outside, sidestepping, keeping his body as close to the fence as possible, he noted the locations of the huts and cages, casting an occasional glance at the rear guard tower as he approached it. His progress was slow and deliberate as he carefully checked the ground before each step.

The prisoners' cages—he counted seven, one smaller

than the others and set off by itself—were clustered under a stand of trees on one side of the compound near a large hut which appeared to be the guards' quarters. As he stood at the section of fence nearest the prisoners, he had a clear view of four of the cages and the dark shapes occupying them.

Another smaller hut—the camp commander's, he surmised—was across the compound to the left of the entrance gate below the front guard tower.

He knew when he passed the latrine area at the rear section of fencing, and farther on, stopped to study a two-and-a-half-ton truck parked behind what looked like a small supply shack from the empty crates stacked against it. The truck had once belonged to the United States Army and had a .30-caliber pedestal-mounted machine gun on the back.

Nothing moved inside the fence, and he continued on to the other side, determining the best points of entry and formulating a plan of attack. He glanced at his watch and estimated that there was approximately an hour left before first light.

Smashy watched the clearing through the night-vision goggles.

"Any sign of him?" Donatelli whispered to him.

"Not yet."

Galimore sat next to Donatelli, his weapon in his lap. His body tensed and he jerked his head to the left, grabbing Houser's arm and squeezing it. Houser alerted Donatelli in the same manner, and Donatelli Smashy. The men silently scanned the immediate area and listened intently.

Two Vietnamese soldiers were less than twenty yards away on the trail that led from the small village a mile

236

north of the camp. Their path would lead them past the team, passing close to their positions. They were well hidden by heavy cover and would not be detected, but each man realized the potential danger the two men posed, and knew what had to be done.

If the soldiers were allowed to reach the clearing and continue on to the camp, they might stumble into Callahan who was still reconnoitering the compound, or was possibly on his way back across the clearing.

The soldiers were returning to the camp after a night of drinking and gambling in the local village. Houser observed they had their weapons with them—Russian SKS rifles, slung over their shoulders. He pointed to Galimore and signaled the others to stay down. He crawled through the underbrush toward the trail, Galimore with him. The rustle of their movements went unnoticed by the chattering soldiers, now within ten yards of the team.

Houser tapped Galimore on the shoulder and pointed to the man on the outside, indicating that he should take him. Rising slowly to their feet behind two large mahogany trees at the edge of the trail, they unsheathed their knives.

The soldiers passed by, too far out of reach to assure silencing them instantly. There were still fifty yards of jungle trail left before it turned and entered the clearing.

Houser and Galimore began stalking their prey, placing the balls of their feet first, then the heels, matching them stride for stride to muffle the sounds of their footsteps. Moving parallel to the trail, they parted hanging tangles of vines and resisted the overpowering urge to brush away the mosquitoes that settled on their faces and hands.

Twenty yards down the trail one of the soldiers stopped to relieve himself while the other stood idly by, looking directly at his pursuers without seeing them.

Houser and Galimore, only a few yards away, their hearts pounding from the rush of adrenaline, waited anxiously for the man to turn his attention back to his companion. The moment he did, they closed the distance.

Galimore cupped his hand over his startled victim's mouth to smother his cries, then jammed his knee into the small of the back as a fulcrum from which to jerk his head backward, exposing the neck.

He drew the razor-sharp blade deeply across the throat of the frantically struggling man, cutting both arteries and severing the windpipe. The attack had been perfectly timed, swift and precise. For a few brief moments the blood spurted freely and forcefully from the arteries, then slowed as the body went limp. Once released, the soldier collapsed heavily to the jungle trail.

Galimore had been so thoroughly engrossed in the attack that he had not seen the struggle between Houser and the other man.

Houser had disarmed him with no alarming cries loud enough to reach the camp, but the man had managed to throw Houser off balance and drive an elbow into his stomach. The panic-stricken soldier ran down the trail toward the clearing, Houser in pursuit but losing ground, not yet fully recovered from having the wind knocked out of him.

Upon reaching the clearing, the soldier turned to look back as he ran, and stumbled, falling into the high grass.

Houser was on him before he could get to his feet, pinning him to the ground facedown. Reaching to cup his hand over the man's mouth, he was bitten, the teeth sinking deeply into the flat edge of his hand.

As Houser recoiled in shock from the painful bite, the

soldier squirmed and flipped onto his back, tossing his attacker off to the side.

Houser didn't see the knife until it was too late to block the thrust, but the man was thrashing wildly and the blade only scraped his rib cage. Quickly rolling onto his knees, Houser straddled him, and with a powerful downward stroke drove his knife through the eye socket into the brain.

His hand had only partially covered the soldier's mouth, and a sharp, screeching cry of pain broke the stillness and carried across the clearing. Houser jammed his hand under the man's jaw and shoved his head backward. Withdrawing the knife, he slashed it across his throat. A bright red geyser of blood shot up into his face and mouth.

Releasing the man, Houser knelt on all fours, gulping for air. His stomach heaved and he vomited violently.

Galimore appeared at his side and pulled him down on the ground. The soldier's cry had awakened the guard in the tower near the gate, and Galimore could see the shadowy figure moving about.

They lay motionless for a few moments, and hearing no sounds of alarm from the camp, Galimore signaled Houser to stay low and crawl ahead of him back to the jungle trail. Grabbing the soldier's limp, lifeless body by the shirt, Galimore dragged him along.

Back under cover, they pulled the bodies off the trail and hid them in the underbrush. Galimore tore the shirt from the back of one of the soldiers and wiped the thick coating of blood from his hands. Houser did the same, dampening the cloth with the moisture from a broad-leafed plant; he cleaned his face and worked at removing the blood caked between his fingers. His hands were still shaking, but he was gradually regaining his composure.

The years of academic life, of caring for the sick and helpless, the precision of surgery, and the pride in accomplishment were a millennium removed from the brutal necessity of what he had just done. He opened his shirt to check the damage from the knife, and found a long surface cut that had already stopped bleeding.

When they returned to the team, Donatelli motioned them to his side and whispered, "We got trouble. The tower guard's awake and Callahan is right below him."

Smashy stood against a tree at the edge of the clearing, the night-vision goggles trained on the front tower and the fence below. He could see the upper half of Callahan's body above the grass. The floor of the tower was only three feet above the fence—eleven feet above the ground. The slightest noise could be heard from that distance by an alert and wary guard.

Smashy had seen the guard stand up after the soldier cried out. He stood in the tower and looked in all directions, watching the clearing for a long time before settling down, unsure of what had awakened him: a prisoner's nightmare, a wild animal, or something he had imagined. But he was alert and suspicious, and any further disturbance could make him sound the alarm.

Callahan thought his heart was going to pound through his chest. He breathed deeply and exhaled slowly to calm himself as he stood flat against the fence, listening to the shuffling footsteps of the tower guard directly above him.

He considered making his way back along the fence toward the rear of the compound and out into the high grass, crossing the stream farther down where it turned back into the jungle. But as his nerves steadied, he began to think more clearly. If he made one misstep, any inadvertent sound that revealed his presence in his attempt to get back to the team, he would have to open up on the guard and compromise the mission, possibly causing the death of Frank Detimore and the other prisoners. And even if he made it to the team undetected, the guard, if he remained alert, presented a dangerous complication in getting the men into position for the attack on the camp. He had to be eliminated. Now.

The side of the tower was approximately five feet high, and set back from the fence. To get a clear shot at the man without exposing himself first, he would have to get him to lean over the side and look down.

Callahan calculated the distance to his target. He was six feet two inches tall, and with his arms extended over his head, he estimated the tip of the Walther's barrel would be seven or eight feet from the guard's head if he leaned out of the tower far enough to see the section of the fence immediately below him. A .22-caliber long-rifle round at that distance could provide the necessary penetration to kill instantly if the shot was precisely placed.

The angle and position of his target offered him only two choices. If the man was looking directly down on him, he would aim for the eye, and hope that any dying reflexes would not be transmitted to the man's trigger finger—if it was in place.

The other choice, the shot he hoped for, was just behind the ear, slightly lower than the ear opening. A no-reflex kill: death would be instantaneous. The round would penetrate to the base of the brain and sever the spinal cord.

Wiping the perspiration from his forehead with his sleeve, he slowly removed the pistol and silencer from the shoulder holster. He fumbled clumsily, almost dropping the weapon, stopping twice to gain control of his trembling hands. His mouth was dry and filled with the coppery taste of fear. He held the pistol tightly against his chest as he threaded the silencer in place.

Stepping six inches from the fence, he arched his back and looked straight up. Leaning backward and resting the top of his head against the fence, he extended his arms and gripped the pistol with both hands.

Again his hands began to shake, and he had to lower the weapon and fight for control. Breathing deeply and evenly, he forced himself to concentrate on what he had to do.

The soft, high-pitched whimpering sound he made immediately attracted the guard's attention. He waited until the man's movements masked the barely audible click made when he cocked the hammer, and steadied himself when he heard him move toward his side of the tower.

Perspiration ran down his face and into his eyes, and he blinked repeatedly to clear his vision. He made the puppylike sound again.

The guard leaned out of the tower, but not far enough for Callahan to get a clear shot. He could only see the hairline and part of the forehead. He waited anxiously, not daring to risk the possibility of a nonfatal shot.

He made the sound again, and this time the guard leaned farther out, exposing himself from the shoulders up. He presented a full-face view, looking directly down at Callahan. Jack went for the eye shot and squeezed the trigger.

The silencer hissed and spit and the guard slumped, his arms and head dangling over the side. He didn't fall in either direction; the rough-cut edge on the side of the tower had snagged his clothing under the arms as he slid backward, keeping him from dropping back inside.

Jack froze in position, afraid the metallic clank of the slide as it went back to pick up another round might have awakened someone in the officers' hut just twenty feet inside the fence, directly behind him. But there was only the buzzing and chirping of the insects and the sound of the wind rustling the grass, and in the distance, the faint sound of the smoothflowing stream.

Stepping out a few feet from the fence, he studied the body in the tower. The guard's head was hanging down and away from the available light, and Jack could not tell if his aim had been true. His hands had been shaking slightly when he fired and he had no way of knowing if he had missed the eye, or if the round had penetrated to either side and angled or deflected, merely knocking the man unconscious. Callahan decided he couldn't take the chance. He had to risk the noise of the slide for a second shot, having all the time he needed to line it up.

Positioning himself for a clear shot at the side of the guard's head, he took careful aim and slowly squeezed the trigger, putting the second round behind the ear.

Standing silently for a few moments, he heard a cough and a soft groan from inside the officers' hut, then nothing more. His legs weak and rubbery, he slid into a crouch against the fence, collecting himself before moving off.

Proceeding slowly along the fence, he turned the corner and continued on to where he could see into the rear tower. Once certain that the guard had not been awakened, he backed away from the compound and crept off into the grass toward the stream. Gritting his teeth, he slid silently into the frigid water.

"We hit them now," Jack said, brushing some leaves and vines from an adequately lighted spot near the edge of the clearing.

The team gathered in a tight circle as Callahan placed

rows of twigs on the ground to designate the compound fence, and broke up a piece of bark to represent the huts and cages.

"The prisoners' cages are on this side of the compound under some trees," he said, pointing, "about twenty meters from the rear guard tower and on the same side. The large hut for the guards is here." He placed a piece of bark a short distance from the cages.

"How many guards?" Houser asked.

"Twenty at most. Unless they're sleeping on top of each other.

"The small hut here," he continued, placing a chip of bark to the left of the entrance, "is probably the commanding officer's hut, and maybe for one other officer as well."

He placed the rest of the chips, pointing out the supply shack, the truck, and the latrine area. "Questions?"

"Why don't we wait until the prisoners are up?" Donatelli asked. "Wait till they all come down to the dock to wash up? Then we can see what we're shooting at."

"No," Jack replied. "We don't know that that's a daily routine. I'd rather know where everyone is, and concentrate our fire in a few areas. I don't want any stray rounds hitting our guys. Right now the guards are all sacked out in their hut which is set away from the cages."

"How thick is the fence?" Smashy asked.

"Six or seven inches in circumference. It's bamboo."

"Where do you want it blown?"

Jack hesitated for a moment, finalizing his plan of attack and deciding on target assignments. "Donatelli, you will place a charge here," he said, pointing to a section of fence directly opposite the guards' hut, halfway between the prisoners' cages and the guard tower. "Houser and

I will be with you. I'll use one of the M16s with the grenade launcher to pop a high explosive round into the rear tower.

"Smashy, it will be the same procedure on your side. I want your charge placed between the front tower and the CO's hut. We'll synchronize watches so we'll breach the fence at the same time.

"Joe," he pointed to Galimore, "you'll be with Smashy. Put an HE round in the front tower just for good measure; I want that machine gun disabled.

"Once inside we'll go directly to the guards' hut and start tossing in grenades. It's only fifteen meters from the fence so we ought to catch them jumping out of their bunks. You guys head for the CO's hut and do the same. And Smashy, take care of the .30-caliber on the truck."

"How far from the fence is the CO's hut?" Galimore asked.

"Maybe twenty feet. There's no power or communications line into the camp, so there's probably a field radio in that hut. Get it before anyone reaches it.

"I want all weapons on full auto. Kill everything that moves that isn't one of ours, and make it fast and violent."

After the synchronizing of watches, the team knelt, tensed and ready at the edge of the clearing. The horizon was edged with a trace of light, and a heavy mountain mist hung in the air.

Smashy took off his jungle hat, reached into the cargo pocket of his pants, and pulled out his green beret. Placing it on his head, he tapped Callahan on the shoulder.

Jack turned to face him and stared at the black, gold, and red flash of the 5th Special Forces Group on the front of the beret. "Leave it to a lifer," he said, shaking his head.

"If I don't make it out of here," Smashy said, "at least I want them to know who tried."

17

Donahue propped his head up with an elbow and watched the guard fumble with the clasp and lock before releasing the leg irons and swinging the door open.

"Di! Di!"

Frank Detimore put on his sandals and climbed slowly out of the cage, momentarily bracing himself against a tree until his legs responded to the change in position.

Donahue followed, dropping to his knees as he came out, grabbing hold of the bars to pull himself to his feet.

The feigned weakness was to convince the guards that the half-rations the two men had received since their escape attempt were having the desired effect. The days of torture and beatings had weakened them somewhat, but Maffey and Hendricks had stolen enough rice—and occasionally raw vegetables and pieces of fruit—to provide them with the same nourishment as the other prisoners.

"Di! Di!" the guard said again, placing the butt of his rifle in Donahue's back and shoving.

"Slant-eyed roach motherfucker," Donahue said, his voice hoarse and raspy from an injury to his larynx caused by a blow from Latrine Lips.

"Shut mouth! No talk!"

"Yeah. Yeah. Whatever happened to 'Good morning, Corporal Donahue'?"

"That's enough, Mike," Detimore said. "You're not one of his favorite people."

"Could've fooled me," Donahue said. "He keeps this shit up when I write my book he's out of it."

"Di! Di!"

The two prisoners walked past the still-sleeping men in the other cages. Frank noticed that Dan Lucere's blanket had slipped off during the night. He didn't know how much longer he could keep the wasted man alive, or for that matter how he had kept him alive this long. There had to be something deep inside the man, some invincible will to live, a courage and strength undiminished in his soul despite the brutality and deprivation he had suffered.

He had thought the same of Donahue after his recovery from the tortures following their attempted escape. Following a period of deep depression and self-pity, the tough young Marine had returned to his former self. But Frank soon recognized it for what it was: a different courage; the courage of no longer caring, of being beaten and abused to the point where fear and desperation no longer existed. He believed that Donahue had accepted that he would die here, and was determined to control how it happened. Perhaps not the method, but the terms—he would no longer relinquish his pride and self-respect to his tormentors.

Latrine Lips had seemed to recognize it, too, and had stopped seeking him out for special attention. Content with an occasional slap or kick when Donahue was most unresponsive to his commands, he otherwise left him alone.

But Frank had seen the same frightening methods used in the prisons in the north during the war. The NVA in charge of the prisons would allow their victims a respite, long enough to regain their equilibrium and believe they had seen the worst of it. Then they would begin again, with treatment more vicious than before. He suspected that that had been Dan Lucere's fate and that Latrine Lips had the same in mind for Donahue.

After a stop at the latrine, the two men continued walking toward the woodpile. Something caught Donahue's attention through the slits in the fence near the rear guard tower; he stared intently at the spot, then looked away. A few yards farther, and again, a fleeting dark shadow against the lightening background registered in his peripheral vision. He glanced in the direction of the fence, then at the guard who was leaning against a tree ten yards behind them.

"Hey, Top," he whispered. "You see that?"

"See what?" Detimore said, stacking wood in his arms for the cooking fire.

"Something just ran past the outside of the fence."

Frank looked but saw nothing. "Probably a monkey."

Donahue looked again and shrugged. "Yeah, probably."

Standing at the woodpile along the back section of the fence, gathering an armload of firewood, Donahue's eyes were again drawn to movement outside the compound. This time there was no mistaking what he saw. He recognized the distinctive silhouette of a man.

"Jesus Christ!" he said, dropping the wood.

"What's wrong?" Frank asked. "Your arm bothering you again?"

"There's somebody out there, Top," he whispered. "And it ain't no monkey. Not unless it's a thyroid monster."

Donahue pushed Frank away from the fence in the direction of the guard. "We gotta move. I think that guy was packin' a charge against the fence."

Frank looked over his shoulder and caught a glimpse of a hurriedly retreating figure. "Son of a bitch!"

"Come on, Top," Donahue said, picking up the pace in the direction of the guard. "If something's goin' down I want to be close enough to jump that bastard."

The two men were halfway to the guard when the shock waves from an explosion picked them off their feet and tossed them to the ground. A brilliant white flash peaked and faded, casting a surrealistic glow over the camp.

Donahue looked up to see the rear guard tower disintegrate and a limp, legless body propelled into the air, landing a few feet from where they had been thrown by the force of the blast.

A split second later another explosion ripped apart the front tower, catapulting its occupant into the clearing.

Three men sprinted through the gaping hole in the fence, almost firing before identifying the two men clad in black as prisoners. They didn't see the man who was guarding them. The explosion had thrown him against the side of the supply shack where he lay momentarily stunned.

"Stay down! Stay down!" Callahan yelled as they ran toward the guards' hut and tossed in grenades. The explosions over, they rushed the doorway and filled the hut with automatic fire. Detimore and Donahue stared blankly at each other, stunned by what was happening around them and immobilized by the terrible swiftness of the attack. Then instinct and training took over, and they were on their feet and moving.

Frank spotted the stunned guard's AK-47 on the ground in front of him, and dived for the weapon.

The guard got to his knees and crawled around a corner of the supply shack before Frank could fire.

"Top!" Donahue shouted. "The window!"

Detimore turned and saw one of the guards crawling out of the rear window of the hut. He took aim and raked him with a burst from the AK-47, blowing away half his face.

Donahue grabbed the weapon dropped by the dead man and followed Detimore toward the supply shack in pursuit of the guard who had gotten away.

The camp was filled with the deafening roar of successive grenade blasts and the rapid cracking of automatic rifles. Thick black smoke rose from the burning huts and the acrid smell of battle lingered in the damp air.

Galimore waited until the dust and smoke had cleared in the officers' hut, then stepped cautiously inside. He quickly scanned the office, spotted the radio lying on its side beneath a shattered table, and riddled it with a quick burst.

He approached the doorway to his right at the back of the office. The door had been blown off its hinges and the room was a shambles. Part of the roof had caved in and a large hole in one wall was burning around the edges. Another wall was completely blown away and open to the outside.

As he inspected the rubble, he heard a noise from the adjacent room, and moved into the office, staying against the wall as he approached the doorway. In a lightning-fast move, he kicked open the partially demolished door and dropped into a crouch, spraying the room with sustained fire.

When there was no answering fire, and nothing moved, he stood and glanced about the room. Through the torn mosquito netting on the window above the bunk, he saw a man running through the opening blown in the fence, disappearing from sight before he could fire.

Smashy was on his way to the truck to knock out the machine gun when he heard Galimore shout. He turned to see the soldier, naked from the waist up, run out into the high grass. He fired and missed and gave chase.

Bad Eye was almost at the stream when Smashy reached the clearing. He had a clear shot, and fired as he ran after him.

Two rounds hit low behind the fleeing target, and then a metallic *thud* was all Smashy heard.

"Son of a bitch!" The M16 had jammed. He slammed the butt on the ground and worked to free the bolt. By the time he had it operational, Bad Eye had slid down the stream bank.

Smashy slowed to a walk and advanced cautiously. A small hole in the ground caught the heel of his boot, twisting his injured knee and causing him to stumble. As he lurched upward to keep from falling, he saw Bad Eye rise from the edge of the stream, a pistol in his hand.

Before he had time to react, Bad Eye had fired twice. The first shot grazed the side of his head and creased his skull. The second tore into his shoulder, spinning him around and knocking him to the ground.

As he started to get up, he saw Bad Eye crossing the stream, and tried to raise his weapon. A wave of dizziness and nausea swept over him and he collapsed onto his back.

Galimore had run through the CO's hut and out the door, heading toward the clearing when he heard the pistol shots. As he turned the corner, a burst from the .30-caliber machine gun sent him scurrying back for cover.

Callahan and Donatelli were checking out the guards' hut when they heard the unmistakable sound. As they ran outside, the ground around them erupted in fountains of dirt. They dived for cover behind the hut, out of the line of fire. Houser, who had been on his way to the prisoners' cages, turned and hit the deck, rolling in beside them.

Jack ran to the other end of the hut and peered around the corner. A guard was on the back of the truck manning the machine gun. Two armed prisoners were crouched behind the supply shack, unable to move, for the guard could swing the pedestal-mounted weapon 360 degrees and for the moment, he had them effectively pinned down. They could not get a clear shot at him without exposing themselves.

Callahan saw the guard swing the machine gun in a wide arc and open up on a ragged line of trees between the truck and the CO's hut. A moment later he saw Galimore move from behind a tree and sprint to another one closer to the truck.

The guard fired another burst, then swung back to chew up a corner of the supply shack, barely missing Donahue, who was about to rush him.

Galimore advanced again, and the guard swung back to him and fired, returning immediately to fire into the supply shack and the guards' hut.

Jack signaled to Houser and Donatelli. "The next time Joe moves—" he called out.

They understood and nodded.

Galimore had been purposefully drawing fire. He got to his feet behind a broad-based teak tree, and readied himself for his next move. Slapping a full magazine into his weapon, he broke cover, firing as he ran.

The guard had anticipated his move. He was quick, but not accurate, and he missed, tearing chunks from a small tree behind his target.

Callahan, Houser, and Donatelli were up and running the instant the guard turned his attention to Galimore. They closed the distance and hit the man with a barrage of fire that slammed him into the side panel and off the back of the truck where Donahue, who had advanced with them, riddled him again as he hit the ground.

Jack looked around him. "Where's Smashy?"

"A Viet in the officers' hut got through the fence," Galimore said. "Smashy went after him."

As the team started across the compound, Smashy came through the hole in the fence holding his hand tightly on his shoulder, blood streaming down the side of his face.

"Fucker got away, Jack," he said. He threw the M16 to the ground. "Piece of shit jammed on me."

Houser examined his wounds. "The head wound is superficial. The shoulder is an in-and-out; didn't hit the bone. Come on, I'll patch you up."

Jack checked the time. The raid had taken seventeen minutes. If the man who had escaped could make eight-minute miles, they still had at least an hour before he reached the army base, another twenty or thirty minutes before a reaction force could reach them. With the helicopter sitting ten minutes away on the Laotian border, the unexpected turn of events posed no immediate threat. In his planning he had considered the possibility of somebody from the nearby village running to the army base when the sounds of the raid reached them.

"Joe," he said. "Get the chopper on the radio. Tell them the area is secure and to get in here."

"Let's get the prisoners out," Donatelli said, walking toward the cages.

Callahan didn't answer. He was looking at a man standing behind Smashy: gray-haired and clad in filthy, frayed black pants and shirt, his sunken cheeks covered with white stubble, and his large rheumy eyes telling of pain and suffering. A broken nose disfigured his gaunt face, and when he smiled, Jack saw that only a few rotted, broken teeth remained in his mouth. The resemblance to the man he had known twelve years ago was faint, but—

"Frank? Jesus Christ . . . ah, Jesus Christ."

Detimore could not control the tremors that shook his frail body. Choked with emotion, he merely nodded his head and embraced his old friend. The rest of the team crowded around him, staring in disbelief at his condition, then hugged him and shook his hand.

"You know these guys, Top?" Donahue asked, intrigued by the reunion.

"Yeah. We heard the hoot owl together a few times." He put his arm around Donahue's shoulder and said, "Fellows, this is Mike Donahue, a good trooper."

Donahue grinned and snapped to attention. "Corporal Michael Francis Xavier Donahue, United States Marine Corps. I really appreciate what you guys just did, but I gotta tell you, Force Recon could've cut your time in half."

Frank laughed, brushing away the tears. "He never quits."

Donatelli approached from the direction of the prisoners' cages, a grim expression on his face.

"You're not going to believe this, Jack. Phil, you better get over there."

Houser finished dressing Smashy's wounds and went over to the cages. Donatelli smashed the locks off the doors, grimacing at the sight of the men inside.

Harry Cambell sat in a corner of his cage, confused and dazed by what had happened. He stared wide-eyed and frightened at Donatelli, and made no move toward the open door.

"Come on, Mac," Donatelli said. "Nobody's going to hurt you. You're going home."

"Jesus Christ!" Houser said as he stood before Dan Lucere's cage. "How long has this man been like this?" he asked Frank.

"Two years."

"How the hell has he stayed alive?"

Frank told him.

Houser's shock was genuine. He had seen most of the horrors of war, but nothing like the stark inhuman reality of the men in the cages.

"Praise the Lord," Hendricks said as he climbed out of his cage, finally allowing himself to believe what had happened. "Praise the Lord—and you, too," he told Callahan.

Houser noticed the swollen joints in Harry Cambell's arms and examined them closely, attributing them to vitamin deficiency. "Beriberi," he said to Callahan. "Is there any B_1 in the camp?" he asked Frank Detimore.

"In the CO's hut," Frank answered.

"I'll see if any of it survived," Donahue said.

"What's wrong with him?" Jack asked, looking at Maffey who was smiling and staring blankly.

"An educated guess is acute brain syndrome, brought on by a starvation diet," Houser said. "When I told him who we were, he said he couldn't come with us because today was the day he went down to the stream to wash."

"No. He ain't got no syndrome," Hendricks said. "He's with Jesus now."

Maffey looked up from where he was sitting outside his

cage, continuing to smile. "I'm all right. I just thought I was dreaming this whole thing."

Houser stared at the two men and shook his head sadly. "Goddamnit!" he said to Jack. "Have you seen the marks on these men? And what happened to that poor bastard's face?" A wave of revulsion swept over all of them as Frank told about the rat feeding on Dan Lucere.

Callahan glanced at Lucere, then winced and looked away as a vivid memory of his team sergeant at Mai Loc, his face torn away by a shell fragment, flashed before him. He turned his attention to six Montagnard prisoners grouped in front of the cages, grunting out a discussion of their situation. As he walked toward them, they grinned and nodded. A few of them came forward and shook his hand—a gesture alien to their culture—telling Callahan they had been in the company of Americans before.

"We can take you as far as Thailand," Jack said.

One of the men, tall for a Montagnard, introduced himself as Toong, and spoke for the group.

"We go to mountains. Find friends," he said, reaching for Jack's hand and pumping it mechanically. He noticed Smashy's green beret and smiled and pointed to it. "You leader?"

"No. The captain is," Smashy said, jerking his head toward Jack.

Toong turned to Jack. "Toong thank you, *Dai-uy*," he said, using the Vietnamese word for captain. "I fight with Mike Force at Nha Trang in war. Kill many VC."

Callahan smiled and gestured toward the guards' hut. He had noticed that some of the weapons stacked near the back of the hut were not damaged. "You can take some weapons with you."

"Things in supply shack. We take some, too?"

"Sure."

Donahue poked about in the rubble in the office of the officers' hut. The fire had burned off most of the thatch roof and one wall, then smoldered on the damp bamboo before going out.

The shelves of medical supplies were in splinters from the grenade blasts, and Donahue stooped and used his hands to sift through the remnants, finding small shards of broken B_1 bottles, but none intact. Spying an unbroken bottle of Ba Mui Ba beer, he popped the cap off on the edge of the battered, overturned desk. Taking a mouthful, he shuddered before swallowing and spit the warm, bitter liquid across the room, throwing the bottle after it.

"Goddamn monkey piss."

Alarmed by a sound that came from the small room off the office, he swiftly unslung the captured AK-47 from his shoulder and stood silently—listening. He heard nothing more, but moved cautiously into the room.

The side of the room with the wall blown away let in the growing early-morning light. The center of the room where the roof had collapsed was a heap of rubble. Donahue looked around, then shrugged, attributing the sound to settling debris, and had turned to leave when something caught his eye. A portion of a hand protruded from beneath an unburned section of roof that had fallen on an overturned bunk in the corner.

The young Marine tensed. Moving toward the hand, he kicked away the large piece of thatch and pulled the bunk away from the corner. His initial shock turned to vengeful menace.

Cowering before him, fully conscious, was Latrine Lips, his left leg shattered and bleeding.

Donahue glared at the defenseless man and slowly, purposefully, placed his weapon against the wall halfway between them. He sat on his heels, his back against the wall, and spoke casually, almost amiably to his hated enemy.

"Hey, Lips. How's it goin'?"

Donahue kept one eye on the AK-47 as he reached for a thick piece of wood that had been part of the roof support. A sardonic smile creased his face as he gestured with his head and eyes, daring the terrified man to try for the weapon. Latrine Lips made no attempt.

"No. I didn't think so. No guts, no glory, Lips." His voice was low and even, a frightening monotone; his eyes fixed and expressionless. "So. How's my favorite slope this morning? Huh?"

Latrine Lips, wide-eyed with terror, glanced at the weapon within his reach, then at the twisted grin on the face of the man he had tortured and brutalized. He pulled himself farther into the corner.

"Come on, motherfucker. You always have somethin' to say to me." Donahue raised the charred club, and reaching out, let it drop on the large, jagged piece of bone jutting out from Latrine Lips' thigh.

The frantic man screamed in agony.

"Payback is hell, Lips."

Latrine Lips pleaded in a muted, half-choked voice.

"Huh, motherfucker? Huh? What did you say? I can't hear you, Lips! *I can't hear you!*"

He dropped the club on the leg again, this time adding force to the downward motion. Latrine Lips screamed hysterically.

Hendricks appeared suddenly in the blown-out opening in the wall. He smiled and nodded. "Oh, yeah. An eye for an eye," he said, entering the room. "Judgment Day. I knew it. I knew it."

Donahue stood and raised the club, ready to bring it down on Latrine Lips' head. He hesitated and let it drop to his side.

"No," he said. "You're not gettin' off that easy. No way."

Picking up the AK-47, he handed it to Hendricks. "Keep an eye on him. I'll be right back. And don't kill him, he's mine."

Hendricks pointed the weapon at the cringing man's head, listening impassively as he pleaded for morphine.

"Jesus didn't get no morphine on the cross. I sure as hell ain't givin' none to you."

Donahue came back into the hut carrying a can of gasoline he had taken from the supply shack.

Latrine Lips watched in horror as Donahue poured the contents of the can over his body. He began screaming when Donahue reached for a glowing splinter of bamboo on the wall of the hut. He struggled to get to his feet, but Hendricks kicked him back into the corner.

Callahan and Frank Detimore, drawn by the screams, reached the hut to find Latrine Lips writhing and shuddering spasmodically as flames enveloped his body. The long trailing screams ended with a short guttural gasp.

"Scratch one slope motherfucker," Donahue said to Frank as he walked out of the hut and across the compound.

Jack stared at the blackened corpse in the corner of the hut. "Jesus."

"He deserved it," Frank said. "And worse."

*　　*　　*

Galimore sat on the tailgate of the truck, the radio handset to his ear. "Koala Bear, this is Wolfpack. The area is secure. Repeat. The area is secure."

"Wolfpack, this is Koala Bear. We have a problem."

Galimore froze. "What problem? Over."

"Our chopper is down. Over."

"What the fuck . . . Koala Bear, this is Wolfpack. What do you mean 'down'?"

As the radio operator at Murdock's camp in Thailand explained the situation, Galimore felt a knot form in the pit of his stomach. The Huey helicopter they had sent out to wait in position at the Laotian border had never made it. A few minutes out from the camp its transmission had disintegrated and it had to make an emergency landing. They were making arrangements to send the Chinook, but would not be able to get them for at least three hours.

"*Shit!* Koala Bear, we can't sit here for three hours. Charlie will be on top of us before then."

"Wolfpack, Koala Bear leader suggests you return to drop zone. Will extract you there."

"Goddamnit! "

"Can you proceed to drop zone? Over."

Galimore signaled to Callahan who had heard bits of the conversation and was on his way.

"The chopper never made it."

Jack's face remained expressionless while a blind rage flashed in his eyes as Galimore filled him in.

"Tell them we'll be at the drop zone, and they goddamn well better be there."

Galimore relayed the message.

"Roger, Wolfpack," came the reply. "Drop zone in three hours. Call upon arrival. With a little luck we may be en route."

"Assholes," Galimore muttered. "World's full of incompetent assholes."

"How the hell are we going to make it back to the drop zone in three hours?" Phil Houser asked. "It took us two and a half to get here ourselves and most of the way was downhill."

Callahan pointed to the old army truck parked near the supply shack. "The map shows the road leading west from the camp pretty much parallels our course back for about half the distance. We'll use the truck as far as we can, then head into the jungle. There're a number of trails we can take."

Houser shook his head. "I hope to God nobody gets on our tail in a hurry. Most of these guys aren't going to be able to move too fast, and we're going to have to carry the catatonic."

Jack looked at his watch. The raid had begun thirty-five minutes ago. He doubted that the man who had escaped had reached the army base, and estimated they had at least another half hour before the enemy troops were mobilized and in pursuit.

"We'll make it. Let's get everybody loaded on the truck."

Frank Detimore, standing with the team, had not said a word while he listened to the conversation between Callahan and Galimore. He quickly realized the opportunity the complication presented.

"Did he say they were bringing in a Chinook?" he asked Jack.

"Yeah. It's on a supply run. They're calling it back now." He held Detimore's gaze and said with conviction, "Don't worry, Frank, we're going to make it. We've got a good lead on the troops from the army base and they'll have to track us to the drop zone."

But something else was on Detimore's mind. "There are eighteen American POWs in the prison at that base."

"How do you know that?" Jack asked.

"I was in a cell there until two years ago."

"Frank, we can't go after them. There's a battalion at that base. We've got to get the hell out of here."

"There used to be a battalion. There's only a company there now. The rest were sent to Cambodia and Laos; I heard the guards talking about it."

"But that company is between us and the base."

"Yeah. But we can get around them. There's a deserted Yard village about four miles down the road toward the base. If we can get there in time there's a place where we can pull in, get off the road, let them pass us."

"Frank—"

"They're going to be hauling ass here, Jack. They aren't going to be looking for anything on the way. And when they don't find us, they'll head west . . . to the border. Nobody's going to expect us to go in the opposite direction."

Jack stared thoughtfully at Frank, then at Galimore who was listening intently.

"Most of that company will be sent here," Frank said. "There won't be more than twenty or thirty troops left at the base. We can get the rest of the prisoners, Jack. That Chinook can carry forty men."

Jack stood silently for a moment, then asked, "What kind of troops are there?"

"Support troops. It was a quartermaster battalion. A breakdown point for redistributing supplies going into Laos and Cambodia. The remaining company is made up mainly of South Vietnamese conscripts."

"What the hell is a prison doing at a supply base?"

"It's isolated and there was an old French colonial jail there they could use."

"How large is the prison detail?"

"Two officers; six enlisted. The officers carry pistols; the enlisted arms are stacked in a weapons room."

"Where are the prisoners kept?"

"In individual cells. They never get out. Those of us capable of working were sent here. The others stayed."

Jack looked over at Lucere. "They made him work?"

"When he first came here he could. They just never got around to sending him back."

Jack stared off in the distance, visualizing one of the intelligence photographs he had studied. "We had an aerial photo of the base," he told Frank. "It's located on a river—"

"Right," Frank said. "The Song Thach Han. They transport most of the supplies by boat. There's a network of rivers they can follow to Cambodia and Laos."

"If I remember right," Jack said, "the surrounding area is heavily wooded and there isn't enough room inside the compound for a Chinook to put down."

"There isn't," Frank confirmed. "But two miles from the base there's a large field we cleared for farming before we came here. Half the distance can be traveled by truck, the rest is jungle trail."

Callahan took out his map. "Show me where the field is."

Frank pointed it out. It was adjacent to a once-deserted village that had been bombed out during the war. "It's a small village," he told Callahan, anticipating his question.

"They relocated about fifty Vietnamese peasants there. They're not going to have any weapons."

Jack studied the map, then looked away, again picturing the aerial photograph in his mind.

"The photo showed the main part of the base to be enclosed with barbed wire, but a section of it was blocked off with a bamboo fence. There were some buildings inside the fence."

"Warehouses. For supplies," Frank said. "I used to watch the trucks go in and out from my cell window. They stored the stuff there until they were ready to load it on the boats and take it downriver. I can sketch the layout of the base on the way."

"What kind of perimeter defense do they have?"

"Nothing. No towers. No machine-gun emplacements, no mortars, nothing. Believe me, Jack, with most of the company gone that place will be easier to take than this camp."

"You're sure? We'll have to take it in one hell of a hurry. We can't give them a chance to kill the prisoners."

We can do it. The prison building is masonry, but the door is wood. Hit it with an M79 round and you'll blow it into chopsticks."

"I don't know, Frank. We'll need more men to cover everything inside that base. You and the other prisoners aren't in any condition to fight."

"Don't kid yourself. We're undernourished and battered, and we look like hell. But we work hard every day. With the exception of Lucere, we're capable. And talk to the Yards. They'll help us. You know how they feel about the Vietnamese."

Callahan looked at Galimore. "Joe?"

Galimore hesitated, then nodded.

265

"Get the others," Jack said. He spread the map on the ground and determined the grid coordinates of the field near the village. Looking up at Detimore, he said, "Most of what I know I learned from you, Frank. If you think we can pull it off, we'll give it a try, if the rest of the team agrees."

"You gotta ask?" Smashy said.

Donatelli shook his head. "What the hell. In for a penny, in for a pound."

Houser's attention was on Dan Lucere who sat huddled against a tree. He slowly nodded his head. "I'm in."

"The Yards are in the supply shack,' Jack told Smashy. "Tell the tall one—Toong—I want to see him."

Turning to Galimore he said, "Get Murdock's man on the radio. Give him the new coordinates and tell him to put the Chinook in position on the border. We'll call them in when we're near the field."

Toong listened as Callahan explained the situation and asked for his help. After a brief discussion with the other Montagnards he turned to Jack.

"We help. You in deep shit, *Dai-uy*," he said smiling, proud of remembering the phrase he had learned during the war.

"How many of your men have seen action?" he asked.

"Three fight in war. Two I train myself."

"How far from the base are the nearest reinforcements?" he asked Toong.

"Twenty kilometers. Near Quang Tri. Maybe two companies," he told Jack. "Da Nang have battalion, but they not leave. Russians have big secret there."

"Most of the combat-ready troops are in Laos or Cambodia, or up on the Chinese border," Frank added. "The troops at Quang Tri are the only ones with a possibility of reaching us.''

"You can count on them heading in this direction when they hear about us," Smashy said.

"Get the alert frequency off the camp radio," Jack told Smashy. "And see if they have a signal intelligence booklet. We can try and tune in on their frequency. We might be able to keep track of them by picking up their transmissions."

Galimore completed his call to Murdock's camp and reported to Jack. "The Chinook is on its way back to camp to refuel. He says they'll have it in position within three hours.''

Harry Cambell had gone to pieces when he heard the news of the downed helicopter. He stood beside Frank, shaking uncontrollably.

"I'm not going, Frank. They'll torture us when they get us. I'm going back to my cage. They won't hurt me if I'm still in my cage. I'll tell them I had nothing to do with this.''

"Pull yourself together, Harry.''

Cambell began to cry. "Please, Frank. I can't take any more torture.''

Detimore led him by the arm to the back of the truck and helped him in. "Nobody is going to torture you. We're going home. You have my word.''

Smashy and Donatelli collected the remaining undamaged AK-47s and distributed them among the prisoners. Donahue passed out ammunition from the supply shack.

Hendricks and Maffey sat in the back of the truck, following Frank's orders and keeping an eye on Harry Cambell who had twice attempted to go back to his cage.

Suddenly, Hendricks glared at two men sitting near the tailgate, and got to his feet, stomping forward. "Oh, no," he said. "Not them godless traitors." He punched Mahanes off the back of the truck, and kicked Gerber in the stomach. "You ain't goin' with us. You stay here with your friends."

After the raid, Mahanes and Gerber had kept out of sight, hoping to avoid confrontations with the other prisoners, and no one up to now had paid any attention to them.

Donahue leaped onto the back of the truck and grabbed Gerber by the hair, throwing him to the ground beside Mahanes.

"I'm not going to kill you maggots like I said, but Hendricks is right. You're not goin' anywhere."

Callahan ran over to where Mahanes and Gerber were sprawled on the ground. Frank Detimore had placed himself between Donahue and the two frightened men. "What the hell is going on here?" he asked Frank.

"They're deserters," Frank said. "Went over to the VC."

Jack looked at them with contempt, then said to Frank, "They go with us. We'll hand them over to the Army when we get back."

Donahue was furious until Frank calmed him.

"Okay," he said. "But they don't get any weapons. I see one of them sons of bitches touch a weapon I'll blow his fuckin' head off."

Callahan pulled Donahue aside. "This isn't the time for judgments, Mike. We need every man we can get."

"Jesus Christ, Cap'n. They're traitors. I hate them as much as the dinks."

"We need them. We'll deal with them later."

"I'm gonna watch them, Cap'n. I'm gonna watch every goddamn move they make."

Callahan approached Mahanes and Gerber. "You want in on this?"

Both men said they did.

"For the record," Jack said, "you mess up, step out of line just once, and I'll let Donahue kill you."

The sound of a helicopter reverberated through the valley, drawing the attention of everyone but Lucere, who sat huddled in the corner of the truck where Donatelli had placed him. He stared at the floorboards, a deep frown on his face, completely unaware of what was happening.

The Montagnards ran from the supply shack and joined the men at the rear of the truck.

"They're coming!" Harry Cambell screamed. "They're coming after us." He tried to get to his feet, but Maffey held him in place.

"No gunship," Toong said. "Just look see."

Callahan watched the helicopter move along the ridgeline, losing sight of it occasionally as it disappeared behind patches of fog rising from the river. Banking steeply and descending rapidly, it made its approach from the east end of the valley.

It was an old American Cayuse—used during the war for low-level reconnaissance. Small, fast, and maneuverable, it could skim the treetops, following jungle trails and checking enemy positions. Jack remembered the intelligence report on the army base and knew where it had come from.

The helicopter flew low over the compound, pulled up, and traversed the ridgeline again, preparing for another pass.

"That goddamn Viet must have run the distance in record time," Smashy said.

"No," Frank replied. "He probably met up with a supply truck headed in this direction."

Donatelli jumped onto the back of the truck, getting behind the .30-caliber machine gun.

"He's coming right down the same slot," he yelled as he sighted the weapon.

He began firing when the helicopter reached the midpoint of the clearing, keeping up a steady barrage as the small, unarmed craft passed overhead.

He swung the weapon around, still firing as the Cayuse rose, trailing smoke. It seemed to stop in midair, then shuddered and dropped into the jungle at the far end of the valley.

Callahan watched the orange fireball erupt on impact, then turned to Galimore. "See that everyone has a weapon and ammo," he said. "Load up!" he shouted to the ragged group of prisoners standing at the rear of the truck. "Smashy. Get behind the .30-caliber."

"I saw some tarps in the supply shack," Donatelli said. "We can use them for concealment."

"Good," Jack said. "Let's get them."

After throwing the tarps on the back, Jack, Frank, and Donatelli climbed into the cab of the truck. Jack cranked the starter, and on the third try the engine came to life.

"Did the Yards put on the Vietnamese uniforms?" he asked Donatelli.

"Yeah. They didn't like it much. But they put them on."

With the rest of the team and the prisoners and Montagnards on board, Smashy slapped the roof of the cab.

"Ready, Jack."

270

When they reached the front of the compound, Donatelli jumped out of the cab and opened the gate.

"You wanted action," he said to Jack as he got back in, "you got action."

Callahan's face showed fierce determination. His thoughts raced ahead to the problems before them as the cumbersome old truck squeaked and groaned over the bumpy dirt road.

18

Callahan and Frank Detimore sat behind a dense thicket near the side of the narrow dirt road. Donatelli had driven the truck and the rest of the men farther into the woods along the edge of the deserted Montagnard village, parking behind a partially collapsed longhouse.

"How's Betty?" Frank asked, staring intently through the brush down the straight stretch of road.

"She seems fine," Jack said. "That's one hell of a woman you married."

" Yeah. She still beautiful?"

"A knockout."

"And the girls? Did you get to see them, too?"

"Just a photograph," Jack said. "They're as pretty as their mother. They're both in college."

"Jesus," Frank said. "They kept me sane, Jack . . . believing that I'd see them again . . . and the memories." He opened his mouth to speak again, but stopped and looked away.

"What is it?" Jack asked.

Frank turned to him with a pained expression, looking directly at him for a long moment before speaking. "How do I look?"

Callahan hesitated, then shrugged.

"I want to know," Frank said. "I haven't looked in a mirror in seven years. How do I look?"

"Like you've been in a POW camp for twelve years."

"Old? My face pretty beat up?"

Jack nodded.

"I tried looking in the sideview mirror of the truck, but the glass was broken out of it, and the windows. The windshield was too dirty." He gestured toward Jack's rucksack. "Do you have a signal mirror?"

"No," Jack said. "Didn't they give you mirrors to shave with?"

"Once. Seven years ago when an NVA political cadre came to the prison up north. That was it. The rest of the time we shaved without them. I saw my reflection in some still water a few times, but it was too blurred to tell much."

"Don't worry about it," Jack said. "You're still you, Frank. A few months at home with Betty and the kids, some good food, some dental work, you'll get back into shape."

"I don't have to worry much about the dentist," Frank said. "I have all of three teeth left."

A low rumbling noise in the distance caught their attention. A moment later a truck appeared around a curve a few hundred yards down the road.

They peered through the brush, watching the canvas-topped troop carriers as they sped by in the direction of the camp. When the last truck was out of sight and the cloud of red dust had settled, they left the cover of the thicket.

"Five trucks," Jack said. "Maybe a hundred men."

"There can't be more than twenty-five left at the base," Frank said. "If that."

Callahan signaled to Smashy who was standing where the truck had been backed into the woods behind the longhouse.

Donatelli pulled the truck forward. It bucked and swayed over the uneven ground, snapping saplings and flattening the underbrush in its path as it lumbered up to the edge of the road.

Callahan and Detimore climbed onto the back, and called to Donatelli to join them.

Jack sat down and placed the sketch Frank had drawn of the base on the floor.

"Listen up," he said. "Frank's going to give you the layout and then you'll get your target assignments."

The men gathered around as Frank quickly and authoritatively detailed what they could expect to find at the base.

"The headquarters building is masonry," he said, pointing to it on the sketch. "There is one large office you enter through the door. Behind the office are two small rooms. A supply room and a radio room. The radio room is on the right. There's usually no one on duty there, but there probably will be now because of the alert. You've got to get him before he can get out a message.

"The prison is here," he said, tapping the sketch. "There is a grove of trees between it and the HQ building. It's also masonry, with a wooden door. It's all one level. Inside the door to the left is the officers' room, on the right the guards' room and the weapons room. The building is

274

T-shaped. There are cells down the long hall to both left and right. By the time we hit it, the guards will have finished eating and'll probably be lounging around in their room. One of the officers will be on duty, maybe both.

"The barracks are here," he indicated. "Four of them. About forty feet long and twenty feet wide. They are nothing but thatch with bamboo supports. The thatch comes almost to the ground on the sides, but they are open on both ends. There's a double row of hammocks strung in each of them. They will probably be empty, but if not, you can stand at one end and cover anybody inside.

"There are five large warehouses inside the fence in the left rear corner of the base. My best guess is that any troops not sent out on the alert will be in there on a work detail. I don't know which warehouses they will be working in, but I'm pretty sure they won't have weapons with them. Make sure they don't get to them."

"Rick," Callahan said to Donatelli, "you'll have the M60. Take two of Toong's men and Mahanes and Gerber and cover the barracks.

"Smashy—you, Donahue, Hendricks, Toong, and one of his men will take the warehouses.

"Joe. You take Maffey and two of Toong's men and hit the HQ."

Galimore noticed that Maffey's eyes still had a vacant, distant look. "Are you sure he's okay?" he asked Jack. "He's got the thousand-meter stare."

Maffey answered for himself. "I'm okay. Just tell me what you want me to do."

"Houser and Frank and I will take the prison." He pointed to Cambell. "You'll come with us."

Cambell shook his head violently. Hendricks had had to physically restrain him several times to keep him on the truck after they had left the camp. "No! I can't," he shouted hysterically. "I can't do it."

"What do you mean you can't do it?" Callahan asked, bewildered at the man's outburst.

"It's okay, Jack," Frank said. "He's got problems."

"Sorry. You stay on the truck and take care of him," he told Cambell, pointing to Dan Lucere.

"Toong. You drive from here on. One of your men will ride up front with you. Choose someone who can handle the machine gun to stand in the back. The rest of us will be under the tarps until we reach the gate."

"You've got to be kidding about him driving," Smashy said. "You ever been in a truck with a Yard at the wheel?"

"No, why?"

"You're in for a treat."

A trace of indignation showed on the Montagnard's face. "Toong good driver. You see."

"You sure you can handle it?" Jack asked.

"Sure. I drive before."

Jack removed the magazine from the Walther pistol and replaced the two expended rounds. He screwed on the silencer and handed it to Toong.

"There's a round in the chamber. When you pull up to the guard at the entrance, stick this in his face and pull the trigger, then drive into the compound and stop in front of the headquarters building. When we get off, you crash the gate in the bamboo fence as fast as you can."

Toong nodded and grinned, pointing at the silencer. "No noise. Right, *Dai-uy?*"

"No noise."

Smashy had trouble containing his laughter as the truck careened down the dirt road, veering close to the tree line,

276

rattling noisily and tossing the men about. Frank held on to Dan Lucere to keep him from being thrown off the back of the truck.

"You made your point," Jack shouted over the racket. "When we get inside the base, you take over the wheel. That maniac is liable to drive us right out of the compound and into the river."

Jack peered out from beneath the tarp as the truck slowed and approached the entrance to the supply base. Through the slats on the side panels he could see a guard, rifle in hand, standing to one side of the opening in the barbed-wire fence. When the truck stopped, the guard walked over and stood beside the cab. He spoke to Toong and waited for a reply.

Toong released the safety on the pistol and raised it from his lap. Putting his hand out of the window, he held the tip of the silencer a few inches from the guard's head and pulled the trigger.

Four quick rounds tore into the man's forehead. Standing immobile for a brief moment, his eyes went blank, his pupils dilated, and he toppled over backward like a felled tree.

Toong floored the accelerator and raced through to the headquarters building, skidding to a stop.

The men in the back of the truck unloaded, separating into small groups, and ran to their assigned targets.

Smashy jumped into the cab. Taking over the wheel, he sped across the compound toward the bamboo fence.

Galimore took the three steps in front of the headquarters building in one stride and burst through the door, his men behind him.

Callahan, Houser, and Detimore darted through the trees toward the prison. Houser and Detimore took cover behind the last row of trees while Callahan fired a high explosive grenade into the door. The explosion split it in two, blowing it off its hinges and knocking it inside.

They rushed from behind the trees into the building before the smoke had cleared.

Two soldiers ran from the guards' room and Detimore cut them down as they entered the hall.

Jack charged into the officers' room to find two men picking themselves up from the floor where they had been thrown by the explosion.

One of the officers reached for his pistol and Callahan stitched him up the middle with a quick burst that slammed him back against the wall. The other man tried to run from the room, but Jack dropped him after two steps.

Tucking himself into the corner of the outside wall for protection, Jack braced himself for the explosion he knew was imminent.

Houser hit the floor against the opposite wall as Frank tossed a fragmentation grenade into the guards' room and dived back toward the doorway.

The two deserters, Mahanes and Gerber, took the first barracks while the Montagnards took the next two.

Donatelli held the M60 at his waist as he entered the last barracks. Three Vietnamese soldiers stood in the center aisle, their faces masked in confusion. Donatelli blew them off their feet with sustained fire from the M60.

His eyes flicked back and forth along the rows of hammocks and bundles of personal belongings piled beneath them. Reaching the other end, he stepped out into the open and saw the two deserters and the two Montagnards exit the other barracks. They walked toward him, watching the compound for targets of opportunity.

Donatelli drew to a halt at the sight of Mahanes stopping dead in his tracks and pointing his weapon directly at him. He reacted quickly, but not before Mahanes fired.

The rounds from the AK-47 passed only inches to his left and thudded into someone behind him.

Donatelli was only an instinctive reflex away from cutting Mahanes in half with the M60 when he realized that the man had just saved his life. Behind him, a Vietnamese soldier who had left his hiding place in the barracks crumbled to his knees, his weapon firing harmlessly into the ground.

Mahanes fired again as he advanced and kicked the weapon away from the body.

Smashy rammed the gate to the warehouses at fifty miles an hour, driving it into the air and over the back of the truck where it nearly decapitated the Montagnard manning the .30-caliber machine gun; he luckily ducked at just the right moment.

Smashy fishtailed the truck around a corner and sped past the first three corrugated-tin warehouses—huge buildings, at least a hundred yards long and fifty yards wide—before finding one with an open bay.

A group of twelve men stood frozen in position as Smashy drove the truck into the warehouse.

Donahue leaped from the cab, and seeing that the men were unarmed, fired into the ground at their feet. Two of them attempted to run outside, and the Montagnard at the pedestal-mounted machine gun swung the gun around and tore them to pieces, continuing to fire into them long after they were dead.

"Hold your fire!" Smashy shouted as he got out of the cab.

The Montagnard swung the weapon back and prepared to open up on the group of unarmed men.

"I said hold your goddamn fire!" Smashy bellowed again. "Toong, take Sergeant York there off the machine gun and check out the other warehouses. Hendricks, you go with them."

One of the Vietnamese on the work detail began talking rapidly, grinning and gesturing with his hands. The others nodded in agreement and smiled happily.

Smashy understood little of what was said. Donahue filled him in, an incredulous expression on his face.

"The crazy son of a bitch is thanking you. He thinks we came to rescue them."

"Rescue them from what?"

"They're some kind of political prisoners. He says they are South Vietnamese. From Saigon. Some of them worked for us during the war. He says he knew we'd come back for them. The two guys the Yard shot were guards in charge of the detail."

"Bunch of shit," Smashy said. "Tell them to sit in a circle over by the door and keep their hands on their heads."

Houser turned away in revulsion from the small barred window in the cell door, stunned and shocked by what he had seen inside.

An emaciated American prisoner wearing filthy, excrement-stained rags sat in a corner of the cell on a straw mat. His left arm had been crudely amputated and his body and shaved head were covered with festering sores oozing yellow-green pus. He stared out at Houser with the blank, hollow eyes of a man more dead than alive. He made no effort to move and was unresponsive when Houser spoke to him.

"Goddamn son of a bitch!" Houser shouted. "Frank! Frank!" He ran from cell to cell looking inside. There were only seven men in the twenty cells, all of them in the same condition as the first man, or worse. All had amputated limbs. Some sat in puddles of urine and on cement floors smeared with human excrement. Rats scurried to their hiding places as he tried the doors.

In the last cell, a terribly disfigured man gasped a sign of recognition upon seeing Houser's face. Houser watched in horror as the dreadfully undernourished man pulled himself across the floor.

Most of his face had been badly burned and obviously left to heal without treatment. His right leg had been amputated above the knee, and a long flap of skin trailed the stump as he dragged it behind him.

Reaching the door, he tried to pull himself upright, but fell onto his back in the attempt. He lay looking up at Houser and spoke in a barely audible voice.

"Lieutenant Matthew J. Andrews," he whispered. "United States Navy."

The desperation and torment in the man's eyes brought Houser to tears. *"Frank! Frank!"*

Detimore ran from the guards' room to find Houser, his face chalk white, pounding on a cell door and screaming, "Get the keys! Get me the keys!"

"The guards have them," Frank said, following him into the room where Jack stood over the two guards who had survived the grenade blast. One man's arm was badly damaged. The other man had only minor leg wounds.

"How many prisoners?" Frank asked.

"There are only seven left. In the most deplorable

281

condition I have ever seen. *Jesus Christ!* Tell them to give me the keys!"

Frank spoke to the man with the leg wounds. The other guard, a sergeant, shouted at him, telling him to say nothing.

Frank told him to shut up. The sergeant spit on him.

Houser jammed the muzzle of his CAR-15 into the mouth of the sergeant, shattering his front teeth.

"The keys, you slimy son of a bitch! Where are the keys?"

The sergeant glared with defiance.

Houser pulled the trigger, blowing away the back of the man's head.

Callahan flinched at Houser's lightning rage and recoiled from the shock of what he had just done.

Houser withdrew the weapon and turned to the other guard. "Where are the keys?"

The soldier shouted frantically and pointed to one of his dead comrades lying near the door.

Houser crossed the room and turned the body over, tearing a key ring from the man's belt.

Galimore tied a handkerchief tightly around the wound in his forearm. The round had passed through cleanly and the bleeding soon stopped.

Two Vietnamese soldiers lay dead in the office; a third sat slumped in a corner of the radio room, a dozen rounds in his chest.

The radio operator had managed to shoot and kill one of the Montagnards and slam shut the door to the radio room, firing through it and wounding Galimore. He had gotten a call for help through to Quang Tri before Galimore killed him.

Maffey listened to the strident tonal voice coming over the radio, and translated what he heard.

"It's the garrison at Quang Tri. They're calling the troops that went to our camp. They're telling them to come back and that they are on their way here."

"Damn!" Galimore said. "We've got to load up and get out of here."

As Galimore reached the prison, Smashy pulled up in the truck. Toong and one of his men stood guard over the ten Vietnamese in the back.

Smashy got out of the cab and ran inside to where Callahan and Detimore were helping Houser carry the prisoners from the cells.

Smashy was shocked by the condition of the men. "My God, Jack!"

"Give us a hand," Callahan said, a grim expression on his face. "We want to get them outside."

"I've got ten Vietnamese in the truck. They say they're prisoners, and they want to go with us. I think they're full of shit."

"No," Frank said. "They've kept political prisoners here before. They're probably telling the truth."

"Get them in here," Jack said. "We have a lot of litters to carry; we can use the help. Assign two of the Yards to watch them."

"We'd better hurry, Jack," Galimore warned, feeling sick to his stomach at the sight of the men being carried from the cells. "The troops that passed us on the road are on their way back and another company is headed here from Quang Tri."

"Any casualties?" Jack asked.

"We lost one Yard," Galimore said. "Donatelli and

his men are sweeping the camp now, but it looks like that's it."

"We're going to need two trucks," Jack said. "Take the one parked near the barracks and get everybody loaded up and ready to move out."

Donahue burst into the hallway, running up to Frank Detimore. "Top, you and the Cap'n better come with me. Hendricks and me busted the padlocks off the first two warehouses. I think you're gonna want to see what we found."

Callahan stood at the entrance to the warehouse. His heart sank as he looked down the long rows of sealed aluminum coffins stacked five high the length of the building.

He felt the anger rising swiftly within him as he walked down the center aisle reading the name tags attached to the coffins on the lower tiers.

CARLON, T. M. CAPTAIN, USMC. DIED FEBRUARY 14, 1979

DAVIS, J. R. LT. COMMANDER, USN. DIED MAY 12, 1980

MENDEZ, A. H. MAJOR, USAF. DIED AUGUST 6, 1978

"Those rotten sons of bitches!" he said to Detimore. "Do you see these dates? Most of these men died after 1975."

"It's the same in the next warehouse," Donahue said. "There must be seven hundred coffins in all."

"Is there a master list of who these men were?" Jack asked.

"There must be," Frank said. "Probably in the HQ office."

"I'll check it out," Donahue said, rushing off with

Hendricks following, glad to be doing something and to get away from the gruesome scene.

Callahan took a miniature camera from his pocket and began taking pictures of the rows of coffins in both warehouses.

"Peace with honor, Frank? Huh? I'd like to have them explain to me where the hell the honor is in this. Lying bastards!"

"I doubt that this is all of them," Frank said. "There are probably more up north."

Galimore pulled up in the truck he had appropriated from the barracks area. Houser and Donatelli, their faces set in somber expressions of anger, sat in the back comforting the mutilated living skeletons they had carried from the prison.

"We're ready to move out, Jack," Galimore said, glancing inside the warehouses at the stacks of coffins. "That Marine . . . Donahue, he found a complete list of names. Come on, we picked up another radio transmission from Quang Tri. They just put a chopper in the air."

Callahan noticed Frank standing alongside the truck, staring into the sideview mirror. The expression on his face was one of horror.

"Come on, Frank," he said, gently pulling him away from the mirror. "We've got to get out of here."

"Damn," Frank said, shaken by what he saw. "They really did a job on me."

Jack empathized with his friend's pain. "It's over, Frank. It's over and you survived. Let's go."

"Round up some weapons and ammo for the political prisoners," Jack told Galimore.

"It's taken care of."

"Give Murdock's man a call. See if the Chinook left."

"I did. It's on the way. It'll be in position in about thirty minutes."

19

With the last disabled prisoner carried from the truck, Jack assigned the Vietnamese political prisoners and four of the Montagnards along with Mahanes and Gerber to carry the litters.

At the sound of an approaching helicopter, he turned to see another Cayuse flying toward them, following the road at treetop level.

Donatelli thanked God it wasn't a gunship and leaped onto the truck. He swung the .30-caliber machine gun around, but the helicopter banked sharply and flew out of range before he could fire.

"Well, now they know where we are," Smashy said.

"Forget about concealing the trucks," Jack shouted. "Everybody into the woods."

"I'm going to hang back," Smashy said. "Rig up a few surprises."

"I'll give you a hand," Detimore offered.

"Not this time, Frank. It's my turn."

"Then I'm staying with you," Donahue said.

Jack ordered him to join the others, but Donahue refused. "I'm good at this shit, Cap'n."

"You sure you're up to it?"

Donahue grinned. "Hey! You're talkin' to a Marine."

"Jesus," Smashy said.

"Divide the contents of your rucksack among the others and take all the Claymores with you," Jack told Smashy. "Get Donahue an M16 with a grenade launcher. You take the M60."

Smashy gathered the weapons and explosives, taking two bandoliers of grenades for himself and giving Donahue two.

Jack sent Frank, Cambell, and Hendricks to the front of the column with Houser and Donatelli, while he and Galimore brought up the rear behind the litter bearers with Toong and Maffey.

A dim green-tinted light filtered through the triple canopy of the towering trees onto the damp shadowy trail. The surrounding jungle was matted with dense underbrush and thick vines, and Callahan decided against putting out flank security, realizing they would never be able to keep up. The column moved slowly as the litter bearers struggled up the steep slope.

Smashy and Donahue followed closely behind until reaching a small stream where they stopped and waited until everyone had crossed. As the last man disappeared around a bend in the trail, Smashy entered the waist-deep water.

Jamming a piece of wood into the stream bank a foot below water level, he tied one end of a thin nylon line to it. Crossing to the opposite side of the stream, he firmly secured a fragmentation grenade in the bank at the same depth as the stick, tying the other end of the trip wire to the grenade pin and drawing it taut. The line cut across the stream at an angle, intersecting the most likely crossing point for anyone using the trail.

"One of Charlie's old tricks," he told Donahue. "Thought I'd give them a dose of their own medicine. It'll get them right where they live." He set up three more grenades in the same manner before they left the area and moved up the trail.

Smashy felt his shoulder throbbing and opened his shirt to check the wound. The dressing was still in place, but the wound was bleeding again. Applying pressure to it, he kept moving until he found a suitable location for what he planned next.

Cresting a steep rise, the trail leveled off and ran straight for approximately fifty yards. Stopping and kneeling at the edge of the jungle, he took off his rucksack and removed four of the Claymore mines.

"You familiar with these?" he asked Donahue.

"Sure. They go boom and people fall down dead."

Smashy shook his head. "They teach you Jarheads to attack a tank with a knife and that's it, right?"

"The M18A1 Claymore," Donahue recited. "One point five pounds of explosives projects seven hundred 10.5 grain steel balls over a sixty-degree arc for a distance of fifty meters at a height of one to two meters."

"Close enough," Smashy said. "You know what we're gonna do here?"

"Yeah."

"You know how to set it up?"

"Yeah."

Donahue took two of the Claymores and went back down the trail thirty yards from Smashy. Placing a mine ten feet into the woods on each side, he angled them toward the trail so the paths of their projectiles would cross and saturate the area. He ran the detonation cords back through the underbrush to where Smashy had set up the other two Claymores in the same manner, effectively covering the entire level section of the trail.

Smashy strung the green monofilament trip wire across the trail at ankle height. The enemy troops could safely pass the first two Claymores, drawing them into the heart of the trap, but the lead man, upon hitting the trip wire at the other end, would trigger the improvised firing device and detonate all four mines, blasting everyone behind him within range.

If the troops were not widely spaced, the deadly mines could kill or incapacitate fifteen to twenty men. The residual benefit was the psychological effect on the remaining troops—slowing them down as they advanced cautiously.

With the trap set, the two men ran a quarter mile ahead to a section of the trail well suited to an ambush.

A narrow passage led to a steep rise with excellent commanding terrain. At the bottom of the rise, Smashy set up the last two Claymores, running the detonation wires up the hill, twenty-five yards away, where he and Donahue would wait under cover.

After the first booby trap, the soldiers would be watching for trip wires. This time he would make the electrical connection himself, hand-detonating the mines at the precise moment he chose. They would open up with the M60 and the grenade launcher before making a rapid withdrawal to join the rest of the team.

Donahue put a full magazine in the M16 and placed a half-dozen grenades next to where he sat while Smashy positioned himself with the M60 and reloaded the box magazine to capacity.

"You stick close to me, Badowski. I'll show you how Force Recon does it."

"I can't wait."

"What kind of name is that—*Badowski?*"

"Polish."

"You know how many Poles it takes to make popcorn?"

"That goddamn joke is ten years old."

"I've been in the slammer for eight years. What do you want from me?"

"I want you to shut up and watch the trail."

Donahue pointed to Smashy's green beret. "That's a silly lookin' hat, you know that, don't you? Makes you look like a goddamn Frog."

Smashy studied Donahue's battered, misshapen face. "That guy you set fire to back at the camp, he do that to you?"

Donahue nodded.

"You should have slow-roasted the fucker on a spit."

"If we'd had the time I would've."

The two men fell silent at the muffled sounds of distant grenade blasts.

"They're at the stream," Smashy said. "Should be about ten minutes before they trip the Claymores."

Donahue shifted his position and loaded a round in the grenade launcher while Smashy checked to make certain the box magazine was feeding properly.

Seven minutes later a loud blast resounded through the jungle, followed by screams of pain and frantic shouting.

"Couple of minutes," Smashy said. "You ready?"

"I'm ready."

"I'm gonna let about four or five of them through and

get partway up the hill. When I fire the Claymores, you take them out first with a buckshot round."

When the first enemy soldiers appeared at the bend in the trail, Bad Eye had the point. Donahue recognized him immediately.

"Bad Eye," he whispered. "Come to papa, you sorry motherfucker."

"Who's Bad Eye?"

"CO at the camp. The guy who put the hole in your shoulder."

Forty yards away, Bad Eye moved slowly along the trail, carefully placing each step. The men behind him were bunched close together, obviously inexperienced in patrol procedures.

Donahue sighted his weapon and waited calmly.

A steady stream of soldiers crowded the trail as far as Smashy and Donahue could see—all carelessly following too close, their eyes on the ground, terrified by the fate of their comrades only minutes before.

Smashy let Bad Eye and the next four men start up the hill, then detonated the Claymores. A violent hailstorm of steel balls blew across the trail, ripping into the frantic soldiers.

The three men closest to the blast were killed immediately, their clothing torn from their bodies. Another man turned in small circles, screaming and holding his hands to his bloody, shredded face before Smashy shot off the side of his head with the M60.

Donahue fired the grenade launcher. The round impacted only inches from where Bad Eye stood immobile with fear. The force of the explosion picked him off his feet and tossed him into the underbrush, his upper body still visible from the top of the hill. Donahue took careful aim with the

M16 and put two rounds into the already dead man's chest.

"And that's all she wrote," he muttered.

Swinging back to the trail, he raked the bodies of the other men before reloading the grenade launcher. While Smashy opened up on a group of soldiers rushing up the trail, Donahue tossed two white phosphorous grenades in their midst in rapid succession.

Men screamed hysterically, flailing and twisting in agony as the white-hot chunks of phosphorus burned deeply into their flesh.

Smashy poured an endless stream of fire from the M60 into the brush at the bend in the trail, pinning down the soldiers who were attempting to regroup.

"Let's go!" he shouted.

Donahue fired two more rounds from the grenade launcher before following Smashy at a dead run up the trail.

The ambush had netted them at least twenty men, and further slowed the progress of the enemy soldiers.

The men carrying the litters were soaked with perspiration, their muscles straining as they climbed the hill that led to the field on the plateau above. Those on the downhill side of the litters had to raise their ends above their shoulders to keep the men they carried from falling out.

Galimore knelt at the side of the trail and let the column go ahead as he tried again to get the rescue helicopter on the radio.

"Koala Bear, this is Wolfpack. Do you read? Over."

He heard nothing but the faint hollow hiss of static.

"Koala Bear, this is Wolfpack. Do you read, goddamnit? *Over!*"

The voice that answered was not the one he wanted to

hear. He was trying to reach the crew of the Chinook and instead heard the radio operator at Murdock's camp.

"Wolfpack, this is Koala Bear. Over."

"I can't raise the chopper," Galimore told him. "We're a few hundred meters from the extraction area. Send them in. *Now!*"

There was no response.

"Koala Bear, goddamnit! Do you read?"

Galimore recognized a different voice as the reply came. It was Murdock.

"Wolfpack, this is Koala Bear leader. We cannot comply. Repeat. We cannot comply."

Galimore was stunned by what he heard. "Why the hell not?" he shouted.

"The chopper was in position but under heavy ground fire when we were cut off," Murdock said. "We have received no further transmissions. We have to assume they have been captured or killed."

Galimore pieced together the likely scenario. When the alert went out, the Vietnamese must have called in their troops in Laos in the vicinity of the border and concentrated them in the areas they considered most likely to be used as crossing points. They probably saw the helicopter coming in and went after it.

Galimore collected himself and asked Murdock, "Do you have anything else you can send? We have thirty-five men for extraction."

"Is the extraction area suitable for the C-123?" Murdock asked.

"Negative," Galimore replied. "We'll need a Chinook or two Hueys."

"We have nothing available, Wolfpack. Nothing."

"How soon can you get something to us?"

"Possibly tomorrow," Murdock said. "Can you take evasive measures and give us new coordinates then?"

Galimore realized the hopelessness of the situation. It would be impossible to evade the enemy and save the disabled POWs. The rational calm of resignation took hold and he gave his solemn reply.

"That's a negative," he told Murdock.

"I'll do everything I can," Murdock said. "Keep me advised."

Galimore didn't respond. He clipped the headset on his harness and got slowly to his feet. Speaking softly to the mental image of his wife, he said, "I'm sorry, baby. I'm really sorry."

He started at the sound of footsteps behind him and looked up to see Smashy and Donahue running up the trail. The two men stopped beside him, breathing heavily.

"Come on, Joe," Smashy said. "Charlie's only a couple minutes behind. Let's go! The chopper here?"

The look on Galimore's face told all.

"Jesus Christ! They'd better get here in a hurry. There's at least a company back there."

"It's not comin'."

Smashy stared wide-eyed, then glanced at Donahue and back down the trail. "Jesus. We've had it."

At the top of the hill the jungle trail entered the uncultivated end of the field. Twenty-five yards into the boulder-strewn area of low scrub, Callahan and Frank directed the men to defensive positions in a semicircle, placing the disabled prisoners in a group behind them under cover of a cluster of boulders and low thickets.

"Pass the word," Jack said. "Conserve your ammo. Semi-automatic fire and choose your targets."

Houser's face was grim, his eyes hard and determined; he had been deeply affected by what he had seen at the prison. He lay in a prone position beside Callahan, partially protected by a large, flat rock.

"I want you to know," he said to Jack, "I'm not concerned about the road to death anymore. Those bastards made the choice easy."

Callahan turned to Frank Detimore who lay in a shallow depression on his right. "Sorry we let you down, Frank."

"Sorry? Nobody else even tried."

"We failed."

"There isn't a man you rescued who wouldn't rather die this way than rot in a cage."

The Vietnamese political prisoners sat chattering in a group near the disabled Americans. The man who had joyously greeted Smashy at the warehouse crawled over to Callahan and spoke to him in Vietnamese. Frank listened and translated.

"He wants to know if we can show them how to use their weapons," Frank said, forcing a smile. "They've never fired one before."

Donahue overheard the conversation. "I'll give them a crash course, Top."

"Don't show them how to use full auto," Jack told him. "They'll shoot up their ammo in thirty seconds. Just show them how to change magazines and point in the right direction. Then spread them out among the men who know what they're doing."

Donahue hesitated before leaving. "Thanks," he said to Callahan. "You and your men gave it your best shot. Nobody could've done better."

Harry Cambell had been sitting beside Dan Lucere, watching everything going on around him, terrified by what he knew was about to happen. He clenched his fists tightly in an effort to stop his hands from shaking, then jumped to his feet and ran to Detimore's position, dropping quickly to the ground.

"Get back behind the rocks," Detimore ordered.

"I want a weapon, Frank."

Frank stared at the frightened man. "You sure?"

"I want a weapon."

Frank told Toong to give Cambell the AK-47 that had belonged to the Montagnard killed at the supply base.

Cambell took a position next to Detimore as three enemy soldiers reached the end of the trail. Smashy reacted immediately and brought them down with a short burst from the M60.

The troops that were following the lead men dispersed to both sides of the trail and began making their way through the jungle, taking up positions along the fringe of the field.

To the sounds of shrill commands, Jack saw some of the troops grouping for an attack. Sporadic fire began and bullets richocheted off the rocks, chipping away small splinters, while others passed overhead, cracking through the thickets.

The first line of skirmishers ran from the trail, firing wildly and inaccurately from the hip. A machine gun opened up to the left of the trail in support of the ill-fated frontal assault. Eight enemy soldiers were caught in a withering crossfire that stopped them ten yards into the field.

Donahue went after the machine gun, crawling to a concealed position closer to the jungle. Lying on his back, he loaded the grenade launcher with a high explosive round. Taking a deep breath, he got to his knees and fired, immediately dropping back under cover. The grenade impacted short of its target.

"Ten meters more!" Smashy shouted.

As Donahue reloaded, the two men at the machine gun rose from their position. Smashy fired, killing them before they could run.

Toong saw a squad of enemy soldiers moving off to his right flank in preparation for a sweep. He, Galimore, and Hendricks cut down all but two of them who crawled to the edge of the field and returned their fire.

Five more enemy soldiers appeared from nowhere and scrambled in beside them, putting out a heavy volume of fire. One of the men stood and tossed a grenade that ricocheted off a thick vine and landed back at his feet. Galimore and Toong shot the two men who jumped up, and two more were killed by the explosion.

Another man stood with a grenade. Toong rolled to his right and raised himself on one knee to get a clear shot, but before he could fire, a bullet ripped through his chest and out his back and he fell forward onto his face.

Galimore killed the man with the grenade and crawled out into the open to get Toong. He grabbed his leg and cried out in pain as two rounds tore into his thigh and shattered the femur. Toong's body bounced and shuddered as he was shot twice in the head.

Callahan and Detimore laid down suppressing fire as Houser ran, stooped over, to where Galimore had pulled himself back under cover. Donahue and Donatelli both fired grenades into the area and killed the remaining soldiers, blowing their bodies out into the field.

The battle ebbed as the enemy regrouped and began to probe the perimeter for a weak spot. The Vietnamese officers were not using their troops effectively: they were spread too thin and disorganized in their assaults.

Callahan heard the dreaded *thunk!* of a mortar shell leaving its tube, and the whooshing of its trajectory. He felt the shock waves from the powerful explosion, and the smell of cordite stung his nostrils. He looked over his shoulder and saw a puff of grayish-white smoke rise from the point of impact, near the disabled prisoners but not close enough to harm them.

A second mortar was fired from a different position. It exploded on their left flank, killing Mahanes and Gerber and seriously wounding two of the Montagnards.

Donahue and Donatelli divided the twelve remaining grenades between them and fired into the suspected positions. The rest of the men poured a heavy concentration of fire into the two areas, and the mortar barrage ceased while the teams moved to new positions.

The enemy troops maintained a steady stream of automatic fire, and a squad of men took advantage of the team's diverted attention and rushed the left flank, breaching the perimeter where the mortar had weakened the defense.

The Vietnamese political prisoners fired their weapons aimlessly into the air, then threw them to the ground and broke and ran. The enemy soldiers cut them down and killed two of the Montagnards at point-blank range before Donatelli and Houser, aided by Hendricks and Maffey, bolstered the defenses, killing the retreating soldiers with dead-accurate fire.

The men fought valiantly, turning back a series of frontal assaults and attempted sweeps. They were running low on ammunition and had expended the last of the grenades in unsuccessful attempts to knock out the mortar teams. Callahan estimated they had killed seventy or eighty men, but fresh troops replaced them and there seemed to be no end in sight as the main body of soldiers reached the plateau.

The tension mounted during an ominous lull in the fighting as the enemy grouped for a massive assault. The men knew that the end was near. They would soon be overwhelmingly outnumbered with only enough ammunition remaining to bring down the first skirmish line.

Houser glanced to the rear in response to a growing pulsating drone in the distance.

"Looks as though they aren't taking any chances," he said to Callahan. "They're coming in from behind, too."

Jack looked to the far end of the field. The black dots above the horizon grew larger as they closed on the plateau. He counted eight helicopters in the rapidly approaching formation.

"Probably heliborne troops from Da Nang," Frank said. "They really want us bad."

20

The enemy troops were massed and ready for their assault when the helicopters reached the opposite end of the field.

Two Cobra gunships, their pylons loaded with a full complement of seventy-six rockets, led the formation. Dropping close to the deck, they streaked toward the team's defensive positions. Their turret-mounted multibarreled electric miniguns and grenade launchers unleashed a devastating barrage of fire into the edge of the jungle before they climbed swiftly away.

"Morons can't hit shit!" Donahue shouted. "They're unloading on their own troops."

Callahan watched the camouflage-painted Cobras bank into a steep turn and start back toward them, one ship on each side of the field. "Hell," he said to Frank. "Nobody is that bad a shot."

A stream of rockets pounded into the jungle on their flanks, sending the enemy troops diving for cover as the ground exploded around them.

Jack followed the Cobras with his eyes as they climbed to join the other helicopters now circling the field out of range of small-arms fire.

"They don't have any markings," he said.

"I noticed. What the hell is going on here?"

Galimore heard a voice come over the receiver and put the handset to his ear.

"Wolfpack, this is Blackbird. Do you read? Over."

"Who the hell is Blackbird?" Galimore shouted.

"Wolfpack, this is Blackbird. Do you read?"

"Roger, Blackbird," Galimore answered. "Read you loud and clear."

"Keep your heads down, Wolfpack. It's barbecue time. Repeat. Heads down."

"Heads down!" Galimore shouted.

The men didn't hear the two jet fighters until they passed overhead and roared into a steep climb, leaving four deadly silver canisters tumbling to earth behind them.

In front of the team's position, the napalm engulfed the jungle in rolling, billowing orange flames that charred to a crisp everything in its path. Enemy soldiers, flaming like human torches, ran into the field in a wild, agonzied dance, dropping to the ground and screaming.

"Who the hell are you?" Galimore shouted into the radio.

"The cavalry," the lead pilot replied. "Didn't you ever go to the movies? Put everything you have into the woods," he said. "The slicks are coming in."

"We don't have anything left to put in the woods," Galimore told him.

"Hang on," the pilot said.

The two Cobra gunships came down fast, firing rockets and nose cannons into the thick black smoke where the napalm had struck, while two Huey gunships flanked them, their doorgunners firing along the edge of the field.

At the command of the lead pilot, four rescue ships descended and settled to the field. A dozen Thai soldiers wearing black berets and armed with automatic rifles and M79 grenade launchers leaped from the first two helicopters. They hit the ground running, setting up defensive positions and laying down suppressive fire as Callahan pulled his men off the line to load the disabled prisoners.

The helicopter crews stared in disbelief at the condition of the men being handed to them. Callahan picked up Dan Lucere from where he sat against a rock, unscathed and unaware of the battle raging around him.

With the last of the disabled men on board the rescue ships, the Thai troops backed slowly toward the helicopters, firing as they withdrew.

The Cobra and Huey gunships made strafing runs along the perimeter of the field, and the enemy fire diminished to sporadic bursts.

Galimore ran, limping painfully, toward the lead helicopter. His leg gave out and he fell to the ground and began to crawl.

Donatelli and Smashy ran to his side, each taking an arm, dragging him to the door, and helping him inside. Smashy quickly scanned the area looking for anyone left behind. No one other than the Thai troops remained outside the helicopters.

"Everyone's on board!" Callahan shouted.

As Smashy turned to dive through the door, two powerful blows staggered him, knocking him into the side of the helicopter.

"Ah, shit!" he said as he stared at the holes in his chest, then slid to the ground.

Callahan went out after him and took a round in the arm as he put Smashy over his shoulder and tossed him through the door, climbing in after him as the helicopter lifted off.

The two rescue ships with the team and the prisoners raced from the area as the gunships made another pass in defense of the Thai troops now scrambling into the remaining helicopters.

Houser pulled Smashy away from the door and knelt beside him. He saw the small holes in his shirt where the bullets had entered the chest cavity and immediately began administering albumin blood expander, tearing open the bloody shirt to get to the wounds.

"It hurts like hell," Smashy said. "Give me some morphine."

"Sorry, Smashy, I can't. Not with a chest wound. It'll slow down your breathing."

Smashy was bleeding profusely, and at Houser's instructions, Donatelli sat behind him, elevating his head and shoulders to keep him from drowning in his own blood.

The bullets had penetrated the chest below the heart. They had torn through both lungs, then smashed through a rib in the back and glanced off, stopping as they embedded in the muscle tissue.

Smashy's breathing was labored and irregular. A froth of bright red blood bubbled from the holes in his lungs. Houser quickly cleaned the wounds and used pieces of wrapping from the sterile bandages to block the air passages created by the bullets. He then applied an airtight bandage over the wounds.

Instructing Donatelli to continue to keep Smashy's head and shoulders elevated, Houser went over to where Callahan sat near the door, and examined the wound in his upper right arm. The bullet had gone clean through, just missing the humerus and nicking a large vein. Houser placed a tourniquet above the wound to stop the bleeding, and put compress bandages over the entry and exit points.

"How's Smashy?" Jack asked.

Houser shook his head. "He's got two sucking chest wounds. One lung has collapsed and the other one is filling with blood, and he's going into shock."

"Will he make it to the hospital?"

"No. I can't stop the internal bleeding, and if I treat him for shock the lung will fill completely up."

Jack went to Smashy's side.

"I'm dyin', Jack," he said, a gurgling sound mixing with his words.

"I know."

Smashy started to laugh, but the pain was too great. "You never were much for bullshit."

"Is there anything I can do for you?"

"Yeah. Make sure Marge and the kids get my money."

"I'll take care of it."

Smashy coughed and a trickle of blood ran from the corner of his mouth. "We had some good times, didn't we?"

"The best."

The light began to fade in Smashy's eyes as he looked up at Donatelli and winked. "We did it. We pulled it off."

"Yeah. We did it." His voice choked with emotion, Donatelli said softly, "I'll miss you, Smashy."

Smashy's head flopped limply to the side. His lifeless eyes stared blankly at the floor of the helicopter.

Donatelli reached out and gently placed his hand on the pale waxen face below him and slowly closed the eyelids.

"I'm sorry about your friend," a voice said from behind Callahan. Jack looked up to see the auburn hair and hard blue eyes of the CIA agent he had confronted at the warehouse in Bangkok.

"He was a good man, and a good soldier," Jack said, suddenly realizing the implications of Stevens' presence.

"*You* brought the rescue team in?" Jack asked.

"With a little help."

"I'm glad you're not the type to hold a grudge."

"You mean that business at the warehouse?" Stevens smiled. "You don't really think you took my men out that easily, do you?"

"You knew we were coming?"

"It didn't take a nuclear physicist to figure out you'd be back. After hearing what your friend the doctor said at our little showdown that morning, I checked the contents of the crates. They told me pretty much what you had planned. Then I got your names from customs and called a friend of mine at the DIA. He filled me in. Asked me to keep an eye on you."

"How did you know we wouldn't kill your men that night?"

"We had a tail on Froggy. When he picked up the Ketamine and surgical masks, we put it together. That stuff's a hallucinogen, you know. The boys had some bad dreams."

"How did you know where to find us?"

"We monitor all radio traffic in this area. We heard your transmissions and got the coordinates when you called them in."

Jack got to his feet and warmly shook Stevens' hand, flinching from the pain in his arm. "Thanks. We owe you."

"What you owe me is to forget that you ever saw me. We weren't here."

"How many men did Murdock lose?"

Stevens hesitated before answering and Jack grew suspicious of the pause.

"How many men did he lose?"

"None."

"He told my radioman that his Chinook was taken at the border."

"The Chinook never left the camp. The crew had picked up heavy Vietnamese radio traffic and refused to come in."

"I'll kill that lying son of a bitch!"

"No you won't. He's no goddamn good, but he does things for us no one else will do. When we're through with him I'll give him your regards . . . your warmest personal regards."

Jack looked out the door of the helicopter and saw the two jet fighters streak by and climb to cruising altitude.

"Our escort," Stevens said.

"Where are you taking us?" Jack asked.

"To a hospital in Bangkok for a couple of days. Then the Air Force will take you back to a military hospital in the States."

"Who do I say got us out of here?"

"Murdock."

"The hell I will!"

"You will. As you said, Callahan, you owe me. You'll be debriefed by the DIA in Bangkok and they'll break the story to the press when you're on your way home."

"I'd like to give the advantage to a Canadian journalist from the *Toronto Herald* before the wire services get it."

"Why's that?"

"He's the man who got Frank Detimore's letter out."

"Give him a call when we get to Bangkok. And remember—Murdock. Not us. I want your word on that."

"You have it."

21

The families of the POWs crowded the flight line as the Air Force plane rolled into position and stopped.

The men on stretchers were carried off first and swarmed by wives and parents and teenaged children who had been prepared by the Defense Department for what they would see, but were still horrified by the condition of the nearly unrecognizable men.

Harry Cambell stood in the aisle of the plane beside Frank Detimore. "I'm ashamed of myself, Frank," he said. "I don't know how I'm going to face anyone."

"With your head held high, Harry," he said, clasping his hand. "When the chips were down, you did what had to be done. Not everyone can say that."

"Are you coming, Jack?" Frank asked as he walked out onto the steps leading down from the plane.

"No," Callahan replied. "This is your moment. Enjoy it. I'll see you in New Orleans later."

Jack stood in the doorway of the plane and saw Betty

Detimore and her children and parents standing off to the side at the bottom of the steps. Four other people stood with them, relatives of Frank's, he guessed. He watched Betty's face and saw what he knew would be there. She was shocked by Frank's condition, but it only showed for a brief moment before the joy and love beamed through. As Frank reached the bottom of the steps she rushed toward him, embracing him and kissing him passionately. The girls were doing their best to wait patiently, but could no longer contain themselves and ran to him, enveloping him in their embraces.

Jack smiled at the sight of Hendricks being smothered in the arms of a huge woman wearing a bright orange caftan while a tall, thin man with a weather-beaten face stood quietly by clutching a Bible in his hands.

"I want to thank you again, Cap'n," Mike Donahue said as he reached the doorway. "You guys did a hell of a job."

"Is your family down there?" Jack asked.

Donahue shook his head. "I was raised in a Catholic orphanage by a bunch of mean-ass nuns. I hope the hell none of them are down there. The last thing I need is a ruler across my knuckles."

Callahan laughed. "You have any plans?"

"Yeah. I think I'll stay in the Corps. They made me a staff sergeant. Believe that shit? Promoted me all the time I was locked up. Got a lot of money comin', too. Seven years' worth."

"You take care of yourself," Jack told him.

"I'll do that, Cap'n. *Semper Fi.*"

As an Air Force band played "God Bless America," Callahan joined the rest of the team. Dressed in civilian clothes, they left the plane with the crew, avoiding the

310

press and television cameras barricaded a respectful distance away from the prisoners and their families. Inside the Flight Operations Center, the Air Force had arranged for them to meet those who had come to greet them.

Galimore was nearly knocked off his crutches as his wife and daughter rushed to his side. Angela Fisher cried tears of joy at the sight of Houser, and leaped into his arms, and Donatelli was embraced by his girl friend as his father stood proudly by.

After the introductions and the congratulatory remarks, Callahan quietly said good-bye to the team. Each spoke of a reunion, knowing that they would resume their lives and probably never see each other again.

A young Air Force sergeant, filled with awe and questions about the mission, drove Jack to the nearest commercial airport where he boarded a plane to take him to where he had one last duty before returning home.

Callahan avoided the electronically controlled gate at the front of the house and under cover of darkness, scaled the rear wall of the property, dropping quietly into the courtyard.

A light was on in the large room off the wrought-iron balcony and the French doors were open to the night breeze. Silently climbing the stairs to the balcony, he waited in the shadows until Justin Hanks, seated behind his desk, had finished his telephone call.

Seeing Callahan in the doorway, Hanks fumbled to open a small drawer in the desk, answering Jack's question as to whether he had been in contact with Murdock.

Hanks' hand gripped the silenced pistol as Jack reached the desk, slamming the drawer shut and breaking the frightened man's wrist.

Hanks cried out in pain and struggled to free his hand.

311

A blow broke the bridge of his nose and knocked him from the chair to the floor. Jack opened the drawer, bending the broken wrist backward and taking the pistol. He removed the magazine and ejected the round from the chamber, tossing them into the courtyard, then threw the weapon into a corner.

"That was a stupid move, Hanks. A very stupid move."

"Be reasonable," Hanks pleaded, unsure of what Callahan intended to do. "Murdock has been severely reprimanded. He will receive no more business from me."

"Reprimanded!" Jack spat out the word. "You're indirectly responsible for the death of one of my men . . . a friend, and you talk to me about reprimands."

"I am not responsible for your friend's death. It was—"

"When you took the money, you took the responsibility," Jack shouted. "He was your man, under contract to you, following your orders. You've been in this business long enough to know the rules."

"But I had no way of knowing he would not fulfill his obligations."

"That's the only reason you're still alive."

Jack pulled Hanks to his knees and dragged him across the floor, lifting the heavy man with ease and shoving him into a chair.

"I figure you owe me thirty thousand dollars for the part of the mission that wasn't completed," he told Hanks, throwing a slip of paper into his lap. "I want the money in that man's account within twenty-four hours."

"I'll take care of it immediately," Hanks said, holding a handkerchief to his bloody, swelling nose. "You have my word."

"Your word is worthless," Jack said, walking over to the ornately carved table where the display of centuries-old

312

Chinese porcelain vases was neatly arranged. He picked up the largest vase and tossed it into the air, catching it before it hit the floor.

"*Please!*" Hanks whined. "Those vases are priceless."

Jack tossed it again and caught it. "There's also a woman's name and address on that piece of paper I gave you," he said. "She's the ex-wife of the man who was killed on the mission. He had two children who live with her. I thought you might like to set up a trust fund for them, something to make their lives a little more comfortable."

"Of course," Hanks replied, his eyes riveted on the large vase in Callahan's hands. "I'll arrange it."

"How much?" Jack asked.

"Twenty thousand dollars?" Hanks offered.

Jack set the exquisite vase back on the table and picked up a poker from the stand by the fireplace. He stood before the table holding the long iron rod like a baseball bat. "How much was that?" he asked again, slowly swinging the poker in the direction of the vases.

"Please, Mr. Callahan. Be careful."

"How much?"

"What figure did you have in mind?" Hanks asked meekly.

"A hundred and seventy thousand," Jack said.

Hanks blanched at the amount. "With what I must return to the other man, that is the entire amount you paid me."

"That's right," Jack said, raising the poker.

"*All right!*" Hanks shouted.

Jack put the poker down and went over to Hanks, grabbing him by the hair and jerking his face upward. "Now let me explain the rules to you. If you renege, I'll

313

be back. And I'll break not only the vases, but every bone in your goddamn body. If you send anyone after me, I'll kill them. Then I'll come after you. Understand?''

Hanks nodded, flinching as Jack let go of his hair.

Before leaving the room, Jack stopped in the doorway and turned back to Hanks, who remained in the chair, holding the blood-soaked handkerchief to his nose.

''Just between you and me, my preference is to kill you. I hope you give me a reason.''

Driving home from the Aspen airport, Callahan reflected, with a sense of satisfaction, on his brief visit with Frank and Betty and their family. He had politely refused Harley Crawford's persistent, at times adamant, offers to come and work with him and Frank; but he did accept an invitation to join them for a salmon fishing trip to a private club in Canada, and he looked forward to it with relish.

Pulling into his driveway and getting out of the car, he walked slowly along the path through the woods to Maggie Hill's house.

Boomer sat at Maggie's kitchen door, having heard the Jeep Cherokee arrive—a sound he had listened for each day—pounding his front paws on the floor and whining at fever pitch. Maggie glanced out the window and saw Jack approach. Boomer did a series of exuberant twirls until Maggie opened the door, then dashed down the steps and raced to the woods, joyously leaping into the air and landing in Jack's outstretched arms.

Maggie came out as Jack reached the steps, the ecstatic animal racing around him in small circles. She saw the solemn expression on Callahan's face, and had the answer she had been afraid of hearing. The names of those involved in the rescue of the prisoners had not been released

314

by the Defense Department at the request of the team, but the press had reported that one of the team had been killed on the mission.

"It was Smashy, wasn't it, Jack?" Maggie asked quietly.

Jack nodded. "He died the way he wanted to," he said. "That mattered a lot to him."

"He was special," Maggie said.

"Yes, he was."

"I need a hug. God, do I need a hug."

Jack embraced her, holding her tightly. "I'm sorry, Maggie."

"Have dinner with me tonight," she said. "I have a Beef Wellington in the oven."

"That's a good place for it," Jack said with a grin, kissing her gently on the forehead. "I think I'd rather take you out. I've had enough dangerous living for a while."

Maggie smiled through the tears that welled in her eyes. "You're a sweetheart, Callahan. A goddamn sweetheart."

"I know."

LUCIANO'S LUCK

1943. Under cover of night, a strange group parachutes into Nazi occupied Sicily. It includes the overlord of the American Mafia, "Lucky" Luciano. The object? To convince the Sicilian Mafia king to put his power—the power of the Sicilian peasantry—behind the invading American forces. It is a dangerous gamble. If they fail, hundreds of thousands will die on Sicilian soil. If they succeed, American troops will march through Sicily toward a stunning victory on the Italian Front, forever indebted to Mafia king, Lucky Luciano.

A DELL BOOK   14321-7 $3.50

JACK HIGGINS

bestselling author of *Solo*